Magic Coming Undone

By
Faith Prince

Chapter 1

Zoeli

The floor falls out from under me. Gravity throws me down, arms flailing in the pitch dark, sailing through an eternity of nothingness.

SPLASH. I hit water, mouth wide open. I cry out, lungs filling up as I sink into the inky blackness. I choke, vomit burning the back of my throat.

Frantic, I paddle my arms and kick my legs, searching for the surface. It's like weights are tied to my hands and ankles. Even as my muscles burn from the effort, I descend, deeper and deeper. I shiver, ice cubes sliding on my skin. It's no use. If I don't drown, I'll freeze to death.

Zoe, what's going on?

The voice comes out of nowhere. Who's that? I feel like I should know, but I can't think clearly. My brain is molasses, slower and thicker than the liquid suffocating me.

What's wrong?

It's like a lightbulb flicks on.

Just like that, I remember who the voice belongs to. More than that, I remember who I am. I'm Zoeli, the underdog witch who showed up to battle, fierce as an untamed warrior. Ready to destroy, I did even more than that. I annihilated. I took the enemy down, one by one.

Zoe, answer me! Damian's voice echoes, ricocheting in the recesses of my heart. It hurts, but feels so damn good. Our relationship is complicated like that.

When I fell in love with Damian, I didn't know that he was already engaged to my cousin, Caliah. Most days, I tell myself that I hate him. Other days, I find myself wrapped up in his arms, pretending that I've discovered an alternate reality where we could be together without the whole universe falling apart. Afterwards, I hate myself for being so damn weak.

Like I said, this shit's complicated. Especially since this pesky telepathic connection makes it difficult to go no contact.

Still, I'm grateful for his voice reminding me of who I am. I'm a fighter. Even when the odds were stacked against me, I never gave up. And I'm damn sure not going to lay down and die today.

I propel my arms, driving them through the murky liquid. Hands push me back down. Hundreds of them. Maybe thousands. Fingers coil around my wrists, ankles, and thighs. I thrash, pulling away, but there's too many. More disembodied hands reach for my throat. I shout, gel-like fluid and ice rushing into my windpipe.

I jolt up, vocal cords vibrating as I scream. My hands fly to my neck, surprised to find that I'm dry. I suck a full breath into my unobstructed airway, heart rattling against my rib cage. What just happened? There were so many hands…

"Are you okay?" I jerk towards the very real voice, not nearly as familiar as the voice inside my head.

A sliver of moonlight illuminates the stone walls. Reflexively, I grab the ratty blanket from my lap, pulling it under my chin. The thin fabric and moth holes hardly protect me from the cold. I shiver. The dungeon floor beneath me might as well be a block of ice.

As the fuzzy-head feeling fades, the world comes into focus. Kian, one of the more tolerable guards, watches me from the other side of the katium bars. At first glance, all I see is black pupils in white eyeballs. His irises are so pale that they're almost invisible.

"I'm, um..." I say. "I must've had a bad dream." My teeth chatter, puffs of white escaping with each word.

"You're freezing," Kian observes. He looks to be around my age. He must've been hired right out of high school.

Across the hall, another prisoner shuffles, her nightgown trailing behind her. Helen clamps her bony fingers around the bars. She sneers at me, baring jagged yellow teeth. I hold my gaze steady, careful not to flinch. "Filthy half-breed," she hisses. Given that her white nightgown is blackened with dirt and her hands look like they haven't been washed in a decade, the irony isn't lost on me. I tell myself it's projection, but there's more to it. In this twisted magical culture, even low-life pure-breeds feel they have the right to denigrate me. There's nothing more disgusting than being part-human.

I keep my chin high. "I'm fine," I tell Kian. My night terrors are embarrassing enough. The last thing I want is pity. Even if I'm falling apart, I'll pretend that I'm not. For myself, but mostly for Saria. I glance over at the heap in the corner. My sister isn't doing well. It's up to me to keep up our morale.

With a quick nod, Kian spins around. His footsteps disappear down the hallway. In the corner, Saria rustles underneath her blanket. "I'm so cold," she says.

I slide next to her and pull her close. Head on my chest, my sister clings to me. When we were kids, we used to cuddle like this. In a soft bed, watching movies and giggling, her warmth oozing into mine. I don't remember her feeling so small and frail. She's skeletal, her collarbone sharp against my ribcage.

"Hey." Kian's back, holding a comforter in his fists. "This might help."

I eye him suspiciously. In here, I've learned to trust no one. Once, a guard named Alex offered me an extra slice of bread. Naive and stupid as I was, I walked right up to the bars. As soon as I was close enough, he snatched the bread away and pinched my ass.

If I didn't fear being separated from my sister, I would've reached through the bars and showed him how it feels to be violated. Instead, I'm keeping a list of men to kick in the balls. I'll take care of them when I get out of here. I hope that I don't have to add another name tonight. I thought that Kian was one of the decent ones. "Where'd you get that from?" I ask. "That isn't for the prisoners."

"It's mine," Kian says. "But you can have it."

"I didn't know that guards were allowed to give prisoners their personal items."

"We're not," Kian says. He pushes the blanket through the bars. It bunches up on the floor, half in and half out of the cell. "So, if you don't hurry up, I might get in trouble."

Beside me, Saria shivers violently. I might be falling right into a trap, but if he's sincere, this could save my sister from freezing to death.

Without any magic flowing in her veins, Saria's more susceptible to the elements. That's my fault. A few months ago, Saria and I weren't on good terms. I stole all of her magic, leaving her in this vulnerable state. If she dies here, I'm to blame.

I pull the blanket the rest of the way through. "Thank you," I say. It's soft and fluffy. I can't wait to snuggle up with it.

Kian stares curiously, like I'm on exhibit at a zoo. A scar slices through his left eyebrow. "I don't understand why everyone's so afraid of you," he says.

"They estimate that I killed over one hundred at the battle. Single handedly." Maybe I sound cocky, but hey, I'm speaking facts. I earned it.

"Yes, but you fought on our side. You helped us win," Kian says.

"And this is the thanks I get." I gesture to the concrete floor and rusty excuse for a toilet. When I lift my arm, a heinous odor hits my nose. I stink.

Saria and I aren't treated like the other prisoners. They don't let us out to use the communal showers. Once a month, a female guard aims a hose through the bars and sprays our naked bodies with freezing cold water. It barely rinses off the top layer of grime.

Kian's fists clench by his sides. "I want you to know that not everyone is okay with this. Aurelians are waking up—" Voices echo down the hallway. Kian jerks his head towards the sound. "I'll see you." He whispers, turns, and disappears down the hall.

Wheels clatter on the dungeon floor. Two guards pass by, pushing a rolling dumpster. They leave it against the wall, just outside of our cell. Great. As if the odor in here wasn't bad enough.

I drag the comforter to the corner where Saria is curled up in the fetal position. As I tuck the blanket around her, a shadow hops in my peripheral vision. A small brown bird wriggles through the bars. A nightingale.

I put my hands on my hips. "What are you doing here?"

A cloud of purple mist swirls: transparent, then darkening, concealing the nightingale. As the mist dissipates, Damian materializes. He towers over me, his biceps stretching his black t-shirt. "Are you okay?" Damian asks. "I sensed something was wrong."

"It was just a bad dream," I say.

"I was worried," Damian says, his voice husky. When we did the spell to connect telepathically, I had no idea that he was engaged. After my mom chose to marry a human, our entire family was banished from Aurelia. Until a few months ago, I'd never even met his fiancé, my cousin, Caliah.

Damian lifts his hand. I don't jerk away fast enough. His fingers graze my cheek. It's the lightest touch, but enough to make my heart race. Knees wobbling, I rip my gaze away. I stare at the cracks on the floor.

I like to think that I'm strong, but everyone has their weakness. Damian is mine.

He reaches towards me again. I step aside, dodging his touch. "Damian, we can't…" I say.

"Zoe, I love you."

"Have you told Caliah that?" Two steps back is all it takes for my back to be against the wall. This cell is too small to keep my distance. "Have you told your parents?"

"Zoe, you know it isn't that simple."

Of course it's not. It's illegal for pure-blood witches like Damian to fraternize with half-breeds like me. If his parents found out about his feelings for me, he'd also be locked up in this dungeon. He'd never become king. Caliah and Damian would never reign, and Aurelia would never change. The corruption and bigotry would continue indefinitely.

Our love can never be.

"Can I please hold you?" Even in this frigid cell, Damian's voice sends heat through me. I look up, my cheeks flushed. It's a fatal mistake. His black eyes bore into mine, drawing me in. "Just for a little while," he says.

I stand stock still, drinking him in. He's tall and built, casting an enormous shadow in the moonlight. I study his angular jawline and masculine features. "Please," he says. I once found his huge black eyes intimidating. Now, they're wide, pleading. It's hard to believe that this hulk of a man is begging me to hold him.

My defenses crumble, scattering in shambles around me. I melt into his arms.

Chapter 2

Saria

I wrap the fluffy blanket tighter around me, grateful for Kian. As far as guards go, he's not too bad. I'm still freezing, but it helps.

A few feet away, Damian sits against the wall, Zoeli curled up in his lap. When she told me it would never happen again, I knew she was lying.

Even though I'm happy for my sister, I feel a pang of longing. I miss Logan. My heart aches when I think of him: his hazel eyes, goofy smile, the way his bulky glasses always slide down his nose. I wonder if he still thinks about me, or if he's moved on with someone new. I've lost track of time. Damian tells us that it's been four months, but it feels like I've been trapped in this hellhole for an eternity.

Although in some ways, I'm freer than I used to be. Not too long ago, I was living a fake life. After I ended a superficial relationship and cut ties with a phony friend, I told Logan that I had feelings for him. Things seemed better than ever before. That was before I was arrested and thrown in the witch slammer.

"Is there any chance that we'll ever get out of here?" I murmur.

"Your court dates are next week," Damian says. "And I'm doing everything I can to ensure a fair trial. I'm even helping my father select the jury. I pretended to be interested in how these things work…you know, for when I'm king."

In seven years, when Damian turns twenty-five, he'll take his father's place on the throne. Hopefully we don't have to wait until then to get out of here.

Zoeli runs her fingers along the concrete. "I wish my magic could make this whole place tumble to the ground."

Damian strokes her hair. "You'd have to be a goddess to have that kind of strength."

"Could a goddess really do that?" I ask.

"With one snap of her fingers." Damian snaps to emphasize his point. Since Zoeli and I weren't invited to attend Enchantments Academy, we lack basic knowledge about the supernatural world. Damian's visits often turn into impromptu history lessons. He doesn't seem to mind. I think he'd recite Aurelia's constitution if it meant he could be close to Zoeli.

"Can we ask a goddess for help?" It might be a stupid question, but it pops out of my mouth. "After all, aren't we their descendants?"

"Yes, but we're also descendants of demons, their arch enemy. They won't help us."

"Are any other super-naturals as powerful as the gods?" Zoeli asks.

"Some very, very old vampires may come close, but most of them were wiped out during the war. If Amos is still around, he's well over two thousand years old. It's possible that his power could rival a god's."

"Would he help us?" I ask.

Damian barks out a laugh. "Never ask a vampire for help. They're evil."

"All of them?" I ask.

"Some may put on a good show, but they're empty inside," Damian says. "They don't have the capacity for love or empathy."

"How do you know?" Zoe asks. "Have you met many vampires?"

"A few. After the Great Witch-Vampire War, we agreed to stay away from each other. Since I'm going to be king one day, sometimes my father takes me to meetings to show me how it's done. Once, he brought me to New York to meet with a vampire. Red owns a bar where they don't just serve drinks. The customers become the feast if you know what I mean."

I gasp. "He uses a bar to lure victims?"

"My father spoke to him about the carnage going on over there. He wasn't really worried about the humans lives as much as he was worried about rousing suspicions. If humans discover vampires, it won't be long before they discover us too. Even though we're more powerful than humans, they have nukes. They also outnumber us. Our kind has suffered enough in wars."

"What was he like? The vampire Red?" Zoe asks.

"Red's one of those charismatic types that'll have you fooled into thinking he's a decent guy. Of course, he denied all wrongdoings."

"How can you judge someone you barely know?" Zoeli pulls away from Damian, her eyes narrowed.

"Zoe, they're ruthless killers. They can't be trusted."

"A few months ago, you said the same about humans. You painted all humans to be violent witch-hunters."

"And what I said was wrong, Zoe, but this is different." Damian shakes his head. "Vampires don't need to murder humans to survive. They could feed from animals. They could even have a taste of human blood without killing them. Red and his crew drain humans dry because they like it. They get pleasure from taking lives."

I shudder. I'm not sure if it's from the cold or the conversation. Around the corner, a door slams shut. We all freeze. "Who's that? I set a sleep spell on the guards that should last–" Damian looks down at his watch. "Oh, shit. I lost track of time."

Footsteps pound against the concrete, coming closer. If they catch Damian inside our cell, he's screwed. He'll never see Zoe again. He could even go to prison. A flash of purple mist, and Damian is gone. Footsteps quicken, growing louder with each step. A nightingale darts across our cell and slips between the bars.

Tactical boots clack against the dungeon floor. Zoe is already in action, ripping the contraband comforter off of me. She piles it in the corner, covers it with a ratty prison blanket and sits on top. I plop down beside her.

Just as the guard approaches, the nightingale disappears inside the rolling dumpster. I hold my breath, hoping that Damian wasn't seen.

The guard leans forward, peering between the bars. His hooded gaze darts from me to Zoeli. "What's going on in there?"

Zoe raises her brows. "Just another lovely evening at the Nightingale Inn, sir." Her fingers lace through mine.

"I heard a male voice." The guard puts his hands on his hips. Across the hall, Helen stirs. I squeeze Zoe's hand, my heart lodging into my throat. Is Helen awake? The last time Damian put a sleep spell on her, she was groggy for days. Helen rolls over and snores. My breath releases, a white cloud blowing from my lips. It's so cold without Kian's blanket.

"There's no one here," Zoe says. "Just two filthy nimwits." Aurelians use nimwit as a slur for witches with human blood. Before I came to Aurelia, I thought nimwit was a silly word. That was before I heard the way they say it here: spit from their lips, dripping with hate and disgust.

"Hmmphh," the guard huffs. He turns around, his boots clacking on the concrete as he walks away.

I glance over at the dumpster and wrinkle my nose. "Poor Damian," I whisper.

"There's been a few times I wanted to toss his ass in a trash can." A smile touches Zoe's lips. "I guess karma handled that."

Chapter 3

Damian

This jury selection process is a joke. It takes everything in me not to slam my fist on the table. I refrain because they'll kick me out. My best chance of helping Zoe is to play it cool and hope they hear my suggestions.

My father, the king, sits at the head of the table, scanning a list of names. "We're settled on representatives from three royal families: Suzette Fox, Henry Hawke and Weston Lyon." I suppress a groan. Suzette is almost one-hundred years old and is conservative as they come. A known bigot, Henry isn't shy about expressing his disdain for humans. Weston is the best of the three, but that isn't saying much.

Only one year older than me, Weston has a reputation for having a chip on his shoulder. He claims that the election was rigged, and his family was gypped out of the throne. He isn't shy to declare that the Lyons would be better leaders. More than once, he and I have almost come to blows. If anything, he might take the Crowe's side just to defy the Nightingale regime.

The court magistrate and my father's closest advisor, Elric Hawke, nods. "These are excellent picks, and also great optics. We have diversity in gender, race, socioeconomics and age."

"But not thought," I mutter under my breath.

My father lifts his brows. "Excuse me, son?"

I stare into the face that is so much like my own and wonder how I ever justified his heartlessness. "I wouldn't want anyone to accuse you of being biased, that's all. I think we need a few members who lean on the progressive side."

"If I didn't know better, I'd think that you were trying to tip the scales in Zoeli's favor." My sister Fallon stares daggers at me across the table. I can read between the lines. She *does* know better. Not too long ago, she caught me and Zoeli making out under a waterfall. If I disrupt the jury selection process, she'll expose my secret.

"I heard rumors about you and the nimwit." Elric taps his skeletal fingers on the table. He studies me with beady black eyes. "Is there any truth to them?"

"No chance." I shake my head. "Mom asked me to watch over her. She was an assignment, that's all."

A long crease grows between his silver brows. Elric doesn't look convinced.

"I despise filthy nimwits as much as you do." I blurt out.

Elric runs manicured fingernails along his pointy chin. "Hmph," he says.

My father nods. "Now back to the selection."

* * *

A few hours later, I'm on a mossy rock, guzzling a beer. My cousin Colson tosses a rock on the pond. It skips across the surface, making the shape of the Nightingale crown. The five-pointed crown ripples and fades. Colson takes a swig of his beer. "What's the matter, man? You seem off."

I shrug and down the rest of my beer. I can't stop thinking about the jury selection. No one listened to a word I said. The panel who will determine Zoe's fate is composed of assholes, bigots and imbeciles.

"Is it that girl, man?" Colson's lips press into a line. "The nimwit."

I clench my fists. If Colson wasn't family, I would knock him the hell out. But he's more than my first cousin. Colson's like a brother to me. We've been best friends since the moment I was born. Literally, there's photos of two-year-old Colson holding me on his lap at the birthing center.

Besides, I understand why his perspective is skewed. It's what we were taught. Through both subliminal and overt messages, we learned the pecking order: royals, witches, duds and then humans. From an early age, it was drummed in our ears. We were told that half-breeds are an abomination and should be referred to as nimwits. Spitting at duds was a rite of passage.

It's fucked up. The most mind-boggling part is that when you're in it, you don't even recognize how fucked up it is. It seems normal. That's the scariest part.

"Don't call her that," I growl.

"That's what she is." Colson smirks.

"I have to go," I say. If I don't get out of here, I'm going to rearrange Colson's face.

"Dame, come back man. I was only joking around."

I move through the trees, kicking rocks, calves burning as I hike up the trail. As I make my way over the hill, Nightingale Palace rises above me in all its majestic glory. Stone walls curve around lush gardens. Crystal roofed turrets glisten in the cotton-candy sky.

Knights hold open the doors as I enter. A butler bows. "Your majesty, how may I be of service to you?"

"I'm okay." I move fast. The hallway is a blur of gold trim, crystal sconces and extravagant artwork.

On her hands and knees, a maid scrubs the marble floors. As I approach, she jumps to her feet and curtsies. "Good evening, your majesty."

I offer a curt nod as I pass. I'm not in the mood for pleasantries. I make my way up the winding staircase and into my suite. I toss my phone on my dresser and collapse in bed. Mind racing, I stare up at the gold tile ceiling. All I can think of is Zoeli. There must be a way to get her out of this mess. I take out a notebook with the intention to jot down ideas. An hour later, the page is still blank.

Someone knocks on my door. "Who's there?" I'm not in the mood for visitors. I frown as the door slides open. I didn't say to come in.

Caliah stands in the doorway. She looks like a runway model dressed in a matching set: a blue crop top and tight pants that accentuate her long, lithe figure.

She twirls a strawberry blonde curl around a French-tipped fingernail. "Hey, sorry for just showing up. I tried to text you." Her voice trails off.

My phone is still across the room, laying on my dresser. I haven't checked it in hours. The only person who matters doesn't need a phone to reach me.

"I missed you. I hope I'm not bothering you." Caliah's turquoise eyes are wide like saucers: sad and unsure.

I put my notebook aside, overcome by guilt. I haven't been good to Cali. "Sorry about that. I've just had a lot on my mind." We used to be close friends. When our engagement was arranged, I thought we would be more. I never expected to fall in love with Zoeli.

Caliah slides next to me. She fits perfectly in the crook of my arm, gazing up at me adoringly. She places one hand on my thigh and leans in for a kiss.

Her eyes are closed, but I keep mine open. Curly tendrils frame her heart-shaped face. Her full lips part, inching towards mine. She's gorgeous. Her lips brush mine. I pull back.

Her eyes fly open. "What's wrong?"

"I'm not feeling well," I lie. "I don't want to get you sick."

"I'm not worried about that." Caliah smiles. "If I get sick, it'll be worth it." She leans in again.

My heart pounds. How much longer can I keep up this charade? If I tell her about my feelings for Zoe, what will happen next? She'll be furious, that's for sure. Rightfully so. If she tells my parents, I'll be in huge trouble.

Worse, my father will make sure that I never see Zoe again. When my father wants someone to disappear, they tend to turn up dead, whether they're in prison or not. Zoe's death would be declared accidental or a suicide. I'd know better, but I'd never be able to prove it. My father's team covers their tracks well.

Her lips press against mine, but I'm frozen, like a statue. I turn away, her lips grazing my cheek. "What's the matter?" Caliah's eyes turn glassy.

"I'm sorry, Cali." I hate that I'm hurting her. I hate even more that I'm not going to stop. There isn't any other choice. At least, not until Zoeli's out of jail and I can keep her safe. "I'm not in the right head-space."

"What's on your mind?" Caliah asks.

"The Crowes' trials are next week," I say.

Cali nods. "I know you care about them." She stares at the mattress, pinching the silk sheets between her fingers. Caliah knows that I'm friends with Zoeli. I'm not sure if she suspects anything more. "They're my cousins. I care about them, too." She fails to mention that she only met them a few months ago. They barely know each other. Yet, her big turquoise eyes seem sincere. Hell, she probably does care about them. Caliah cares about everyone.

I'll never forget the first time I noticed Cali. In third grade, Hollie Reed was a bully. She pushed Darla Cook, a dud, into a ditch at recess. Our whole class laughed as Darla struggled to climb out, her hands and knees swallowed by muck.

Caliah elbowed her way through the crowd and leapt into the ditch. A moment later, she reappeared, arm around Darla, mud caked on her flower-print skirt. Hollie Reed waited at the top, her hands on her hips.

I stepped up, like I should've in the beginning. "Cut it out, Hollie," I said. "It isn't cool to be a bully." Even back then I knew my power. I'm the prince, the king's only son. If I told Hollie to stop, she would. Yet, Cali had more guts than me. She inspired me that day. Since then, she continues to impress me with her compassion and the way she always lends her hand to those in need.

"I sat in on jury selection." I tell Cali. "The Crowes don't stand a chance."

"Who's on the jury?"

I tick off the seven members representing the seven royal families. "Suzette Fox, Henry Hawke, Weston Lyon, Joslyn Wolfe, Liam Deere, Lorelai Crowe and Connor Nightingale."

"That's absurd!" Caliah folds her arms across her chest. "Who the heck is Lorelai Crowe?"

"Some ninety-year-old hag who's still furious at Zoe's mom for tarnishing the Crowe name. She doesn't even come from your bloodline of Crowes. She's sure to vote guilty." I say.

Cali paces the length of my bed, back and forth, fists balled at her side. "Is there anything we can do?"

I shake my head. "I tried."

Cali's cheeks are red, her jaw clenched. "When I'm queen, I'm going to dismantle this crooked court system. First of all, every citizen of Aurelia will be eligible to serve on the jury."

"Every citizen?" My brows knit together.

Cali puts her hands on her hips. "Why not?"

"Because…" I pause, thinking. "That's just not how things are done. Juries have always been made up of seven members, one representing each royal family."

"Just because something has always been done a certain way doesn't make it right. If you're a tax-paying citizen, you should have a say in our justice system."

My eyes widen as I consider what she's saying. "Every tax-paying citizen? Even the duds?"

"Yes," Cali says, her turquoise eyes meeting mine, daring me to challenge her. When she's all riled up like this, I have to admit that she's pretty damn sexy. Cali's passion for helping others is what drew me to her. The other girls I dated from school were self-absorbed and shallow. They liked me for all the wrong reasons: the power, status, riches, and opulent palace. Cali's something different. "Even the duds," she continues. "They're citizens and entitled to equal rights."

"Their lack of magic makes them susceptible to mind meddling. We couldn't trust them to serve on a jury."

"There are ways around that and you know it! They could wear mind-protection charms–"

"Those charms expire after a few days. What about trials that last for weeks?"

Caliah waves her arms wildly. "There's potions and spells and other safeguards we could put into place."

"You're talking about using a lot of money and resources," I point out.

"I never said that doing the right thing would be easy or cheap." Cali holds her chin up high. "What about those ruby-encrusted thrones your parents just had made?"

"What about them?" I ask.

"Do you think that they were a wise use of taxpayer dollars?"

I shrug. I know my father is a corrupt piece of shit. It still feels like a betrayal to say it out loud. "Not exactly."

"When I'm queen, taxpayer dollars will be used to help the people. I'll be just fine without a fancy chair. I'll sit on the floor if it means that everyone's treated fairly."

"You're good, Cali," I say. If I let her, she's the type of woman who could change me for the better. In almost every conversation we have, she helps me see the world through a new lens. "Deep down to your core, you're good."

She climbs back onto the bed and straddles me: her hips around my pelvis, her breasts dangling centimeters above my mouth. "Would you?"

"Would I what?" I ask. It's hard to think clearly right now. Against my will, my body is reacting to Cali's body on top of mine.

"Would you give up your ruby-encrusted throne for the betterment of your people?" Her breath tickles my neck.

"I'm not sure." I smirk to let her know that I'm teasing. Or am I? "You have to admit that I would look incredibly handsome on that thing."

"You sure would." Caliah leans forward, her breasts grazing my face, her manicured nails traveling down my chest.

"I'm pretty confident that the people would agree that such a sight is worth draining their wallets, wouldn't you say?" I ask.

Cali giggles. Her hand moves lower, grazing the inside of my belt. Her perfume is making me heady: spicy and sweet, cinnamon and vanilla. She slithers lower, looking up at me with a smoldering blue-green gaze. It's okay if I have a little bit of fun, right? Zoeli would never have to know…

Thinking of Zoe brings an unwanted image to mind. I imagine Zoe doing what I am now, her body pressed against another man's. Just the thought is like a wrecking ball to my heart.

I would kill him.

I snap back into reality. *What am I doing?* I push Cali away. I let things go too far.

"Damian?" Cali's voice trembles. "Did I do something wrong?"

A tear rolls down Cali's cheek. I'm such an asshole. "Cali…" My voice trails off. I want to tell her the truth. I really do. Maybe I should just get it over with. I take a deep breath, considering. Sure, she'll be pissed off, but she'll get over it. She won't do anything to hurt me or Zoe. Right?

"I love you," Caliah says. My heart drops into my stomach. If I confess, I won't only be breaking her heart. I'll be destroying her dream of becoming queen. I'm the heir to the throne, not Caliah.

I close my eyes and see Zoe's aquamarine ones. My mouth opens, then clamps shut. Even though I trust Cali, something tells me that I'm better off keeping this to myself. For now. After Zoeli is released from jail, I'll make this right. Somehow.

"I'm sorry," I say. I don't say the rest out loud. I'm sorry that I'm in love with someone else. I'm sorry that I'm leading you on. I'm sorry that your heart is collateral damage in this treacherous game.

"It's okay," Caliah says, wiping her eyes. "Do you want to hang out and watch a movie? I promise I'll keep my hands to myself." She giggles nervously, looking down at her wringing hands.

"Sure," I say. "Let's go downstairs to the theater room where we can watch it on the big screen." In a room with wide open doors, I add silently. The king, queen, princess or any number of castle staff could enter at any time. We'll have to behave.

"Sounds great." Cali's smile doesn't reach her eyes.

Chapter 4

Zoeli

Kian stares with his strange eyes. The faintest blue ring frames his black pupils. At first glance, it doesn't look like he has any irises at all. "Today's your court date," he says.

"I know." I stand, brushing off my new orange prison jumpsuit. Last night, Esther, the grouchy female prison guard, spent a whole ten minutes hosing us down with freezing cold water. She scowled the entire time, like it personally pained her to grant us the privilege of cleanliness. "Wash up, nimwits!" Esther barked. "It doesn't matter how hard you scrub. You'll never eliminate the foul stench of your human blood."

At least I'm relatively clean, and in a few minutes, I can walk out of this wretched cell. Granted, I'm going to a courtroom where I'm sure to be heckled, ridiculed and berated. Still, I'm happier than I've been in months. For a few hours, I can breathe air that isn't contaminated by mold. Hey, the bar is low around here. I'm even stupid enough to hold onto an iota of hope that maybe, just maybe, I'll be found not guilty and get to go home.

Kian raises his hand between the bars. "I'm so sorry, Zoeli." My jaw falls open as I notice the black object in his hand. He aims the gun at my chest, point blank range. "I'm just following the king's orders." He pulls the trigger.

It hits me in the heart. My legs collapse beneath me. The world fades into blackness.

* * *

I jolt up with a start and clench my chest. My skin and clothing are intact. There's no blood, no bullet wound. Did I have another bad dream?

I look up. Saria's gone. In her place, a television sits on a folding table. On the screen, people mill about the bustling courtroom, dressed in their finest suits. My lips part in awe. Even though Damian described the courtroom's opulence, he didn't do it justice (pun intended). He couldn't have. No existing words could illustrate the extravagance of this place.

Marble tiles glitter like they're speckled with diamonds. Jurors maneuver inside the mahogany jury box, settling onto blue velvet cushions of their throne-like chairs. On the front wall, thousands of sparkling gems create an enormous n above two massive thrones.

A man with long hair tied in a ponytail at the nape of his neck holds a microphone. A black suit and crisp white shirt cover his long, skinny frame. "Please be seated." Spectators scramble to find a seat on the exquisite mahogany benches. The wood is adorned with gold-filled depictions of the royal animals. The announcer smirks, relishing in his power. A few spectators slide over to allow Aunt Gwenna and Caliah to squeeze in by an intricately carved golden fox.

"As most of you know, I am Elric Hawke, court magistrate." Elric reminds me more of a snake than a hawk: beady eyes, lanky body, triangular-shaped face. A thick silver stripe contrasts with his otherwise black hair. "Today, we are very fortunate to have all members of the royal family in attendance. Everyone, please take a moment to welcome Princess Fallon." Elric stretches his elongated neck to peer over the crowd.

In the back of the courtroom, two fully-armored knights open the arched double-doors. Fallon struts in, clad in a blood-red sheath dress. She wears a sunburst-style crown: long golden spikes and marcasite jewels brush back her long black hair. The audience applauds, murmuring their approval. Fallon is drop-dead gorgeous.

"Prince Damian." Damian walks in. My man is devastatingly handsome in a tailored black suit. A simple gold crown sits atop his wavy black hair. As he passes, a few whistles break through the applause. Damian's lips curve into his trademark lopsided grin. My heart aches.

"Queen Taya." The queen steps inside: regal posture, chin lifted high. Two servants trail behind her, holding her tremendous blue velvet cape. A gold belt cinches the waist of her blue satin gown.

"All rise for King Keifer Nightingale." The magistrate raises his arms, and everyone stands up. The king enters, a white gloved hand holding an ornate golden scepter. Servants fuss around him, brushing his white fur cloak. On his head, his crown shimmers, encrusted with hundreds of diamonds.

At the front of the court, ruby-handled swords were welded together to create thrones for the king and queen. Beside them, the prince and princess settle onto smaller bejeweled thrones. Damian's throne glistens behind him: swirls of gold and blue crystals.

"Please be seated," the magistrate says. Three prisoners enter, shackled and flanked by guards. My heart skips a beat when I see my mom. I've missed her so much. Hunched over, her hip bones are visible beneath her orange prison garb. I wonder if she's been all alone. She must've gone crazy worrying about me and Saria.

The prisoners shuffle forward: Saria, Mom and a woman who I don't recognize. Iron rings hang from their necks. Chains crisscross their chests and clamp around their wrists and ankles. The guards prod them into wooden chairs and then hover behind them.

"Our first case today is Ms. Rosa Halliwell, charged with theft. I call the first witness, Lady Adelyn Nightingale, to the stand."

Nightingale? I reach out to Damian telepathically. Is she related to you?

A distant cousin. On the screen, Damian stares straight ahead, unblinking. No one would have a clue that he's communicating with me.

A middle-aged woman stands, brushing off her royal blue pencil skirt. I've noticed that the king's supporters wear blue to represent their solidarity. It's like a gang. Her patent leather heels click against the marble tiles. She slides into the witness stand, smoothing a few tendrils that escaped from her French twist.

"Lady Nightingale, I understand that Ms. Rosa Halliwell was an employee at your residence."

The witness nods. "Yes. She was my housekeeper for almost a year before I caught her in the act."

"How did you discover that she was stealing from you?"

"I trusted Rosa. Even when I felt sure that a few dollars were missing from my wallet, I chalked it up to a cashier miscalculating my change. When one of my precious rings disappeared, I figured that I must've misplaced it.

"When she asked for a raise, I became suspicious. The audacity! Rosa's a dud." Adelyn Nightingale chuckles, raising her white gloves to her lips. "She's lucky to be employed at all. What's wrong with this generation? Even duds feel entitled! As you can imagine, I was aghast by her ingratitude. I decided to set up security cameras and caught that dirty thief red-handed.

"When I showed Rosa my video evidence, she couldn't deny it. She claimed that she was planning to replace it when she could. She begged me not to turn her in."

"What did you do?"

"I called the police. Criminals deserve to be arrested and tried for their crimes. This is a civilized society, after all."

"Thank you for your testimony, Lady Nightingale." As Adelyn leaves the witness stand, the magistrate spins on his heel. "I call the defendant, Ms. Rosa Halliwell, to the stand."

Rosa inches forward, head low, chains dragging on the floor. A guard shoves her. She trips, falling onto the witness chair, smacking her chin into the microphone stand. As she rights herself, no one moves to help her. No one asks if she's okay.

This is going to be brutal.

When Damian told me how criminal court works in Aurelia, I was horrified. There are no defense attorneys. The magistrate, a direct employee of the king, runs the court. He calls the witnesses. He asks the questions. This is what they call a "fair trial."

"Ms. Halliwell, are you aware that you are being charged with multiple counts of theft?"

"Yes, sir." Rosa Halliwell doesn't look much older than me. One long light-brown braid drapes over her shoulder. Hands in her lap, she fidgets with the end of her braid.

"Are you aware that there is video footage that shows you stealing money from Lady Nightingale's purse?"

"Yes, sir, but–"

Elric holds up his hand: long, skeleton-like fingers inches from Rosa's face. "Ms. Halliwell, it was a yes or no question. I didn't ask you to elaborate." Elric leans on the witness stand, his fingers sliding along the beveled wood. "Ms. Halliwell, do you admit to stealing from Lady Nightingale?"

"Yes, but–"

"It was a yes or no question," Elric hisses. "I will not tolerate disrespect in this court." His silver brows lower over his beady eyes. "Especially not from a dud."

Rosa's mouth snaps shut. The slightest hint of blue glints in her eyes. It's so fast and faint that I wonder if I imagined it.

Elric stumbles like he was pushed. His long ponytail flails out behind him: a flare of black and silver. Crack! His nose slams into the floor. Blood puddles on the glossy white tiles, pooling in cracks between them.

King Keifer jolts to his feet. "Medic, now!"

A woman walks down the center aisle. A gauzy purple skirt billows around her legs. Her silver suitcase rolls on the tile. She kneels beside Elric, dozens of bangles sliding down her arm. They clink as she rubs circles on the back of his head.

That's Jaiyana. She's the most powerful healer in Aurelia.

Rosa did this. She knocked Elric down.

Impossible. She's a dud.

Elric's unnaturally still: arms sprawled out, legs bent at awkward angles. Jaiyana opens her suitcase, rummaging through a pile of rocks and potion bottles. She grabs two crystals, holding one in each palm. She rolls her hands above Elric, making figure eights.

His legs twitch. Elric pushes up, rising to his knees. Dark red blood is caked on his nose and chin.

"What happened to him?" The king asks.

Jaiyana tosses the crystals into her suitcase and stands. "Your majesty, I believe it was a magic attack."

"Who dared to assault my magistrate in my court?" King Keifer glares at the crowd.

"It was her!" A woman rises in the audience, pointing at the witness stand. Rosa shakes her head, cheeks red, eyes wide with terror.

"Don't be absurd. She's a dud." The king waves his arm, his fur cloak flailing open. "Whoever did this will be caught and prosecuted to the fullest extent of the law." He addresses Elric. "Are you ready to continue?"

"I just need a moment to clean myself up." Elric says.

"The court will take a short recess," King Keifer announces. "Then we'll resume with the scheduled trials."

My father's pissed off. This is very, very bad.

I haven't noticed anything different from his normal disposition. I wasn't aware that he has the capacity for other moods.

He's happy sometimes, usually when he gets his way. But it doesn't take much to piss him off. Once, the chef burned my father's breakfast. He sentenced a homeless woman to twenty-five years for shoplifting a sandwich.

I see. He has three moods: pissed off, very pissed off, and villainous gloating.

My mom usually keeps him in line, but she was out sick that day.

Now, Queen Taya whispers in the king's ear, her left hand on his forearm. On her ring finger, a huge diamond glistens. I still can't understand how she tolerates that monster.

My father loves my mom. As awful as he can be, he's good to her.

I didn't mean for Damian to hear that, but sometimes my thoughts slip through.

Taya's fingers lace through her husband's. As she talks, a strand of black hair falls over his eyes and one side of his mouth lifts into a lopsided smile.

I can't deny the uncanny resemblance between Damian and his father. My heart launches into my throat, constricting my airways. Am I seeing a glimpse of my own future? I know that Damian can be hot-headed and selfish. He's been indoctrinated in an ignorant ideology that he's working to unlearn, but he isn't like his father. Right?

Elric re-enters the courtroom, smoothing the lapels of his black suit. "I'm ready to continue, your majesty." The king calls for order. Rosa stares at her hands.

"Did you steal from Lady Nightingale more than once?" Elric hovers over the witness stand.

"Yes, sir–"

"How much did you steal in total?"

"Um." Rosa pauses. "I'm not sure."

"Approximately."

"Maybe around five thousand," Rosa mumbles. The crowd gasps. "I was going to return it when I could. I needed the money! My husband–"

"I have no further questions." Elric cuts her off.

That's it? I don't condone stealing, but context matters. I'd like to hear her side of the story. Elric turns to the jury. "At this time, members of the royal jury are invited to ask questions. Are there any questions at this time?"

I can hear my breath, rattling in my chest. The silence seems impossible. I have dozens of questions.

Finally, an old woman clears her throat. She looks like a witch from the movies: graying skin, hook nose, oversized chin. "Lorelai Crowe, do you have a question?" Elric lifts his silver brows.

She leans forward, gnarled fingers gripping the edge of the jury box. Her nose brushes the microphone. "I have a comment, sir." She wags a claw-like finger at Rosa. "If we don't stop them, duds like her will be the downfall of our society. Their jealousy provokes them to commit crimes against us. They have no place in Aurelia. They should all be imprisoned or banished to the human realm."

"Whoop! Whoop!" An audience member cheers, inciting a smattering of applause and hoots.

"Thank you for sharing your thoughts, Ms. Crowe." Elric nods. "Anyone else?" After a moment of silence, he turns around. "Very well."

"I have a question." A juror raises his hand. Wild dirty-blonde curls hide his forehead.

"Weston Lyon." Elric slithers around the jury box. "What is your question?" The last time I saw Weston Lyon he was covered in tawny-yellow fur. He pounced, golden mane blowing back, claws extended at Damian. I grimace at the memory. If I'd known what I was capable of at the time, he would've been lion meat.

"Ms. Halliwell." Weston's golden eyes turn to Rosa. "What did you do with the money?"

"My husband has a neurodegenerative disease. After his hands started shaking uncontrollably, he lost his job at the factory and his health coverage–"

"Answer the question, Ms. Halliwell." Elric interrupts. "We don't have all day."

"Lady Nightingale doesn't offer a health plan."

"Answer the question." Elric leans on the witness podium.

Rosa recoils. "My husband, Theo, needed a healer." Her voice cracks. "We have a two-year-old daughter and we can't afford–"

"Enough, Ms. Halliwell." Elric's fist flicks open, his open palm inches from her face. "Are there any further questions?" His snake-like gaze moves from juror to juror. Each one shakes their head.

"If I'm imprisoned, who will take care of my daughter?" Rosa's voice rises in a shrill crescendo. "When my husband gets sicker, he won't be able to work. My baby will be homeless on the streets. And if he dies–"

"Ms. Halliwell, if you continue this disruption I'll add contempt of court to your charges." Elric hisses. Elbows on the witness stand, he leans in close enough for Rosa to feel his breath.

King Keifer rises. "Let us take a half-hour recess while the jury deliberates. When the jury returns, we'll announce the verdict and move on to the Crowe trials."

Chapter 5

Saria

"The jury has reached a unanimous decision in the Halliwell case." Henry Hawke's putty-like nose looks like it was mashed onto his flat face. "Guilty." My heart drops.

There's a medley of whispers, hums, and a shriek "Justice has been served!" In the back row, a cherub-faced child leaps against the restraints of her father's arms. "Mama! Mama!" The father clutches her to his chest, his light-brown eyes rimmed with red.

The iron ring around my neck is agony. When I lift my head, pain radiates down my spine. I'll be lucky to make it through the day without a broken neck. I drop my gaze, but the little girl's tear-streaked face is emblazoned in my mind.

"The king and queen will determine Ms. Halliwell's punishment," Elric announces.

My neck throbs. Underneath my wrist shackles, my skin itches. King Keifer's voice booms into a microphone. "As my wife and I discussed this case, my compassionate queen reminded me to be sympathetic to the strife that Ms. Halliwell's family has endured. Rather than impose the maximum penalty of twenty years for stealing from a royal, Ms. Halliwell will serve five years in Nightingale dungeon."

Five years? That still seems harsh.

Queen Taya rises. "During Ms. Halliwell's prison term, medical care and healer expenses for Mr. Halliwell will be covered by the Nightingale reign."

"Thank you so much, Queen." Rosa's voice is thick with unshed tears.

"Take her to the dungeon." The king orders, his tone sharp.

Guards in tactical boots dart across the floor. A child wails. "Mama! I need you Mama!" The guards drag her mama across the court, their hands clenched around her upper arms. Angry red marks peek out from behind her iron shackles.

Arched doorways open wide. The guards shove Rosa to the other side. With a loud boom, the doors slam shut. "Mama!" The little girl cries.

Beside me, my own mother stares straight ahead, her lips a straight, determined line. She lost a ton of weight in prison. Collarbones poke out from beneath her prison jumpsuit. Yet, there's extraordinary strength in her green eyes.

"Next up, we have Alaina McKinney-Crowe, who's being charged with multiple counts of healing humans in the human realm. In addition, you're charged with multiple counts of using sorcery in the presence of humans." Elric announces.

Even though it must hurt like hell, Mom holds her chin high. I wish I had a tenth of her grit and courage. I still have so much to learn from her. Tears well up in my eyes. I need my Mama, too.

"I call the defendant, Ms. Alaina McKinney-Crowe, to the stand."

Mom trudges to the witness stand, chains sliding on the floor alongside her.

"Ms. Crowe, is it true that you used magical healing powers on humans while working as a nurse at Mountainside hospital?"

"In the ER, I'd often see victims of car wrecks. Many were young and healthy. Without my intervention–"

"It was a yes or no question, Ms. Crowe. Healing humans is illegal without prior authorization from the king. Did you receive the required authorization?"

"With all due respect, there wasn't time. In emergency medicine, every second counts. If I waited–"

"When I ask a yes or no question, I expect a yes or no answer. Do you understand, Ms. Crowe?"

Mom stares daggers at the magistrate, her eyes narrowed. There is a long pause before she opens her mouth to speak. "Yes, sir."

"As you know, these laws exist for a reason. Witch hunters are a real threat to our kind. In recent years, the number of witch hunters have grown exponentially. Some want to run experiments on us, but most just want us dead. By exposing your abilities to humans, you put all of us at risk."

"I put myself at risk. No one else."

"Witch hunters are ruthless. If you were captured, enduring days or months of agonizing torture, it's only a matter of time before you'd divulge identities and locations."

"I would not! Besides, I was careful. No one knew–"

"There are many reports of miraculous recoveries under your care, are there not?"

"Yes, but no one suspected–"

"Nonsense! If any witch hunters caught wind of this–"

Mom faces the jury, her eyes wide. "Without my help, they would've died! Some of my patients were children! As their parents and siblings wept at their bedside, how could I stand by and do nothing?"

"So you admit to valuing the lives of humans over protecting your own kind?"

"I didn't say that–"

"I can't say that I'm surprised. You're a human-lover, after all. Marrying and interbreeding with a human is the ultimate betrayal. Even after being punished, you continue to disrespect our laws and way of life."

"Loving my husband shouldn't be a crime."

"I have no further questions. You've admitted to your crimes." Elric faces the jury. "Do you have any questions at this time?" Every member of the jury shakes their head. "Excellent. We'll take a short recess while the jury deliberates."

Less than five minutes later, the jury reaches a verdict. When Henry Hawke clears his throat, his turkey neck jiggles. "Guilty."

My tears spill over. I can't hold back anymore. "Mommy!" I don't care that I sound like a baby. If I wasn't restricted by chains, I'd throw myself on the ground, kicking and screaming. I'm going to lose it. I think that I already have.

Queen Taya rises. Her bejeweled crown sparkles atop her wavy brown hair. "At this time, the Nightingales pardon Ms. Alaina McKinney-Crowe on all charges presented to this court today. Her previously enacted punishment, including the curse that prevents her from shifting and banishment to the human realm, will continue indefinitely."

A murmur worms through the crowd. A woman clutches her chest, like she might keel over from shock. Another stomps out of the courtroom, her face twisted up in disgust.

Elric scratches the sharp line of his chin. "Queen Taya, both the king and queen must be in agreement to grant a pardon."

"Yes, Mr. Hawke. I know the law."

"Your majesty, if Ms. McKinney-Crowe is released, she'll continue to act in ways that jeopardize the safety of our community."

King Keifer leans forward on his throne, stroking the golden nightingale on the tip of his scepter. "Mr. Hawke, in this courtroom, my wife and I make the decisions. Please see that Ms. McKinney-Crowe is escorted back to the human realm."

"Yes, your majesty."

As several silver-clad knights guide my mom out, tears flow down my cheeks like rivulets.

Taya is going to help us. We have a chance.

Chapter 6

Zoeli

My sister stammers one-word responses, her lip quivering. It's painful to watch. Saria used to sashay around town, her entourage parading behind her, like her shit didn't stink.

After I wiped out her magic, Saria's facade fell apart. Underneath, she was insecure and scared, but determined to rebuild herself from the ground up. She was still laying her foundation when we were thrown into the dungeon.

The first time a guard spit at us through the bars, I gave him the finger. Saria curled up in a ball and cried. Her groundwork crumbled. After four straight months of torture, her body and spirit broke.

"Is it true that you disclosed confidential information to a human by the name of Logan Archer?"

"Yes, but–"

Elric talks over Saria. "Is it true that you used magic in public spaces with humans present?"

"I -I was c-c-areful."

"It's a yes or no question." Elric leans on the witness stand and taps his foot.

Saria flinches, jerking back. "Y-yes."

Elric turns to face the jury. "By disclosing her identity to humans, Saria has compromised our secret and made us vulnerable to being discovered by witch hunters. If there aren't any questions, I'll excuse the jury to the deliberation room."

As Lorelai Crowe rises, she wags her corpse-like finger at Saria. "Deplorable. You and your human-lover mother have tarnished the Crowe name!"

In the blink of an eye, the jury returns with a guilty verdict. My stomach churns. I swallow to keep the bile from coming up.

Queen Taya is our only hope. She convinced her husband to pardon our mom, but I'd be a fool to believe that lightning could strike twice. The best we can hope for is a reasonable sentence.

Queen Taya stands, her blue velvet cape swinging behind her. "Given that Saria's magic has been stolen from her in its entirety, there is no longer any risk of her exposing our lifestyle to humans." Queen Taya clears her throat. "After careful consideration, the king and I have determined that Saria has already suffered the appropriate consequence of her crimes. Under the condition that Saria will remain powerless permanently, abolish her practice of witchcraft, and never speak a word about the witch community again, Saria may return to the human realm."

Elric's mouth opens and then snaps shut. He shakes his head, mumbling in gruff tones under his breath.

My twin smiles for the first time in months. Tears slide down my face. I want to lift her in the air, jump up and down, and scream with joy.

"Are you in agreement with our terms?" Taya asks.

"Y-yes, your majesty." Saria squeaks out the words. "Thank you, Queen Taya. I am grateful."

Taya nods. "Very well, then." She gestures to a guard. "See her out."

As the knights guide Saria toward the door, King Keifer raises his hand. "Saria." King Keifer's voice booms. My heart thumps. The knights turn Saria around to face the king. "If you violate any of our conditions, we won't be easy on you next time. Understood?"

"Yes, your majesty." Saria's voice quivers.

King Keifer points his golden scepter at the door. "Get her out of here. Fast. Before I change my mind." The knights thrust open the doors. Sunlight beams in, and then my sister is gone.

I throw my hands up in triumph. I thank Taya. I thank God. My mom is free. My sister is free. I pinch myself to make sure it's real.

"Next up, we have the trial for Zoeli McKinney-Crowe." My smile falters. Now it's my turn. Good things come in threes, right? Or was that bad things?

I love you. You got this.

I lift my chin, prepared for whatever is to come. I love you too.

My future queen.

My screen splits in two. On the left side, I still see the courtroom. On the other side, I see a live video image of myself. I gasp at my reflection. I look like hell ran over: ratty hair, dark bags beneath my eyes, acne-ridden skin. I can't believe that Damian kissed that.

You're beautiful.

You're delusional.

"For public safety, we had no choice but to conduct this trial virtually. Zoeli is ferocious, relentless, and unpredictable. In addition to stealing every ounce of her twin's power, she possesses a copious store of blue magic." In the audience, eyes widen.

What a crock of bullshit. I'm not a danger to anyone in that courtroom, and the magistrate knows it. The only threat would be to their egos if I managed to subdue them and escape.

"Ms. Crowe, do you understand the charges against you?"

I stare into the camera, careful to keep my voice steady. "Yes, sir."

"Did you perform an unauthorized evulsion on your twin sister, Saria?"

"Saria admitted to abusing her power. The queen seems to believe that my actions were warranted."

"That wasn't the question, Ms. Crowe. The law states that an evulsion must be pre-authorized by the king and queen. Were you granted prior permission?"

"Sir, I was banished from Aurelia at birth due to my perceived genetic deficiencies. I don't have access to any form of communication with the Aurelian government."

"Since you're incapable of answering a simple question, I'll answer it for you. Ms. Zoeli McKinney-Crowe performed an unauthorized evulsion."

I fold my arms across my chest. "The queen just stated that the evulsion was an appropriate punishment for Saria's crimes."

"That was not for you to determine."

"I'm simply quoting the queen, sir."

Elric's beady eyes narrow. "You've also been charged with multiple counts of bewitching humans and using sorcery in the presence of humans."

"I was never taught how to control it. If I'd been allowed to attend Enchantments Academy, I would've–"

"It's not our responsibility to educate nimwits."

"Sir, if educating us is such a burden, you have no right to punish us. Aurelia has agreed to stay out of vampire matters. Why don't you do the same for half-breeds?"

"Vampires are an entirely different entity. Your mother's a witch." Elric juts out his pointy chin.

"Either I'm one of you or I'm not. I've been excluded from your schools. I'm not permitted inside your country. I can't even date a witch. You only claim me when you want to use your laws to punish me."

When Elric turns to face the jury, his long black-and-silver ponytail slithers like a snake. He leans on the jury box, eye level with the jurors. "This witness has shown disdain for both Aurelian law and culture. Like most humans, Zoeli is deeply envious and harbors resentment towards our kind. Her jealousy, recklessness and store of blue power makes her a threat to our community."

"Bullshit!" No one hears me. They shut my microphone off.

"I have no further questions." Elric says.

I'm proud of you. You killed it, Zoe.

More like got myself killed.

I've never seen Elric without a comeback. You stumped him.

When all else fails, make the woman look jealous and unhinged. It's a tried-and-true strategy that the patriarchy has used throughout the ages.

Henry Hawke smooths his mustache, his putty-like nose leaning into the microphone. "I do not believe that we need to deliberate on this one. We, the jury, find Zoeli McKinney-Crowe guilty on all counts."

I hold my breath. Every juror nods in agreement. Queen Taya is my only hope.

King Keifer steps forward, the golden nightingale on his scepter wrapped tightly in his fist. His lips curve into an all-too-familiar half-smirk. Like father, like son. My heart lodges in my throat.

"Zoeli McKinney-Crowe." The king speaks slowly, relishing each word. "You are sentenced to twenty-five years in Nightingale Dungeon for your crimes."

Twenty-five years? In this hell-hole? I turn to Taya, praying that she'll object. The queen stares down at her hands, brown waves shrouding her face. She doesn't stand. She doesn't say a word.

I never really expected anyone to save me. That's fine. I'll rescue myself.

I throw blue power at the bars, at the stone walls, and the concrete floor. I imagine ripping this place to shreds, tearing every piece apart until it's nothing but a pile of rubble on the ground. Then, I'll rise up from the ashes.

I use so much force that I can actually see blue waves shooting from my hands, but nothing happens. The intact walls laugh at my futile efforts. Every facet of this dungeon has been embedded with katium, the mineral that's impenetrable to magic.

But I don't stop. Every ounce of rationality leaked out of my brain the moment I heard **twenty-five years**. I hurl magic at the bars: fingers stinging, sweat spilling down my back.

Zoe, stop. You're going to hurt yourself.

I can barely hear Damian's voice over the ringing in my ears. I collapse against the wall, sliding to the floor, my eyelids heavy.

I love you, Zoe.

You should move on, Damian. You deserve to be happy.

I'm happy with you.

How? I'm filthy. I stink. I'm a prisoner. Caliah is beautiful, kind and free. You can be with her outside of these wretched cell walls.

His silence has weight. I can feel it pressing down on me, hindering my airways. At that moment, I know that I didn't mean it. I want him to argue back. I want him to say that he doesn't want Caliah.

But no one in their right mind would wait **twenty-five** years. It wouldn't be fair of me to ask that of him.

I choose you. Dirty, soiled, and with a rotten stench. You. Only you.

I bark out a laugh. You're crazy.

Crazy enough to get you the hell out of there. It's my only mission. I won't stop until you're free.

But you can have anyone in the world. Anyone you want.

Oh, I know. Women fall at my feet regularly.

Ha! You'll never find me groveling on the ground.

It's only a matter of time. You'll fall so deeply in love with me that you won't even know which way is up.

You arrogant bastard.

I prefer your majesty, but that also has a ring to it.

It's getting harder and harder for me to keep my eyes open.

Get some rest, my love.

Exhaustion takes me.

Chapter 7

Damian

At the corner table in the back of Enchantment's Academy library, my phone vibrates. I check Colson's text message.

What are you up to tonight? Austin and I want to check out that new club. The old Damian would never pass up a night out with my two best friends. I definitely never turned down a party to hit the books. But… this isn't an ordinary study session.

I'm at the library. I have work to do.

Seriously?

Sorry man.

Loser.

I sigh and open a tattered old spell book. Dust tickles my nostrils. I sneeze, blowing my handwritten notes across the table.

"Damian?" A female voice says.

"Hey, Ms. A!" My favorite teacher, Ms. Apotheker walks in my direction, fringe dangling from her suede vest.

Brow furrowed, she checks her watch. "What are you doing here so late?"

"Studying," I say. Ms. A raises one eyebrow, as if to say that she doesn't believe me. I can't say that I blame her. Come on, who wants to spend their weekends memorizing potion recipes?

Even though I can't remember the chemical composition of katium if my life depended on it, my report cards boast straight As. After all, I'm the prince of Aurelia. When I finish high school, I'm all but guaranteed admission to Enchantments University, our own version of an Ivy League institution. Even if I jerk off all day, I'll graduate with a 4.0.

Is the system corrupt? Yes, but since I'm the one benefitting from it, I haven't put up a fuss. If Zoe knew, she'd rip me a new one. She's into integrity and fairness and all that. It's something I admire most about her– Caliah, too. I'm still a work in progress. They're both better than me.

Ms. Apotheker peers over the pile of books. "What is it that you're, er," Ms. A lifts one corner of her mouth. "Studying?"

"I was looking into, um," I pause. Ms. A's my favorite teacher. She's also one of my mom's closest friends. I trusted her enough to ask her to help Zoeli learn to control her powers. But this is different. What I'm plotting now is so criminally egregious that I'm not sure if she'll back me. "Reversing spells," I say, trying to keep my tone as casual as possible.

"Reversing spells," Ms. A repeats, sliding into the chair next to me. "What class is that for?"

I can't lie. Ms. A knows the curriculum like the back of her cauldron. "It's a personal project."

"Hmmm," Ms. A pauses for a moment, considering, and then raises her shoulders in a half-shrug. "What do you want to know?"

Score! "I understand that in order to reverse magic the entire spell must be conducted backwards."

"That's correct," Ms. A says. "It's very difficult to accomplish. Every action conducted in reverse undoes each original action. It must be precise: every word, ingredient, stir, and pour must be as if someone pressed rewind on a motion picture. What spell did you cast that you'd like to undo?"

"I didn't exactly cast it." My voice trails off.

"I see." Ms. A rests her chin on her palm. She studies me with intense blue eyes, her brows lifted. Deep creases mar her forehead. "Reversing magic done by an unrelated witch is theoretically possible. It's been done a handful of times, if you believe the tales. Some believe it's never happened at all."

"What about related witches? I read that it's possible to reverse spells cast by direct family members."

Ms. A nods slowly. "I see you've been doing your research. The closer the genetic ties, the more likely the reversal is to work. There are, of course, moral, ethical and legal considerations. Reversing magic without the spellcaster's permission or the king's order is against Aurelian law." She sighs. "What has Fallon done this time? Rather than getting yourself in trouble, talk to your mom. Taya can usually talk some sense into that reckless girl."

Of course, Ms. A would assume this has something to do with Fallon. No one would ever imagine what I'm really up to. It's crazy. It's absurd. "This isn't about Fallon," I say.

Ms. A leans back in her chair. "What's going on, Damian?"

"Don't worry about it. I'll figure it out."

She crosses her arms across her chest. "Let me level with you. If you get caught attempting to reverse spells, you'll be in deep shit. I know you're the prince and all, but you don't have the right to mess with other witches' magic."

"What if that magic is causing harm to someone you care about?"

Ms. A fiddles with her crystal bracelet. "Damian, what are we talking about here? Spells heal, protect, and bless others. Certain spells can make objects fly, impact the weather, or even make things invisible, but let's be clear about one thing, spells do *not* cause harm. If someone is using magic to hurt or punish, that is a curse, otherwise known as a hex."

I shrug. "If you want to be technical."

"This is more than a technicality. First of all, the process to undo a curse is very different from reversing a spell. More importantly, witches cannot hex someone without the king and queen's approval. If someone is going around hexing others, the court needs to be notified immediately. They should be arrested and tried for their crimes."

I look down at the page in front of me. Ms. A will never approve of my plan. I'll have to figure out how to undo a curse on my own.

"Damian, this is a serious matter. The king needs to know. He will take care of it."

"He knows," I say, keeping my eyes down. I flip the page. "And he isn't going to do a damn thing about it."

"Your father knows." Ms. A repeats, her brow creased. "Are you sure about that?"

I guffaw. Leaning back in my chair, I meet her eyes. "He's the one who did it." I shouldn't have blurted it out, but it's too late now.

Ms. A's mouth falls open and then snaps shut. Her eyes are wide like saucers as realization dawns in them. "Damian, you can't." Her voice trails off.

I look back down at the book, my mouth a firm line of determination.

"It's impossible," she says, shaking her head.

I turn the page. I'm crazy enough to get it done. Someway, somehow.

Ms. A shuffles through the piles of books until she finds the right one. She grabs it and flicks through the pages. "Magic doesn't like to be used for evil. Benevolent spells last long-term, sometimes indefinitely. On the other hand, curses used to burn out fast. The universe recognizes negative energy and snuffs it out." Ms. A slides an open book in front of me. In pictures, several sorcerers surround a cauldron. One sprinkles ingredients in the steaming pot. Another stirs. "Then, our ancestors discovered how to create a lasting curse." Ms. Apotheker points to another picture. A witch pours liquid from the cauldron into a small red bottle. "By sealing the potion inside a bottle made from demonite, the curse is preserved."

I nod. I remember learning about this in class, but a little refresher doesn't hurt. For once, I wish I paid less attention to girls and more to my studies.

"While the potion is inside the bottle, it's stabilized." Ms. Apotheker continues. "To break the curse, you must break the bottle." She flips the page to a picture of an enormous vault. "All government-ordered curses are kept inside the Capital Vault. It's secured by eighteen-inches of steel, massive locks, and ten skilled guards ordered to protect the vault at all costs. They have permission to use magic to maim and kill." She points to another picture. Small red bottles line metal shelves. Hieroglyphic-like codes mark each curse. "Inside the Capital Vault, the names on each bottle are encrypted. Even if you somehow managed to make it past all the layers of security and break a bottle, you'd have no idea if you were freeing the Crowes or allowing a serial rapist to use his dick again." Ms. A folds her hands together. "Sorry to be crass, but that is the reality of it."

I sigh. It does seem useless, but I refuse to give up. This is for Zoeli. I have to try. "Isn't it possible to undo a curse in the same fashion as reversing a spell? By doing every step backwards."

"It has been done." Ms. A admits. "But the odds are dismal. Out of thousands of attempts, there's been a few reported successes." She drums her fingers on the table. "It must be precise. Your power must be equivalent to or greater than the power of the witches who cast the original hex." Ms. A shakes her head. "Curses ordered by the king are completed by seven sorcerers, one from each royal family. While you may be an immediate relative of one participant, you're not related to any of the others. Besides, your power can't compete with the power of seven."

"Says who?" I joke, curling up one side of my mouth.

Ms. A playfully hits me on the back of the head. "While there are limits to your power, there's no limits to your conceit."

"What if I got six others to join me?" I ask, lowering my voice. "Six witches from the right bloodlines, one from each royal family."

Ms. A bursts into laughter. Her smile falls when she sees my expression: stone-cold serious. "You've got to be kidding me."

"The other option is trying to break into the vault. Out of the two, this one is less likely to get me or anyone else killed."

"Where do you think you'll find six royals willing to participate in this insanity?"

I shrug. "I have a lot of friends."

"Friends who are willing to break the law? Defy the king? Risk their own freedom?"

"For me?" I flash my best dazzling smile. "Don't underestimate my charm."

Ms. A shakes her head. "Be careful."

"Don't worry about me, Ms. A." I sound more confident than I feel. If I tell the wrong person, I could get thrown in jail. A lump of doubt crawls up my throat. Can I really pull this off? In my mind's eye, I see Zoeli curled up on the dungeon floor. Even freezing and hungry, blue flames flicker in her aquamarine eyes. How much more can she take? She's the toughest person I've ever met. Maybe even tougher than me, although you won't catch me admitting that out loud. But she isn't invincible. Eventually the isolation and abuse will wear her down. I won't stand by and watch her fire burn out. Damn it all. If I have to risk everything, that's what I'll do.

Ms. A rifles through a stack of books, reading each title and then tossing a few aside. She holds up a black leather book. Gold Letters across the front read, Curses and Punishment. She flips the book open to the table of contents. Her finger slides down the page. She stops halfway down. "This is it. Chapter twenty-three." Her finger underlines the chapter's title,

Cursing the Shapeshifter: How to Deny their Right to Shift. I skip to page 407, ignoring the earlier chapters that cover warnings and ethical considerations.

"There's several curses in this chapter." I guess I'll have to try them all, one by one. This could take a long time, maybe years, considering that many require a particular phase of the moon, constellation present in the sky, or alignment of a planet.

Ms. A bites her lip, reads and then turns the page. "A colleague of mine was there when the curse was done. Afterwards, we discussed it." She flips the page, her gaze darting from line to line. "This is the one." She taps page 413.

"Thank you." I tuck the book inside my backpack. I'll study it later. All night, until I have every nuance memorized. "Do you think it'll work?"

"Nope." Ms. A shakes her head.

"Then why did you tell me?"

"Because I know you. No matter what I say, you're going to try. You're headstrong, cocky, and overconfident to the degree of stupidity. I'm sparing you from wasting a ton of time."

I lift one eyebrow. "Your doubt only drives my determination."

Ms. A throws her hands in the air. "You don't have the potion bottle. You're counting on six friends, likely high school students, to execute a complicated procedure *backwards*. Even if every one of you managed to pull it off, you'd have to collectively be as or more powerful than the original spellcasters to undo their actions." Ms. A stands and adjusts her crochet purse strap over her shoulder. "You're more likely to get struck by lightning."

I grin. "So you're telling me there's a chance."

"Maybe one in a billion."

"Then I'll be the one." Statistics won't deter me. I was never a fan of math. I'll get this done. For Zoeli, I'll do whatever it takes.

Ms. A sighs. "Let's go. The library's closing up." I follow my teacher down the hallway, our footsteps echoing through the archways. "I could get in a lot of trouble for not reporting you." She takes a deep breath. "I could get in even more trouble for helping you."

"It looks like I'll be getting straight As this semester," I joke.

Ms. A slaps me on the back, but she's laughing. We trust each other. That's more than I can say for any of my family members. Even my mom.

We push through the exit. Outside, on the glittering sidewalk, a gust of cold wind smacks me in the face. "Goodnight, Damian." Ms. A crosses the parking lot. Her car's tail lights disappear down the hill.

On the front steps of my school, I scroll through my phone's contacts. I stare at the name, my fingers hovering over the call button.

Caliah Crowe. Cali. We've been friends since childhood. When I close my eyes, I'm transported to a simpler time, when Cali's pigtails bobbed as we raced across the monkey bars. In the summers, we'd fly, side by side, me as a nightingale, Cali as a crow, up and over the mountains. At the enchanted lake, we'd return to our human forms, using rocks as waterslides.

In seventh grade, when Cali's dad passed away, she cried in my arms. By this time, she wasn't a little girl with pigtails anymore. I'd watched in awe as she grew into a beautiful young woman: strong yet delicate, tenacious but sweet. I couldn't deny that I had a crush. When she lifted her head from my shoulder, her black lashes wet, tears flooding her turquoise eyes, it took everything in me not to kiss her right then and there.

Back then, I thought a romance between us could never be. Fooling around would only jeopardize our friendship and make things awkward when we inevitably dated others.

Little did I know that a few years later, genetic testing would prove it was possible to intermix species, at least in our case. When we found out, Cali skipped into my arms, strawberry-blonde curls bouncing. Her breath tickled my ear when she whispered, "I love you."

I didn't have the heart to tell her that I'd fallen in love with someone else.

I've already betrayed Cali in so many ways. She believes that I intend to marry her. I let her kiss me, hold my hand and sit on my lap. We haven't had sex. I intend to keep it that way, even though it's getting harder and harder (pun intended) to thwart her advances.

Now I'm going to ask her to break the law. I have no doubt that she'll do it for me. She'll risk decades in jail and a lifetime of public scorn. For me.

Cali will put her own ass on the line, thinking that Zoeli and I are just good friends.

And if it works, I'll leave her for Zoeli.

It isn't fair.

It isn't right.

But it has to be done.

I press the call button. Cali answers on the first ring.
"Hello, handsome." I hear the smile in her voice.
"Hey." I take a deep breath. "Cali, I need your help."
"Of course. You name it. Anything, my love."

Chapter 8

Saria

Curled up in Logan's arms, a soft blanket wrapped around us like a cocoon, I can almost pretend that the past four months weren't real. Every part of us is intertwined: our legs twisted together, his fingers tangled in my hair. We breathe in unison, our bellies touching with each exhale. He caresses my bare back, sending shivers down my spine.

For a few moments, I'm not haunted by images of dank stone walls, seeming to close in on me. Memories taunt me: guards gawking from the other side of the bars, like I'm some kind of mutant. Some spit at me. My skin crawls as I remember wiping gobs of saliva off my filth-strewn face.

Here, shrouded in Logan's peace and love, it seems impossible that a place so full of evil and hate exists.

Zoe's still there.

Thoughts of my twin keep me awake every night. My soul's ripped in two. What if I never see her again? I know that I couldn't survive a quarter-century in that hell-hole. Even if she lives, she'll be traumatized beyond recognition. *I have to save her.* But how?

"Where were you?" Logan asks.

"I already told you." I close my eyes and recite the cover story created by the Nightingale's. "My parents were having marital issues. Me, Mom and Zoe took off and stayed at a hotel. After a few months, Mom and Dad talked on the phone and worked things out. We packed our bags to come back, but Zoe ran away. We don't know where she is." I open my eyes.

Logan's brows move together. "I know that's what you said, but I want to know the truth."

My mouth opens and closes. Nothing comes out. I can never tell Logan the truth. He already knows too much. Logan's hazel eyes darken. "Someone hurt you."

I shake my head, lowering my gaze. In my mind's eye, a flash of memory. The guards' rough hands shove me into the cell and kick me to the ground. Hours later, tender bruises and purple handprints were strewn all over my body.

And Zoeli's still there. Still enduring the abuse. Tears well in my eyes.

"I'm sorry," Logan says. "I don't mean to press you." His lips are soft against my cheek, kissing me again and again, moving over to my earlobe, and then my neck. Tingles zig-zag down my spine. "There wasn't a moment that I didn't think of you. I never stopped searching for you. I hiked every trail in this town: waded through streams, climbed under bridges and peeked inside caves. I found a few bear dens."

"That sounds dangerous."

"I didn't care. All that mattered was finding you. I barely slept. All night, I tossed and turned, thinking of more places to look. Every weekend, I organized search parties. You have no idea how many people care about you. Hundreds of people showed up. Even Chad and Mallory came out."

I grimace at their names. Not too long ago, I considered Mallory a friend. That was before she hooked up with Chad, my boyfriend at the time. "How are they?"

"They broke up," Logan says. "Chad seemed pretty shaken up when you went missing. I think he still has feelings for you."

I shrug.

"Should I be worried?" Logan asks.

I can't help but laugh. "Are you joking?"

"Well, not really." Logan's shoulders tense up. "Chad is an athlete, popular and jacked, and I'm, well…" He stares down at his lanky frame.

"Perfect," I finish for him. "You're thoughtful, generous and humble. I don't care if Chad can bench press more than you, you're more of a man than he'll ever be." I run my fingers through his sandy-blonde waves. "You are my best friend. You make me laugh. You are everything I need." I press my lips against his.

"I love you, Saria."

"I love you." On his nightstand, my phone buzzes. "That's probably my mom. I promised I'd be home for dinner." I glance at the clock. It's almost seven pm. I hadn't even noticed as the hours slipped away. I grab my phone and press the green button.

"Saria!" Mom sounds frantic. "Are you okay?" She wasn't always like this. I used to be able to be five minutes late without Mom having a meltdown. After all that's happened, I guess I can't blame her.

"I'm fine, Mom. I'm with Logan. I just lost track of time." I unravel myself from Logan's embrace and pull my sundress over my head. "I'm leaving now."

"Drive safe," she says. "And stay vigilant. Pay attention to who's around you."

She doesn't say their names, but I know who she means. Talon, Licinia and their militia are still a threat. No one knows their next move, or if we're a target. In some ways, we were safer locked in the dungeon.

"I'll be home in a few minutes."

Logan shrugs on his shirt. "I can't believe tomorrow's the first day of school."

"I can't either. I missed the whole summer."

"Your birthday's Friday." Logan holds my hand as we leave his room and head downstairs. "I was thinking I could take you out for a nice dinner and–"

"I don't want to do anything," I say. It's not only my birthday. It's Zoe's birthday, too. If she can't celebrate, neither will I.

My mom's sedan is parked on Logan's driveway. Since we came home, I've been borrowing it more often. Mom quit her job at the hospital and hasn't been driving much.

I lean against the driver's side door. "Do you need a ride to school?" Logan asks.

"Me, Keisha and Penny are riding with Giselle. After she was voted the softball team's MVP, her mom bought her a new Mercedes."

"I'm sure that you leaving the team had a lot to do with that."

"Giselle deserves it. She worked hard for it." Unlike me. I used magic to enhance my performance. "But I wish my mom would buy me a Mercedes." I joke. "She told me to get a job."

Logan pulls me in. As we kiss, he lifts me by my hips, pressing my back against the car. I wrap my legs around his waist. Our kiss deepens, tongues twirling, heat rushing through my veins.

As much as I don't want to stop, I have to go. "I'll see you tomorrow," I say. I open the car door and slide inside. Even though I've been to Logan's house thousands of times, I almost never drive here. Usually, I hike through the woods that connect our backyards, climbing over boulders and ducking under tree limbs. That doesn't feel safe anymore.

I pull out of the driveway. In the distance, a glowing orange sun descends, half-hidden by the labyrinth of mountains and trees.

In my rear-view mirror, I see Logan at the end of his driveway, hands in his pockets, watching me go. As the distance between us grows, he shrinks into a blurry black dot, and then he's gone.

My hands are white, clutching the steering wheel. My heart races. I'm okay, I remind myself. I'm only a mile from home.

PTSD is a bitch.

A cloud drifts over the sun. Darkness flickers in the orange-streaked sky. I suck in air, my chest rattling as I hyperventilate. *Calm down.* I focus on my breath, counting each inhale and exhale, slow and steady. I might throw up. I just have to make it home.

Headlights shine in my rear-view mirror. Am I being followed? The car moves close to mine: too close. The glare of headlights prevents me from seeing who's behind the wheel. In a panic, I turn right, even though it's not the way to my house.

The car turns too, its headlights on my tail. They're following me. My heart races. It lodges in my throat, constricting my airways. I hit the gas.

A green street sign appears on my left. My wheels screech as I turn again.

Behind me, it's dark. Then, headlights reappear. No, no, no…

I speed down the residential street; houses blur on either side of me. I turn left, left, right, and left. I have no idea where I'm going. All I know is that I have to lose them.

I taste rubber, toxic fumes soaked up by my tongue. Cold sweat drips down my back. I jerk to the left, another wild turn. I slam the pedal to the floor.

The headlights are gone. I'm not sure when or where I got away.

Panting behind the wheel, I feel more like a petrified animal than a human being. Am I losing my mind?

I lift my foot from the pedal. I'm lucky I didn't crash. I could've killed someone. My arms and legs shake uncontrollably. I roll to a stop, pulling over to the side of the road.

Was I really being followed? Am I just paranoid?

I take deep breaths, filling my belly up with air, until my heart slows down. Where am I? I made so many turns. I drove so fast. I have no idea where I ended up.

Across the street, rose bushes bloom outside a ranch-style home. I recognize the blue siding, white shutters and bird house dangling above the front porch. I'm outside Mallory's house.

The front door opens and a girl steps out. In the shadows, I can't make out who it is. Curly dark hair falls past her shoulders. A form-fitting shirt accentuates her toned body.

The girl strolls to the sidewalk. A street light illuminates her brown skin. I take in her familiar face: big brown eyes and high cheekbones. My jaw falls open.

When Mallory went behind my back with Chad, Keisha was furious at her. Keisha said that their friendship was over. Why was she at her house?

I duck as Keisha passes, careful to not be seen. Tears well in my eyes. It sucked losing Mallory as a friend, but this hurts so much more.

Maybe I didn't expect Mallory to hook up with my boyfriend, but I knew Mallory was a catty, jealous person.

On the other hand, I trusted Keisha. She's always been real with me. She never refrained from telling me the harsh truth when I needed to hear it. She's always had my best interest at heart.

I'm overthinking it. Last week Keisha threw me a welcome home party. When I opened her front door, balloons were floating everywhere. She launched herself at me and wrapped me in a hug so tight that I thought she might break my back.

Maybe she was trying to hurt me.

No, I'm being paranoid again.

There has to be a good explanation for why Keisha was at Mallory's house. She'll tell me all about it tomorrow. Right?

In my hand, my phone rings. Startled, I jump. It slips between my fingers, tumbling onto the floor mat.

I'm a mess. I need to pull myself together. I pick up the phone.

"Saria! Where are you? Is everything okay?"

"Sorry, Mom," I say. "I'll be home in five minutes." I put the car in drive, trying to drown out the screams in my brain warning me that something isn't right.

Chapter 9

Saria

Honk! Honk! Oh, crap. Giselle's here. I race down the steps, zooming past Dad and into the kitchen. I throw a banana in my backpack. I'll have to eat on the go. I don't want to be late on the first day.

When I turn to leave, I notice Mom sitting at the table. She stares vacantly into space. "Mom, are you okay?" It's a stupid question. Of course she isn't okay. Her daughter's a prisoner.

If everything was okay, Zoe would be rushing to school, breathlessly sliding into her seat as the bell rings. Her biggest concern would be practicing for her next show. I had the pleasure of seeing my sister's band, The Exiled Crows, perform. Hours later, we were thrown behind bars.

Mom doesn't respond. Her eyes are open, but I don't think she sees me. Her lip quivers. "Mom, I love you." I put my hand on her shoulder. She's more bone than flesh. I kiss her cheek and taste salt.

I remember when I was a kid, I'd curl up in her arms and she'd promise me that everything was going to be okay. Now I want to do the same for her.

"See you later." Guilt rises like bile in my throat. I can't leave her like this. I stand in the doorway, watching her, feeling helpless.

"Go ahead, Saria." Dad says. "I'm working from home today."

"You've been working from home for weeks." Mom already quit her job. If Dad loses his, we'll be in big trouble.

"Don't worry," Dad waves his hand. "My boss understands. I have all the equipment that I need here in my home office." He pulls an oversized watch out of his pocket. "I want you to wear this."

"Um, I already have a watch." I hold up my wrist, showcasing my dainty gold watch. Tiny diamonds surround its oval face. On the contrary, my dad's gadget is enormous: thick black band, a plastic screen that's twice the size of a smartwatch. It's definitely not my style.

"It's an enertron, not a watch. It detects supernatural activity. I've been working on it for a while now. The technology isn't perfect yet, but I hope that it will help keep you safe."

"Wow." Even though I know that my dad has a really cool career: helping create technology for various purposes from night vision to self-driving cars, I had no idea that he could develop this. I secure the clunky device on my wrist. It weighs a ton, and it doesn't go with my outfit. That's a small price to pay if it saves my life. "Thank you." Maybe it will help with my paranoia, too.

The screen lights up. A green number appears on the screen: 172. "The enertron detects magic on a scale from zero to one-thousand. I've discovered that almost everything creates some supernatural energy, even people and objects thought to be non-magical. You'll probably never see a reading below one-hundred. Right now, it's picking up on waves of energy from me, you, and your mom…" Dad glances through the archway into the kitchen. Mom doesn't look like she has any energy at all. Head in her hands, she's slumped over the kitchen table. In another life, Mom would twirl around that same table, pouring coffee and serving pancakes as Zoe practiced guitar.

"I lost track of what I was saying." Dad rubs his temples. "Oh yes, the readings. Up to 300, I call the safe zone. From 301-500 is called mild risk: there may be a witch or two nearby. 501-750 identifies moderate danger: at least three supernatural beings are in the vicinity. Over 750 is classified as severe danger. This reading suggests that a group of active super-naturals are close."

Honk! Honk! "Thanks, Dad. I gotta go." I pull on my denim jacket, concealing my dad's invention, and dart out the front door. The slap of the screen door shutting rises over the purr of Giselle's silver Mercedes. Keisha smiles and waves from the passenger seat.

I slide into the back seat beside Penny. My redheaded friend throws her arms around me. "We're so happy you're here." She squeezes me tight.

Beep! Beep! Beep! It takes a moment for me to realize that the alarm is sounding from my wrist. I fold up my jacket's sleeve and peek underneath. Numbers flash on the screen: 114,

1533, 666, 1800. The number vanishes, replaced by a word: ERROR, ERROR, ERROR

Penny's hazel eyes widen. "What's that?"

Keisha spins around in her seat, her forehead creasing as she studies the device on my wrist.

Giselle reaches through her curly brown hair to plug her ears. "Can you shut that thing off?"

Can I? Flustered, I press a button on the side of the device. A moment later, the screen turns black. "Sorry," I murmur. "It's just an alarm to remind me to, um, take my vitamins." I reach into my backpack, pull out a tablet, and pop it into my mouth.

Giselle puts her car in drive, seeming satisfied by my lame cover story. We roll down my long, winding driveway.

My parents built our house out of sight: on top of a hill in the middle of the woods. The bulwark of trees shields us from being seen while performing witchcraft.

Canopies of branches and leaves shroud the narrow trail. Giselle's car propels beneath the shadows. Is someone hiding in the woods? The isolation meant to protect us may become our greatest threat.

I need to warn my parents. I pull out my phone and text Dad. *Be careful. As soon as I went outside, the enertron went crazy. Now it says error? I'm worried that someone's on our property.*

Penny sits a little too close. When I face her, her gaze darts the other way. Was she spying on my text message?

No, of course not. It's just my paranoia rearing its ugly head again.

"Your car's amazing, Giselle," I say, running my fingers over the black leather seats. As my friends gush over her new wheels, another thought occurs to me. What if the supernatural presence isn't outside…but in here?

I stare at Giselle: her big brown eyes, straight white teeth, and supermodel smile. If she had supernatural abilities, wouldn't she use them during softball? I saw how much it tore her up when I outperformed her. If she had magic capabilities, she surely would've used them, right?

My gaze flutters to Keisha: her melanin-rich skin and long black eyelashes. My besties are both beautiful, alluring and magnetic, but not witches… right?

I shake my head. I've known Giselle and Keisha since we were in diapers. A montage of memories flash through my mind as I search for the slightest sign: any indication of supernatural phenomena.

My mind wanders back to preschool, the three of us climbing to the top of the jungle gym. Keisha teetered on a narrow beam, lost her balance and fell. In the ER, my mom wrapped her wrist. Mom winked at me, a little secret between the two of us. Keisha's fracture healed in unprecedented time.

In seventh grade, the year that Penny moved to town, Tommy Jenner turned down Giselle's invite to the dance. As Giselle wept, Keisha and I made other plans. We all blew off the dance in favor of a girl's night. Giselle, Zoe, Penny, Keisha, and I danced in my living room. We poorly executed choreography, tumbling over each other, a heap of girls rolling with laughter.

"Saria! Earth to Saria!" Giselle snaps her fingers in front of my face. I blink. We're parked outside Mountainside High School.

"Sorry," I mumble. "I have a lot on my mind."

My phone buzzes in my hand. I open the text message from Dad. *Everything seems okay around here. I'll check out the enertron when you get home.*

I suck in a deep breath that rattles in my core. It's just a malfunctioning device. My parents are safe. I'm with my friends. Nothing bad is going to happen. The words echo in my mind: tinny and hollow like empty lies.

The back door opens. I jump in my seat. In the parking lot, Keisha's hand flies to her mouth. "Oh, Saria, I'm so sorry. I didn't mean to scare you." She helps me out of the car and links her arm through mine.

Giselle takes my other arm. "We know that you've been through a lot. We're here for you."

Sandwiched between my best friends, I have a flashback: guards flank me, rough hands pushing me forward, fingers digging into my bruised, tender flesh. I scream and flail my arms, shoving them away. Keisha stumbles backwards, landing on her butt in the parking lot.

Tears burn the corners of my eyes. What's wrong with me? "I'm sorry. I'm just…" I can't find the right words. They can never know what happened to me.

Back on her feet, Keisha dusts off her behind. "It's alright. You're lucky that I have some cushion back there." She reaches out, tentatively this time. Her hand rests lightly on my shoulder. "I can't imagine what you're going through, but I miss Zoe, too." Keisha's brown eyes are wide and glassy, full of sincerity. "I love you, Sar."

I collapse into her arms. Tears cascade down my cheeks. Giselle and Penny join in, enveloping me in a group hug.

When we pull apart, all our eyes are wet. I can't believe that I ever doubted them. Even after I lost my powers, they stuck by my side. When Mallory hooked up with my boyfriend behind my back, they were there for me.

As if on cue, Mallory passes us, her auburn hair whipping in the wind. Last night, I saw Keisha leaving her house. Today, she struts by without even saying hello. "How's Mallory doing? Do you ever talk to her?" I ask.

Giselle wrinkles her nose. "The backstabbing boyfriend-stealer? Hell no."

Penny flicks her middle finger at Mallory's back. "She can go to hell in a handbasket."

Keisha walks ahead. I take two big steps to catch up with her. "What about you, Keisha? Have you talked to Mallory lately?"

Keisha stares straight ahead. "After what she did to you, I don't want anything to do with her." Chills race under my skin. Why would Keisha lie to me? She pushes open the door to school. "See you later, Sar." Keisha squeezes my hand before she turns down the hallway. She disappears into the sea of students, her head bobbing above the mass of backpacks and moving appendages before she's swallowed up entirely.

Someone slaps me on the back. I jolt forward. "Saria, you have no idea how glad I am to see you!" Chad, my ex-boyfriend, smiles at me. Dimples indent his cheeks. Even though I've moved on, it's nice to know that after all the time we spent together, he cares. "I was shitting bricks when the police questioned me about your disappearance. Do you know what they do to pretty boys like me in jail?" Oh. I should've known. Chad doesn't have the capacity to care about anyone but himself.

Disgusted, I stomp away. Blood pumps hot in my veins. In my mind's eye, fire rages. Between the flames, Keisha bares her teeth. Blood drips from her fangs, splattering on the linoleum floors.

Suddenly, the school hallways are a tunnel to the underworld. I squint, but all I see is red: blood spilling down the corridors, puddling on the floor.

I blink again. The walls chant: red, red, red, blood, blood, blood. Sweat beads on my brow.

"Saria, what's wrong?" Logan closes his locker, his lips a straight line, forehead etched with worry. The golden flecks in his eyes glow like the sun.

The school hallway comes back into focus. There's no blood, no fire. I'm officially insane.

I stand in front of him, not saying a word. My lower lip quivers.

"Oh, Saria." He pulls me into his arms.

"It's all too much," I murmur into his chest.

Hand on my back, Logan guides me into a broom closet. He kicks a bucket and a mop out of the way, locks the door and presses me against the wall. I wrap my legs around his waist. "Distract me. I don't want to know my own name," I say.

Logan kisses my neck. I feel myself coming undone in the best way possible: unraveling. Threads loosen. Knots untie.

I break into pieces: heat, breath, skin, sweat.

I don't produce cohesive thoughts. I couldn't if I tried to.

For a few minutes, I can forget the horror. All I feel is his love.

The bell rings.

I tried my best to be on time on the first day of school. I really did.

It looks like I'm going to be late.

Very late.

To be fair, we are in the school building.

That counts for something, right?

Chapter 10

Zoeli

Rosa hunches over, a hook-shaped finger pointed at me. "Nimwit vermin must suffer! You are not authorized to leave this prison until you remove all the warts and slime in between my toes."

I burst into laughter at her spot-on impression of Lorelei Crowe. "I'm only sentenced to twenty-five years. I'm not going to have time for all of that."

Rosa thrusts her foot towards me. "Lick them clean, nimwit, or spend the rest of your life under the streets with the sewer rats!"

I wrinkle my nose. "I'll take option two."

"What's so funny?" On the other side of the bars, Frederick, one of the more unpleasant guards, sneers at us. "This isn't a party." He makes a show of adjusting his holster belt, his fingers gliding over his gun. It might be more intimidating if it didn't look like it might slide off his gawky frame. "If you keep it up, I'll have to separate the two of you." He smooths his handlebar mustache.

"I'm terribly sorry, sir," I say. "We'll make sure to be miserable at all times."

"Don't get sarcastic with me, nimwit." Frederick hocks up a loogie and spews it through the bars. Mucus splatters on my arm.

I gather saliva in my mouth and aim my lips at Frederick's greasy nose. Rosa catches my eye and shakes her head. If I retaliate, I'll be punished. Even worse, they'll move Rosa. Even in the godforsaken hellhole, she makes me laugh every day. I swallow my spit and mentally add Frederick to my kick-in-the-balls-as-soon-as-I-can list.

Frederick howls with laughter. I bite my tongue until I taste blood, imagining that it's his. Frederick strolls away: whistling, nose up, combat boots clomping on the cement floor.

Rosa dips a washcloth in a bucket of murky water and wipes the spit off my arm.

"I feel like Frederick was the nerdy kid who got bullied," I say. "Now that he has a taste of power, he wants to inflict his pain onto others."

"Not everyone who was bullied wants to hurt others," Rosa says. "If anything, it makes me more empathetic to others because I know how it feels. As a dud, I was tormented relentlessly."

"I'm sorry. Kids are so cruel."

"It started in second grade. In elemental forces class, we were practicing using magic to set fire. I failed, so my classmates thought it would be funny to light my hair on fire. Even kids who I thought were my friends laughed at me." Even though it's dirty and matted, I can tell that Rosa has beautiful hair. She tugs on the light-brown ends, attempting to unravel some of the knots. "Our teacher put out the fire, but the damage was done. I had to chop my hair off above my ears."

"They would've called me a dud too," I say. "When Mom taught us how to make fire, Saria was a pro in no time. I couldn't even make a spark." I shake my head in disbelief. "But all along, I was more powerful than Saria." An image flashes in my mind's eye: Rosa on the witness stand, the faintest glint of blue in her eyes as Elric face-planted on the floor. "Rosa!" I shout in excitement, and then realize my mistake. I lower my voice to a whisper. "You knocked Elric down. You're not a dud! You're like me. You're just having a hard time accessing your power. Blue power is hard to reach."

Rosa chuckles. "That's a nice thought, but it isn't true. I'm as dudley as they come. I couldn't have done that to Elric."

"I saw it in your eyes."

"You have a wild imagination."

"I saw it," I insist. Or was my mind playing tricks on me? "What if everyone's wrong about the duds? What if they're the most powerful of all?"

Rosa raises her brows. "You're kidding."

"I'm not," I say. "I'll show you what Ms. Apotheker taught me."

Rosa sighs. "Zoe, I've tried a thousand different ways. It's a waste of time."

"I'm still learning, but I'll help you the best I can. Please. We have to try."

I'm coming down. Damian's voice interrupts my thoughts.

It's too soon. You were here three nights ago.

Rosa shrugs. "I guess. It's not like I have anything better to–" Rosa passes out mid-sentence, her mouth hanging open.

A nightingale hops between the bars. Purple mist swirls, darkens, and then Damian materializes holding a cupcake. A blue candle pokes out from a glob of white frosting. With a flick of his finger, Damian lights the wick. "Happy Birthday, Zoe."

"Is it my birthday?" I've lost all track of time.

"It sure is. Happy birthday to you. Happy birthday to you." Damian sings in a deep, melodic tone. Is there anything this man isn't good at?

Tears well in my eyes. It's Saria's birthday too. I hope that wherever she is, she's having the time of her life.

"Make a wish," Damian says. As the flame flickers, shadows dance on the walls. The bars shrink and grow: a living cage.

I don't believe in birthday wishes, but in this hopeless place, it's all that I have. I clench my eyes shut. *I wish Saria and I will be together on our next birthday. I wish that we'll be free as birds: free from the dungeon, free from the curse, crows flying side-by-side amongst the stars.*

I blow out the candle.

"I'm going to make your wish come true," Damian says.

When we're this close, it's hard to shield my thoughts. Anger rises in me like a tidal wave. I'm tired of Damian's bullshit promises. When I found out about Caliah, he claimed that he doesn't love her. He swore their relationship is nothing more than a political move for them both. Yet, he's still engaged to her. After I was arrested, he vowed to get me out of here. Five months later, I'm still locked up.

"I'm sorry." Damian's eyes suck me in like a black hole. If I let them pull me deeper, their blackness will smother my anger into a pile of ash. Apologies and declarations of love have worked in the past. Not tonight.

I tear away from his gaze. I'm stronger than gravity. He shouldn't underestimate me. "I don't need you to make my wishes come true," I say, a stubborn edge in my voice. "I can do that on my own."

Damian raises his eyebrows and gestures towards the bars. "It doesn't look like you're doing a great job of that, sweetheart."

"And what have you done, tough guy? Throw around empty promises? Sweet talk and tell me that everything's going to be okay? Saying it doesn't make it true, Damian, and I'm tired of pretending."

"Zoe, mark my words. I'm going to get you out of here."

"I won't hold my breath."

"You're not a damsel in distress," Damian says. "I know that. But I'm still going to be the hero who rescues you."

I fold my arms across my chest and shrug. I'm not as strong as I pretend to be. I'd love to be thrown on the back of a horse and whisked away by my knight in shining armor. I'll never admit that to Yazmin. She'd revoke my feminist card.

Damian holds the cupcake to my lips. I take a greedy bite. Damian kisses me, stealing the icing from my lips. I scarf down the rest, gooey sweetness sticking to the roof of my mouth. Damian licks the crumbs around my mouth.

I never thought I'd be the kind of girl who'd fall in love and become stupid, but here I am.

Chapter 11

Saria

"Happy birthday to you. Happy birthday to you." The candles flicker atop the ice cream cake. I see flames engulfing me, burning me alive. Every day, I teeter on the edge of insanity.

"Happy birthday dear Saria." Aunt Gwenna's raspy voice rises over my parent's and Logan's voices. Light flickers over her beak-like nose.

I'm not sure why she's here. We aren't close. In fact, she spent most of my life despising my existence and the fact that my parent's marriage destroyed her chance to inherit the throne. Maybe now that she's laid the groundwork for her daughter to become queen she's willing to let bygones be bygones. There's one thing I know for sure: if she knew about Damian and Zoeli, she wouldn't be singing right now.

"Happy Birthday to you!" Mom really tried today. She even brushed her hair and put on lip gloss. I appreciate the effort, but she isn't fooling me.

Everyone says that it'll get easier in time. They're all liars.

I paste a fake smile on my face.

"Make a wish," Dad says.

I wish that this will be the last birthday without Zoeli by my side. I wish it over and over and over again like it will make a difference. As if the power of my wish could defeat the Nightingale regime.

I blow out the candles. A blanket of darkness cloaks the room. Underneath the table, Logan interlaces his fingers in mine.

Dad flicks the light back on. Mom slices the cake. She plops a piece onto a plate and slides it to me. I smile even though I want to scream.

My spoon shakes as I bring it to my lips. "Mmm," I say even though I can't taste a thing. I pop another spoonful into my mouth. And then another. Globs of ice cream stick to the roof of my mouth. It seems to thicken as it slides into my throat.

I can't swallow. It's like I forgot how. I try again, but my muscles refuse to cooperate.

My heart races. Cold sweat glides down my back.

Cake clogs my airways. I raise my hands to my neck. I can't breathe.

The cake's been poisoned. The thought comes out of nowhere.

How could my own parents poison me? No, no, that can't be it. It must've been Aunt Gwenna. I gag. A chunk of ice cream rises up, spews from my lips and lands on the table.

"Saria! Are you okay?" Mom's brows shoot up.

Logan grabs a napkin and wipes the ice cream off the tablecloth. With his other hand, he rubs my back. Everyone stares at me, waiting for an answer.

"The cake..." My voice drifts off. "It doesn't taste right," I say.

"Tastes great to me," Dad says, shoveling some into his mouth.

"It's divine," Aunt Gwenna agrees, licking her lips. Logan's plate is empty: streaks of chocolate are all that's left behind. Mom lifts her spoon and finishes the last bite of her piece. They're all fine.

I'm an idiot. More than an idiot. I'm insane. There's nothing wrong with the cake, but there's a lot wrong with me. I drop my head into my hands.

"Oh, Saria." Mom pulls up the chair beside me and puts her arm over my shoulder. "I know, baby. It's so hard."

Tears explode from my eyes. "I'm going to Nightingale Palace right now." I'm incoherent, sputtering words like a maniac. "I'll demand that they release my sister."

"We cannot discuss this in front of the humans," Aunt Gwenna hisses, gesturing to Logan.

"I don't care. I'm going." I stand up, knocking over my chair. It clatters on the floor behind me.

"You'll get yourself killed, you fool," Aunt Gwenna says.

"We need to do something!"

"There's nothing to be done. We're not stronger than the Nightingale regime. When Caliah becomes queen–"

"That's over seven years from now." I slam my fist on the table. Dishes rattle. Coffee sloshes over the side of my cup.

"Saria, take a deep breath." Dad stands my chair back up. "I'm not going to lose another daughter. Please sit down." If Dad's voice didn't quiver, I might've protested. In my entire life, I've never seen my dad cry. He's always been the rock of our family: the voice of reason whenever emotions run high. If he falls apart, the rest of us don't stand a chance.

And the bigots think that humans are weak. Imagine that?

"I'm sorry," I say.

"Don't be sorry." Dad pulls me into his arms.

"I should get going," Aunt Gwenna says. She glances over her shoulder on her way out. "Don't do anything stupid."

I nod, even as a plan is hatching in my mind. A plan that is utterly, unbelievably stupid.

* * *

A few hours later, long after Logan's gone home and Dad's in bed, Mom and I sit up by the fireplace.

"Mom, have you ever met a vampire?"

Mom chuckles. "Why do you ask?"

I shrug. "Just curious." I wonder what she'd say if I told her the truth. I'm looking for some powerful allies to help me fight the Nightingale regime. I heard that vampires, especially the older vampires, can kick some ass. Yes, they might be vicious, bloodthirsty monsters, but hey, desperate times, desperate measures. I'm sure that'd go over well.

A dreamy look washes over Mom's face. "It's so funny how things turned out. After I graduated from Enchantments Academy, I was content to stay in Aurelia. Everything was simple: witches were superior, humans were vermin, vampires were evil, and Aurelia was the best place in the world.

"It was Taya, my best friend at the time, who wanted to go to college in the human realm. She convinced me that it would be an adventure. After all, it was a great big world, much larger than Aurelia. Even if the humans were simpletons, we'd explore the landscapes, soak up new experiences, and learn about nature.

"Boy, was I surprised when I met real-life humans! They weren't all blockheads. Many were brilliant, innovative, and spiritually connected. Even though I couldn't reveal my true identity, I didn't believe that people who'd become my friends would want to kill or experiment on me if they knew I was a witch.

"Once I realized that Aurelians were wrong about humans, I wondered if they were wrong about vampires too." Mom perches on the edge of her chair. "When I told Taya that I wanted to meet vampires, she called me insane. She thought I'd get eaten alive." Mom grins. "I did some crazy things. I never told anyone, not even Taya."

"Don't leave me hanging, Mom. What did you do?"

"There was a bar in New York, just a few blocks away from our apartment. The rumor was that vampires hung out there."

"The bar owned by Red?" I ask.

Mom's brow creases. "What do you know about him?"

"Damian said that they don't serve alcohol there," I say. "They drink the customers."

Mom bursts into laughter. "Is that what Damian told you? Those embellished tales are only catalysts for hate." She shakes her head. "They sure do serve alcohol. They make some of the best cocktails I've had in my life. Bea mixes a mojito that's to die for." Mom grins. "Not literally."

Mom looks happier than she has in months. She's talking about vampires and she's *smiling*. What the fudge-popsicle is going on here? I don't know who's crazier at this point– me or my mom. It's a close one.

"We'd dance all night until dawn when the vampires had to go to their coffins." She's joking, right? But Mom continues, seeming unaware of my jaw dropping to the floor. "Red was quite the character: handsome and charming, but humble, too. It seemed like all of the ladies were in love with him, but it was Amos who stole my heart."

"Excuse me?" I must be hallucinating.

Mom sighs. "I fell in love with a vampire. An ancient one, too. Even though he wasn't conventionally good looking, I was fiercely attracted to him. His brilliance is what captivated me. He read everything he could get his hands on. Amos was a wealth of knowledge: a walking encyclopedia."

"Wait a second," I shake my head in disbelief. "You dated a vampire?"

Mom nods. "We loved each other."

"He didn't bite you?"

"Not unless I wanted him to."

I hold up my hand. "Whoa, Mom! TMI."

Mom shrugs. "You asked."

"You and Amos were in love." I speak slowly, still trying to process all of this.

"Very deeply in love." There's a wistful expression in her eyes.

"Why did you break up?"

"He broke my heart," Mom says. "In the beginning, we both assumed it would be a fling. When our feelings deepened, he knew we'd gone too far. I wanted kids, and that was something that he could never give me. Also, our relationship was illegal, and to complicate matters further, I was a royal.

Amos feared that our love could ignite another war between our kinds. He was alive during the great war between the vampires and witches. In the bloodshed, Amos lost friends who he considered soulmates. He grieved for them often."

"Damian said that the vampires killed during the war captured witches, tied them up, and then threw parties where they'd cheer as they drained witches' blood."

Mom rolls her eyes. "Damian was educated in Aurelia, where history lessons are exaggerated to justify the atrocities committed by the Aurelian army. A very small number of vampires participated in those parties. Yet, when the Aurelian military retaliated, they went after everyone indiscriminately. Vampires who'd never even heard of these parties were slaughtered in their coffins or taken as hostages." Mom shakes her head. "Imagine if, say, an alien species learned about Jeffrey Dalmer, and then decided that the entirety of the human species should be exterminated based on his actions alone. That's what witches did to vampires."

"That's not how Damian tells it."

"He's brainwashed. Enchantment's Academy teaches prejudice towards both humans and vampires. If I'd never ventured out into the world, if I'd never met Amos, I'd never have known better."

"Mom, can't you ask Amos to help?" I blurt out. "He's one of the most powerful super-naturals in the world. If anyone can help, it's him."

"I haven't spoken to Amos in over twenty-five years. After we split up, I stopped hanging out at Red's. A year later, I met your father. I guess I have a penchant for forbidden romance." Mom chuckles.

"We have to find a way to contact Amos," I say. "Does Red still own the bar in New York?"

"They won't get involved. There's a truce between the witches and vampires. We stay out of their business and they stay out of ours."

"Can't we try?" I ask.

"Enough. We aren't going to drag the vampires into this mess. They've endured enough suffering at our hands."

"But if they want to help–"

"After so many years of conflict, hatred runs deep on both sides. Generation to generation, stories have become overdramatized: gorier, more brutal, invoking fear and disgust. In the same manner that witches are trained to hate vampires, the vampire community is taught to hate witches. Red's bar may not be safe for witches anymore." Mom checks the clock. "It's two a.m. We should go to bed."

We climb the stairs, side by side. I feel dazed, overwhelmed by all the new information. I always knew that my mom was rebellious. She married my dad, after all. Still, I never imagined her romance with a vampire.

I turn into my bedroom. "Goodnight, Mom." I slide under my covers, but sleep won't come. I can only think of two things: a bar in New York City called Red's and how to get there without anyone finding out.

Chapter 12

Damian

The full moon shines down like a spotlight in the clearing. We're far enough out in the woods that we're unlikely to be spotted, but just in case, I have a cover story. If anyone asks, we're working on an assignment for Ms. Apotheker's class. I have a feeling that she'll have my back.

Caliah flicks her finger, lighting the fire beneath the cauldron. "We have to do everything backwards, remember?" I snap my fingers and the flames become a puff of smoke. "Lighting the cauldron will be the very last step."

Cali shivers, her hands deep in her pockets. "I'm cold." She nuzzles her head against my sweatshirt. "Where is everyone?"

"Austin's on his way," I say. On cue, leaves rustle. A stag gallops through the bushes, its enormous hooves pounding in the dirt. His majestic antlers reflect in the moonlight, casting sharp shadows that look like monsters' teeth on the ground. "What's up, buddy?" I knew I could count on Austin.

The deer fades, becoming one with the night air. There's a flash of golden light, and then Austin appears, adjusting his navy windbreaker. "I can't believe I let you talk me into this man."

"Thanks for coming dude." Even though Austin wasn't the biggest fan of my idea, he came to help me out. I've done the same for him a handful of times, but nothing on this level of stupid.

Blue eyes peek between branches. A brown wolf's fur ruffles in the wind. Its body blurs, changing shape, morphing into a girl with tan skin and bright blue eyes. "Jas!" Cali skips over and hugs her friend. "I'm so glad you came!"

Austin straightens up. "Hey, Jasleidy." He puffs his chest out slightly, his stare drifting down to her cleavage. C'mon man. Jas is hot, sure, but I need you to focus.

A red fox slinks out from behind an oak tree, green eyes glinting in the moonlight. The fox flattens herself on the ground and melts into a puddle of red liquid. Fiery lava shoots up, takes shape, and solidifies. "I'm here for the party." Layal tosses her bright-red hair.

"Hi Lay!" Cali and Jas run to Layal's side, the three girls giggling under the moon.

"We have a Crowe, Wolfe, Fox, Deere, and a Nightingale." Austin counts on his fingers. "Five members of the royal families."

"Five direct descendants of the original spellcasters." I point out.

"What about the Hawkes and the Lyons?" Austin asks.

"There's no one I could trust." The Hawkes are loyal to the Nightingales to a fault. I can't imagine any of Elric's children, or nieces and nephews, for that matter, disobeying Aurelian law. If my father tells them to jump, they ask how high.

On the other hand, the Lyons despise the Nightingales. There's not a chance in hell that any of Tafari Lyon's kids would do me a favor.

"Everyone, gather around the cauldron." Once we're all standing in a circle, I begin. "First of all, what happens here tonight stays here for life. We can never tell anyone what we did." I catch Austin's eye. "That includes Colson, man."

"You think Colson would rat on us?" Austin asks.

"Of course not. It's just safer if we keep this between us. Also, we don't want to put any of our friends in a position where they'd have to lie to an interrogator. Is everyone clear on this? We take this to the grave." I glance around the group. Cali watches me intently, twirling a strawberry curl around her finger. Jasleidy shivers, arms wrapped tightly around herself. Austin sidles closer to Jas, his eyes still where they shouldn't be. Layal looks bored.

"Okay, let's move onto the logistics," I continue. "I wasn't able to secure representation from all of the royal families. Tonight, I need each of you to perform your absolute best. We're down two, but with optimal force and concentration, I believe that we can still break the curse." The truth is: it's a long shot, but I won't say that. When a coach hypes his team up before a big game, he must display unwavering confidence. Anything less defeats motivation and becomes a self-fulfilling prophecy.

Austin blows out a puff of air. "And I believe cotton candy is made from unicorn farts." So much for morale. Thanks, buddy.

"Actually," Layal flashes a sly smile. "We're only down one."

I raise my eyebrows. What the hell is she talking about?

"I asked a Lyon to join us tonight," Layal says.

My fists clench at my sides. "Layal, I very specifically told you not to tell anyone about this. Were you listening to me?" I should've listened when my father said to never trust a fox.

Layal shrugs, checking her nails. "I must've missed that part."

A golden-haired beast leaps over the bushes, landing gracefully on his gigantic paws. The wind picks up, spinning into a whirlwind. A tornado of black dust conceals the beast. As the cyclone dissipates, Weston appears, veins bulging in his neck.

"Weston Lyon," I say, my lips pressed in a firm line. "What brings you here tonight?"

Weston shakes out his hair. Bronze curls tumble over his forehead. "I believe in the cause. I'm against wrongful imprisonment and all that shit." He smirks.

"Bullshit. You were on the jury." My heart pounds in my ears. "Why are you really here? I know you don't want to help me."

"Not usually," Wes agrees. "But in this specific case, it seems that our motivations align." He grins, rows of pearly teeth glistening in the moonlight. "If your cockamamie plan actually works and your little friend breaks free, it'll make the Nightingale regime look pretty bad, won't it? If your father can't even keep track of violent criminals, how can he possibly keep Aurelians safe?"

Ah, I see. Weston's hoping that Zoeli's escape will galvanize a revolution against the Nightingales. Maybe even provide an opportunity for the Lyons to claim the throne.

It'll never happen. Even if we succeed in breaking the curse, my father has too many supporters. He'll find a way to pass the blame on someone else. After a few charismatic speeches, all will be forgotten.

I shake my head. "If you're not here for the right reasons, then you shouldn't be here."

"Does it matter?" Layal asks. "I'm here because I'm an anarchist and I like to stir shit up."

"I'm here because my buddy's crazy." Austin nods in my direction. "Years ago, we swore that if one of us goes down, we'd go together, so here I am." He throws up his hands. "I'm an idiot," he mutters.

"Same." Jas says, rolling her eyes towards Cali.

"I'm here for you," Cali says, linking her fingers through mine. "And for my cousin Zoeli, too."

"It's not getting any warmer out." Jas rubs her arms. "Let's get this show on the road so I can put my fur back on."

"It's freezing," Layal agrees. "If I'd known this was going to take all night, I would've just given my blood."

"Blood?" Cali's brow furrows.

Layal sighs. "If you're going to be a queen and all, you need to study up. If someone can't make it to the ceremony, they can perform the ritual in advance while their blood drains into a glass container. On the night of the spell, their blood can be transferred to the cauldron."

"A physical presence is more effective than a blood offering," I explain. Taking a deep breath, I think over the options. Even though I dislike Weston, six is better than five. As much as I hate to admit it, he's powerful. With Wes, we have a higher chance of success. I meet his eyes. "How do I know you won't rat on us?"

"Because I'd be ratting on myself. I don't want to go to jail," Wes says.

"Fair enough." I unzip my backpack. Inside, a dozen glass bottles are filled with various ingredients. "Did everyone memorize the spell?" There's a chorus of yeses. "In reverse?" Everyone nods. "Okay. Let's get started."

As I sprinkle ingredients into the cauldron, everyone chants. My gaze darts from witch to witch as they mouth the words. Are they on point? Is everyone trying their best? I wish that Zoeli's fate didn't lie in their hands.

I imagine Zoeli: aquamarine eyes, jet black hair, a smile that lights my soul on fire. I muster every ounce of power in me.

We're doing it. Let me know if anything happens on your end.

Chapter 13

Keisha takes another bite of her hamburger. Beneath the diner's fluorescent lights, dark bags are evident beneath her eyes. "Are you okay, Keisha?" I ask. "You look tired."

"Yeah, I'm alright. I've just been having trouble sleeping, that's all."

"What's keeping you awake?" Giselle asks. She takes a sip of soda.

"Nothing in particular." Keisha stretches her neck, averting her eyes.

"What's wrong, Keisha? I'm worried about you," I say.

"I'm fine." Keisha waves her hand. Her smile looks genuine enough. It might fool someone who hasn't known her since pre-school. It doesn't fool me. "I've just been binge watching shows too late. It's not that deep."

"We should get going," Giselle says. "You need to go home and get some rest." She raises her hand to alert the waitress. "Check, please!"

"I'm going to run to the ladies room." I slip out of the vinyl booth. I stride past tables of raucous customers, laughing and scarfing down fries and greasy sandwiches without a care in the world. I bet their sisters aren't prisoners in an alternate realm.

I push open the door to the ladies room and walk towards the row of stalls. A door flies open, nearly knocking me over. I stumble backwards, steadying myself on the sink's countertop. Yazmin puts her hands on her hips, brown eyes narrowed into slits.

"Hey, Yaz," I say. "I'm sorry. I didn't see you." Why am I apologizing? She's the one who almost took me out. And why does she look so angry? "Is everything okay?" I ask.

"That's a stupid question. My best friend's missing. I don't even know if she's alive."

Yazmin gathers her hair, twisting it into a messy bun. A few purple-streaked tendrils are too short to stay tied up. They come undone, framing her pretty face. She steps in front of me, fury burning in her eyes. Yazmin looks ready to fight.

"Believe me, I know, Yazmin. I miss Zoe every day."

"I'm sure you do." Yazmin's voice drips with sarcasm. "Everyone says poor Saria, her twin sister's gone. Do they all have amnesia? Did they forget what you did to Zoe? Because I didn't." Her tone is laced with venom.

"I did some terrible things, but I apologized to Zoe. We moved past it."

"Bullshit. You were horrible to Zoe. In fact, I wouldn't be surprised if you had something to do with her disappearance." She shakes her head in disgust. "I know that she didn't run away. She wouldn't have picked up and left without telling me."

"Yaz, I promise you that I want her home just as badly as you do."

"Liar." Yazmin hisses. She leans forward, her face inches from mine. "I'm watching you, Saria. If you know anything about where Zoe is, if you're hurting her, I will find out." Her platform heel stomps on my ballet flat. I yelp in pain.

A few months back, I had a similar confrontation with Mallory. I seem to have a knack for altercations in bathrooms. The difference is: I don't want to hurt Yazmin. Yes, she's out of line, but it's because she's hurting. She loves Zoe.

Yazmin spins on her heel and storms out of the bathroom. The door slams shut behind her. My chest is tight with trapped breath. The exhale comes out in a whoosh.

I teeter against the sink. A carousel of horror spins around me: Zoeli's mouth wide-open, a piercing scream escaping her pink lips, black rings surround Keisha's vacant eyes as she shuffles forward like a zombie, blazing fires. Voices chant: red, red, red, blood, blood, blood.

"Hey, Saria, are you okay?" a soft voice asks. A girl slowly comes into focus: converse sneakers, black-and-white striped t-shirt, holey jeans, horn-rimmed glasses. Miranda Keller is a shy, almost timid, girl. When she was younger, she was a frequent target for bullies. Now, she stands over me, fidgeting with her split ends. "I'm sorry to bother you. Um, I mean, I know…" Her voice trails off as she seems to have difficulty finding the words. "Are you okay?" she repeats.

"Yeah." I force a smile. "I think so."

She flashes an apprehensive smile, revealing crooked front teeth. Her gangly arm darts out and pats me on the back. "Um, glad you're alright." She turns too fast, almost tripping over her own feet. As she steadies herself against the wall, her cheeks are red as fire.

"Thanks for checking on me," I say.

Miranda leaves the bathroom without looking back.

* * *

Hours later, when everyone in the McKinney-Crowe household is sound asleep, I slide out from under my covers. It's midnight. While everyone in the sleepy suburbs is tucked in their beds, the nightlife in New York City is just getting started.

I tug on a black minidress and over-the-knee boots. I apply lipstick, adrenaline coursing through my veins. Am I really going to do this?

I don't see any other choice. If I continue to do nothing, I'll lose my mind. Every hour that Zoeli rots in that hellhole, my sanity fades, faster by the day.

I tiptoe down the stairs, careful to skip the steps that creak. I slip out the front door. It clicks shut behind me.

I dig into my purse for my mom's car keys. Her car is parked on the driveway, just beneath my parent's bedroom window. This is the moment of truth.

Inch by inch, I open the door to her sedan. I slide inside and press the button to start the engine. I cringe as the engine roars up. I half-expect to be caught right then and there. I imagine my parents sprinting out the front door, scolding me as they drag me back into the house. If they knew what I was up to, they'd probably chain me to my bedroom wall.

Surprisingly, the house is quiet. No one stirs. The lights stay off. Crickets chirp.

I shift the car in drive and make my way down the dark, winding driveway. I don't turn on my headlights until I reach the bottom of the hill, when my house is long out of sight.

I'm home free.

I load up my GPS and enter the address for Red in New York City. There's no traffic at this hour. In forty-five minutes, I'll be face to face with vampires.

Chapter 14

Zoeli

Let me know if anything happens on your end. Damian's voice echoes in my thoughts. What exactly is supposed to happen? If the curse is lifted, will I even know?

From what Damian tells me, shape-shifters' experiences vary widely. Some endure excruciating pain. Others feel euphoria. Some black out and don't recall the moment when they change bodies. It's impossible to know what my own shift might entail.

The dungeon's silent. Curled up on the floor, Rosa's blanket is wrapped around her like a cocoon. Eyes closed, her chest rises and falls at a steady rhythm.

I lean against the wall and close my eyes. I visualize myself as a crow, wriggling through the bars and soaring to freedom.

Nothing happens. Damian told me that shifting is reflexive for him. It comes naturally without any effort at all. Other shape-shifters report using an immense amount of labor. It's all over the map. I sigh.

For days now, Damian's been practicing the chant, over and over again. I've heard it countless times: both in person and in his head.

I have it memorized. I'm compelled by the desire to say it aloud.

My lips move, soundlessly reciting the words.

sgniw rieht esol llahs worc layolnu nA
sgnis reverof worc lufhtiaf A

I repeat it, louder this time, a whisper unraveling on my tongue.

Tendrils of blue light circle me, glittering as they wind around my feet and move up my legs. Pins and needles start in my toes, piercing open my cells and rearranging the DNA inside them.

Blue beams revolve around me, shooting like comets. The prickling sensation permeates my skin, pushes deep into my organs, and digs into my bones. An orb of shiny blue magic encases me. All I see is glittery blue.

And then it's gone. The dungeon comes back into focus.

The cell seems bigger somehow: wider, taller. The bars seem to extend up into oblivion.

Something tickles my nose. When I try to scratch it, I discover that I have no hands. Instead, I stare at four black talons, perfect for tearing the flesh of prey.

Holy shit. My heart rattles in my chest.

I'm a crow.

Damian did it. I never should've doubted him.

It's time for action.

I squirm between the bars, my wings flattening against the cold metal. And then I'm on the other side. Just like that, I'm free.

I glance back at Rosa, She snores softly, the sheen of moonlight illuminating her skin. I hate that I have to leave without saying goodbye, but it's for the best. Once they discover that I'm gone, Rosa will be interrogated. They'll use magic to extract information from her. The less she knows, the safer I'll be.

I walk along the wall, inching my way down the hallway. I'm so small. It's taking longer than I expected.

In my mind, I review the escape plan. Damian and I went over it every day this week. First, I'll turn the corner, and then find the loose air vent on the ceiling. Once located, I need to fly up, climb inside, and enter the labyrinth of ducts that leads to Damian's bedroom.

I got this. I know that I can pull it off.

Footsteps clap against the ground. I recognize Frederick's high-pitched whistle and heavy gait.

Oh shit.

I look up, desperately searching for the escape hatch, but I can't find it. Where is that damn air vent?

Footsteps are louder now, just around the bend.

In seconds, Frederick will round the corner, and I'll be exposed.

This would all be for nothing.

They'll throw me right back in jail. Guards will hover over me twenty-four-seven. I'll never get out.

I'll never see Damian again.

I have to think fast.

Chapter 15

I'm being followed. At first, I blamed my paranoia. I tried to convince myself that I was overreacting. It's not normal to regard every car that happens to drive behind me with suspicion.

Thirty minutes later, I'm running out of excuses for why this car is still on my ass. I speed down the highway, weaving in and out of lanes, attempting to lose my pursuer.

Yazmin's voice echoes in my thoughts. *I'm watching you, Saria.* Is it possible that she camps outside my house every night, lurking in the shadows, waiting for an opportunity to follow me?

As unlikely as it seems, I won't rule it out. I've discovered that hurt people do crazy things. For instance, sneak off to New York City in the middle of the night to bargain with a vampire who may or may not be a witch-hating bloodthirsty lunatic.

I pull over to the shoulder and barrel down the side of the highway. Drivers honk. One sticks their middle finger out of the driver's side window.

I slide back into traffic, almost sideswiping an SUV. I abruptly take the next exit. My heart hammers in my chest.

I check my mirrors. The car is gone. For now. I drive through the Holland Tunnel. I'm almost there.

A few minutes later, I'm circling city streets, looking for parking. Two young women in minidresses walk around the corner. A blonde stumbles, almost tripping over her platform heels until her friend catches her.

Someone had too much to drink. The sober friend helps the plastered one into the passenger seat of a blue coupe. The brunette slams the door shut and rolls her eyes, seeming annoyed that her night came to an early end. If they're leaving Red's bar, the blonde's antics may have saved their lives.

Mom claims that vampires aren't inherently evil. Damian says that all vampires are sadistic killers. Even though I trust my mom, I'm terrified.

As soon as the coupe pulls out, I take their spot. Sucking in a deep breath, I step outside.

The soles of my boots scuff against the sidewalk. I manage one step forward, and then another. My legs quake as if the earth is trembling beneath me. I steady myself against a building, palms pressed against the cold bricks.

For months, Zoeli was my salvation. Locked in that wretched cage, I almost died of starvation and hypothermia. Without her, I would have. Through chattering teeth, Zoe insisted that she was fine, stomach grumbling as she passed me her food and blanket.

I lift my chin. I can't chicken out. I'm doing this for her. For my twin.

One step at a time. One foot in front of the other. I can do this. I turn the corner.

When I searched for Red's bar on the internet, I couldn't find a website or google reviews. I uncovered the address in a decade's old article titled *Twenty Unique Bars to visit in New York City.*

I can't be sure that the place still exists. Part of me hopes that it doesn't.

In front of the address, a gargantuan man waits. He guards a black door, arms folded across his leather jacket. My heart beats double time.

There's no sign or windows to view the inside. The man looks me up and down, rubbing the stubble on his chin.

"Um, u-u-m." I take a deep breath. "I'm, um, looking for Red. Is this his bar?"

"You're in the wrong place." His brown eyes narrow.

"Oh, um, I-I, I'm sorry. I thought this was the address for–"

"You're not wanted here." The man has a sharp edge to his voice

"O-oh. I'm sorry." I repeat. What am I blabbering about? I need to get the hell out of here while I still can. I spin on my heel and stalk away.

"Was someone looking for me?" The voice sounds like it's right inside my ear, even though I'm almost at the end of the block. I glance over my shoulder.

A man strides my way, his footsteps stealthy and quiet. His pecs strain against his button-down shirt. Muscular thighs are evident beneath his black dress pants. The full moon shines on him like a spotlight.

When he's a few feet away, he holds out his hand. "Miss Crowe, I'm Redvers Castigan, but my friends call me Red. I'm pleased to make your acquaintance."

He towers over me, fluorescent blue eyes glowing brighter than the streetlights. Minus his eyes, he's a black-and-white photo: ghost-white skin, pitch black hair, crisp white shirt, glossy black shoes.

Even though he doesn't look older than me, he exudes a masculine elegance that I haven't seen in boys my age. While Logan is more adorable than handsome, boyish even, Red is the epitome of sex appeal.

Red arches a black brow, his otherworldly gaze drifting from me to his extended hand.

"Oh." I startle, realizing how rude I must seem. I wipe my clammy palm on my dress before shaking his hand.

"Miss Crowe." His eyes are hypnotic. "I'd be happy to show you around the club. Join me." Instead of releasing my hand, he laces his fingers through mine and leads me towards the black door. "Perhaps you'd like to tell me your first name."

I flush with embarrassment. When he introduced himself, I stood there like a moron, my brain the consistency of mush. Wait a second… I never told him that I'm a Crowe. "How do you know my last name?" I don't mean for it to sound as accusatory as it does.

Red's Hollywood-white teeth gleam. No fangs, thank God. "I can smell a Crowe from a mile away, but until I saw you, I didn't realize that you're Lani's daughter."

People have always told me that I look like my mom, but I've never heard anyone call her Lani. "Oh," I say. Why am I having such a hard time coming up with words? How am I supposed to ask him to help rescue Zoeli if I can't even put a sentence together?

"Your name?" Red repeats.

God, I'm such an idiot. "Saria."

As we approach, the bouncer shakes his head. "Red, what are you doing man?"

"It's alright. She's with me."

"Let's go talk, man." Red holds up one finger, indicating that he'll be right back. In the blink of an eye, they're a dozen yards away, their backs facing me.

I shift from foot to foot, wringing my hands as I wait. Although I can't hear most of their whispers, I make out a few words. "Witches…" "The truce…" "An old friend…"

A few minutes later, they're back. The bouncer's lips are set in a firm line as he holds out his palm. "I'll need any phones, cameras or devices that could be used to take pictures and or videos."

It takes a moment for me to realize that he's talking to me. I clench my purse in my fists, holding it tight against my body. I'm not sure why—it's not like I can call Buffy to rescue me. Even though it might be a false sense of security, I'm not giving up my phone.

Red eyes my white knuckles. "Luke, she won't be out of my sight. I'll make sure she doesn't take any pictures."

Luke groans loudly, but steps aside. Red opens the black door, pulling me inside with him. I follow him down a long narrow staircase. The soft glow of wall-mounted candle sconces light the way.

At the bottom of the stairs, Red pushes through another door. Rock music, strobe lights, and laughter assault my senses. Ribbons of laser lights stretch across the impossibly tall ceilings.

The crowd parts to let us through. Everyone stares at Red as we pass. Women bat their lashes and flash coy smiles.

Guys slap him on the back. Red smiles and offers high-fives, acknowledging every patron who shouts his name.

Red leads me to the dance floor. "Do you dance?"

"Um, I was hoping we could talk." I shout over the electric guitars.

"If you come to my club, I must show you a good time. It's a responsibility that I take quite seriously. First, we dance, then we talk." He raises his brows. "Is that okay?"

"Sure." Why not? Maybe if I prove to be a worthy dance partner, he'll hold off on draining my blood. The problem is: I'm not a good dancer.

Red twirls me around. His hips swing to the beat. "Move with me, one, two, three, one, two, three." His feet glide across the floor.

Following his lead is surprisingly easy. My feet seem to move of their own volition. Before I know it, I'm sashaying, laughing and doing the rhumba like a seasoned dancer.

Red lifts me up, spins me around and then dips me low to the floor. When he pulls me back up, he draws me tight against his hard chest. His neon eyes flash in the strobe lights. Am I wrong to notice how hot he is?

"I have a boyfriend." I'm not sure if I'm informing Red or reminding myself.

"We're just dancing. I hope I didn't cross a line." Red half-smiles, looking unsure of himself.

Can vampires be self-conscious? There's so much to learn about these fascinating creatures, but I can already tell that Red will blow every stereotype out of the water. "Oh, no, dancing is fine. I just, um, you know, wanted you to know."

Red nods. "Noted." He tosses me in the air. I twirl like an ice skater doing a triple axel before he catches me.

"Wow," I breathe. "You're a great dancer."

He grins. "I've had one hundred years to practice."

"Red!" A woman in a 1920s flapper-style dress puts her long red nails on Red's shoulder. In her wine glass, dark red liquid swirls. "Who's this?" She takes a long sip, baring her teeth. Red droplets trickle down her fangs.

A chill sweeps through me, like ice cubes slithering down the back of my shirt. Is she Red's girlfriend or something?

"Hey, Bea." Red greets her. "Sari, meet Bea, my assistant bar manager and one of my closest friends. Bea, meet Sari, Lani's daughter."

"Lani." Bea repeats. She studies me, tucking a stray hair back into her sleek chestnut bob. "Ah, I see it now. It's been so long." Bea smiles and extends her hand. "Your mother was a good friend of mine. I'm Beatrice Sinclair." She toys with an antique locket around her neck.

A short, stocky man sidles up, his dark eyes narrowed. He sniffs the air. "Do I smell a crow?" He does not look happy to see me. If I'm killed, tell the police it was a man with slicked back hair and a mole on his chin. My hands are slippery with sweat. "Sari, meet Giovanni Romano. Gio is another close friend of mine." Red says.

"What the hell is a witch doing in here?" Gio growls.

"She's my friend's daughter."

"Not all witches are bad, Gio." Beatrice says. Cocktail rings glisten on every one of her fingers.

"I want her out of here," Gio grunts. "Fool me once–"

"Where are your manners?" Bea slaps him on the back. She leans in and whispers in my ear, her feathered hair clip tickling my cheek. "Don't mind him. His bark is bigger than his bite."

"She's staying." Red's voice asserts authority. What Red says goes.

"You're both idiots." Gio stomps away.

"Sorry about that," Red says. "Forget about him. Let's dance."

The live music (Are they live? Or undead?) is out of this world. The band's eclectic lineup transitions from rock to salsa to hip-hop seamlessly. No matter what genre they play, their music is hypnotic. The singer's long braids sway as she belts out the lyrics. Her soulful voice sends goosebumps up my arms. The guitarist kneels, strumming a haunting melody. I wish Zoeli was here. She would appreciate the hell out of their musical talent.

"They're incredible," I say. "The best band I've heard in my whole life."

"The Dragon's Psalm is one of my favorites, too. They've come a long way from their early days. Five hundred years of practice doesn't hurt," Red says.

I guess being immortal has its perks. "The Dragon's Psalm." I repeat the band name. "They deserve a grammy. How come I've never heard of them?"

"Vampires stay under the radar. If we call too much attention to ourselves, the public will realize that we don't age. Besides, in this digital media era, it's impossible to find fame if you can't take a selfie or shoot a music video."

Even as he focuses on me, Red remains vigilant of his surroundings, finding moments to help his customers. Someone spills her drink: a hazard of vigorous twerking. Red motions for his bartender to mix her up a new one, free of charge. When a drunk guy gets too handsy on the dance floor, Red throws him out– literally. He grabs him by the collar, drags him across the club, and chucks him out the door.

"We don't tolerate disrespect here," Red says.

I slip my phone out of my purse, grateful that Red allowed me to bring it inside. There aren't any missed calls from home. Mom and Dad must be sound asleep. If they knew where I was, I'd be dead. I check the time. It's 3 AM. I can't believe it. Hours slipped by like minutes.

Red's isn't just another dark, sweaty basement club. Here, beams of light zigzag like lightning bolts across the infinite ceiling. The strobe lights blink on tempo. The music is intoxicating: almost euphoric. Red's is a place where you can truly leave your worries at the door.

For the first time in months, I feel calm. I never imagined that I'd like it here. I expected to hate every moment. Yet, I love it. Life never ceases to throw me curveballs.

Red gestures to the phone in my hand. "If you need to use your phone, I can take you to my office. Phones are forbidden in the club. Vampires won't appear in photos or videos, so we can't risk someone trying to snap our picture. If my customers see you with a phone, they might be upset that they were asked to leave theirs at the door."

"Oh, I'm sorry." I slide my phone back in my purse. "I need to go home soon, but I was hoping we could talk."

Red laces his fingers through mine. "This way." As we pass, a gyrating pelvis slams into my backside. I peek over my shoulder and cringe. A red-faced man grabs my hips, grinding his crotch against my skirt.

In a flash, Red's fingers clamp around the guy's wrist. Effortlessly, he flings the man like someone might flick an insect. When the man hits the ground, his shirt rides up, exposing rolls of meaty flesh.

A college-aged boy scurries over. Yellow letters on his black polo shirt read SECURITY. Sweaty curls stick to his forehead. Dark bags hang under the hollowed eyes of his too-thin face. He looks like he skipped a few meals while pulling all-nighters studying for exams. "Nate," Red addresses the security guard. "Get him out." Red gestures to the rumpled man on the floor.

The creep pants, his belly jiggling as he struggles to sit up. "I spent a lot of money in this joint."

"Your money's no good here." Red snaps his fingers. Another man wearing a SECURITY shirt darts over. In stark contrast to Nate, this man is short and stocky, built like a lumberjack. Meaty hands folded, he waits for orders. "Get him out of here," Red demands.

The two security guards hoist the prick up, their faces contorted with effort as they lug him away.

"Are you okay?" Red asks me.

I shrug. "I'm used to jerks sneaking up on me."

"That's unfortunate." Red's lip curls in disgust. His fangs glitter under the strobe lights. "You shouldn't be."

In the far corner, tucked inside an alcove, two jacked security guards patrol a door. As Red and I approach, they step aside.

We enter a long, dark corridor. My heart races. What if I've been fooled? When the candles flicker, it's pitch black. If Red wanted to, he could rip my jugular out. Instinctively, I touch my neck. My pulse flutters beneath delicate skin.

The hallway slopes down, descending into the earth. It smells of moist dirt, like a cemetery with freshly dug graves. The trek seems endless. I almost turn around and bolt.

When we finally reach another door, a security guard nods at Red. "Hey, boss." He offers me a small smile as he steps aside. "You're lucky. I've been working here for years and Red still won't let me party in VIP."

"One day, Dom." Red squeezes his shoulder as we pass.

As we cross the threshold, my heart lurches into my throat. I'm not sure what to expect, but heinous visions race through my mind: vampires feasting on bodies, tearing their limbs apart, and then bathing in pools of blood.

My breath releases when I see it's just another part of the club: smaller, but similar vibe. Spotlights circle the ceiling. Laser lights slither like snakes across the floor. Hips and booties shake.

A woman with impossibly long hair sways to the music, her back to me. As she turns, I see that she has an ethereal glow and skin so light, it's almost translucent. A red drink balances gracefully on her fingertips. She circles all the way around, facing me, staring with crimson eyes. Her pupils glow: red like rubies.

I gasp and cover my mouth, loud music drowning out my scream. "There's nothing to fear." Red squeezes my hand reassuringly. "When vampires have a little too much to drink, our eyes turn red." Red snatches the drink from the woman's hand. "Rhianna, you're cut off."

"Oh, Red, you're killing my buzz."

"I'm looking out for your safety."

"Maybe if you got laid once in a while, you wouldn't be such a stick in the mud," Rhianna says.

"The last time you were under the influence you made some questionable choices. You'll thank me tomorrow evening." Red leads me around the dance floor and into a lounge area with black leather couches. A woman in a sequin dress laughs, dusting off the shoulder of a man in a business suit. She crosses her legs, exposing her stiletto's red bottoms. Dark liquid ripples in her wine glass.

"What is this place?" I ask.

"It's the supernatural only section," Red says. "Mainly vampires, but demons show up from time to time."

I clutch my chest. "Demons," I repeat, my heart like a jackhammer. "Why did you take me here?"

"To talk." Red slips a keychain out of his pocket. "In my office." He gestures to a door a few yards away. I double the size of my steps, stretching my legs as far as they'll go. We're almost there. Red inserts a key in the doorknob and twists.

Red's office has a modern aesthetic: clean lines and sharp edges. The door clicks shut behind him. Red slides into his leather office chair, propping his elbows on a glossy L-shaped desk.

I step onto a black-and-white checkered area rug. Red gestures to the white couch that faces his desk. When I sit down, the leather groans.

"What's going on, Sari?"

"It's Saria," I correct him. I'm not sure if he misheard me when I introduced myself earlier.

"Can I call you Sari?" Red asks. "Everyone I like, I call by a nickname."

I shrug. "Okay." I don't object to the name. It actually sounds kind of cute coming from his lips. It's just that no one's ever called me that before. "But you barely know me."

"I'm good at reading people," Red says. "Your aura's pure, but strong. You're generally benevolent, but you'll fight for the people who you love. You're fierce when you need to be."

My gaze drops to the floor. "I don't know about that," I admit. "When I was a prisoner in the Nightingale dungeon, I all but folded. Without my sister, I'm not sure that I would've survived."

"You're also too hard on yourself," Red says. "You blame yourself for things that aren't your fault. Or maybe they were, but you were a different person then. The guilt drives you insane."

I shrug. "Insane sounds about right."

"Forgive yourself. Everyone makes mistakes." Red studies me, his eyes stripping me down to my soul. "But there's more that plagues you: a deep, dark sadness, like a piece of your heart has been ripped away."

I don't say anything. The tears streaming down my cheeks are all the confirmation that he needs. He's spot on.

"Tell me, Sari. What's your story?"

The words spill out. I start at the beginning. I tell Red about how I used to misuse my powers for my own benefit. How ashamed I am of the way that I treated my sister in the past. I explain the conflict between Talon, Licinia and the Nightingale regime and the circumstances of my imprisonment. I describe the conditions of the Nightingale dungeon: the guard's cruelty, how they mocked and spit at us, the freezing cold floors we slept on and the moldy scraps we ate. Red's lips twist into a frown as I recount the torture I endured, his blue eyes ablaze.

I move on to Aurelia's corrupt court system, and how lucky I am that Queen Taya pardoned me. I choke out Zoeli's sentence, how much I miss her, the visions of her isolation and torment that haunt me day and night.

I tell Red everything. I talk and talk and talk until my throat is sore. Forty-five minutes later, Red knows more about me than my best friends. More than my own boyfriend.

When I'm done, I let out a deep breath, my shoulders falling as the tension releases. Until I started, I didn't even realize how badly I needed to get it out. I just bared my soul to a vampire. As crazy as it sounds, this is the sanest I've felt in a very long time.

"I'll do everything I can to help you," Red says.

"Thank you," I breathe. "Thank you so much."

"I promise that I'll try, but I can't make any guarantees. Vampires aren't allowed to meddle in witch's matters, so I'll have to be discreet."

"What about Amos? Do you think that he'll help?"

"Maybe." Red pauses. "He stopped hanging out here decades ago, after…" Red's voice drifts off. "He was a bit heartbroken."

"Because of my mom?"

Red raises his brow. "I didn't realize that you knew about their relationship. Yes, their breakup was hard on him. We haven't spoken in years, but I'll reach out."

"Thank you," I say again. My phone rings. "Oh shit. My mom's going to kill me." If I don't answer, Mom will call every hospital, police department and news station in the tri-state area. I press the button to receive the call.

"Where the hell are you, Saria?" Mom shrieks in my ear.

"I'm fine, Mom. I'm safe. Everything's okay."

"It's four in the morning! Where are you?"

"I'm sorry, Mom. I'll be home soon."

"WHERE ARE YOU?"

Red holds out his hand. "Give me the phone."

"WHO THE HELL IS THAT?"

I hand Red my phone. He places it on his desk and turns on the speakerphone. "Hello, Lani. It's been a long time."

"Wait a minute… Red?" Mom's voice rises in disbelief.

"After all these years, you still recognize my voice." Red smiles. "I'm impressed."

"You're the only one who ever called me Lani," Mom responds.

"It's been a pleasure getting to know your daughter. She filled me in on your circumstances. I'm appalled by the way the Nightingale's have treated your family. I'm going to see what I can do to help rectify this mess."

"As much as I appreciate your offer, I don't want to put you in danger." Mom sighs. "I told Saria not to drag you into it."

"It's too late for that," Red says. "And I'm glad that Sari came to me. We miss you, Lani. Anytime you want to come out to the club, there's a killer mojito waiting with your name on it."

Mom chuckles. "Not everyone stays seventeen forever, Red. I'm a middle-aged woman now. Most nights, I'm in bed by eleven. Unlike my daughter who seems to think it's okay to sneak out until all hours of the night. You're in big trouble young lady."

Red's forehead creases. "The Lani I know danced until the sun came up. Be easy on your daughter. She's going through a tough time."

"We all are," Mom says. "But my daughter's safety comes first. She's a young woman all alone in the city at night." Mom's voice trails off. "Most parents worry about drunk hooligans wandering the streets, but I have even more at stake. Talon and Licinia are still at large. My uncle's made it clear that he hates my family and wants us all dead."

"Lani, I will personally chauffeur Sari to your front door. Not a hair on her head will be harmed. I promise."

"Thank you," Mom says. "I'll be waiting."

"We'll be there shortly." Red disconnects the call. "Let's go." Red stands up. "Before we're both grounded."

Someone knocks on the office door. Bea's head pops in, dangly earrings swaying. "Nellie Baker is here."

Red raises his brows. "It's been ages since she came around."

"She asked to see you."

Red checks his watch. "I don't have time. I have to drive Sari home. Send Nellie my regards."

To my surprise, Bea hugs me. Her chestnut bob tickles my cheek. "It was awesome meeting you." Her perfume smells like lily of the valley.

"Thank you. Same to you. I had a blast."

"Don't forget to tell your mom that I said hi." When she reveals her teeth, I barely register the blood stains. Instead, I notice the warmth in her smile, the lively spark in her eyes.

Bea's animated and sweet: the exact opposite of what one might expect from a vampire. I realize how foolish I was to be afraid: to prejudge someone based on myths and stereotypes.

Since Damian is the prince of Aurelia, I held him up on a pedestal, trusting his words to be facts. But even royals can be wrong. Even though Damian may have good intentions, his ignorance perpetuates harm and division. By spreading falsehoods that depict vampires as violent, he bolsters hate and fear amongst our kinds.

I follow Red through the club, up two flights of stairs, and back to the city street. Walking along the sidewalk, Red asks, "Where's your car?"

I point to my mom's blue sedan, parked a few yards away.

"That old thing?"

I shrug. When I was learning to drive, I accidentally backed into the mailbox (oops). Another small dent is from a fender bender from years ago. There's rust around the wheel wells. I guess the car's seen better days, but we're not rich. I'm used to driving jalopies.

"Come with me," Red says. "I'm going to bring you home in style."

"Wait, what about my mom's car?"

"One of my staff will drive it home." Red turns into a parking garage. We walk up the ramps, our footsteps echoing in the cavernous space.

Red presses a button on his keychain. The doors to a black Ferrari open like a butterfly spreading its wings. My jaw falls open. "Your car?"

"One of them."

"Wow." I slide in, running my fingers over the luxurious leather. "Your club must do well."

Red shrugs. "I do alright." He guns the gas. We speed down the city streets, gliding around curves, streetlights passing in a blur.

Conversation is easy with Red. He amuses me with stories of eccentric patrons at his club. He tells me about a customer who used to sleepwalk, or rather sleep-dance in the middle of the dance floor, snoring while performing the macarena.

I shake my head and giggle. "You're lying," I say.

Red raises his hand. "I swear on my immortality. She didn't have health insurance, so I paid for her to see a sleep specialist. I was worried that she'd get hurt during one of her episodes."

Sleep disturbances make me think of Keisha. I remember how drained she looked earlier: dark half-moons beneath her eyes, a stark contrast to the vibrant Keisha I know.

I've always been in awe of how Keisha takes things in stride. Even when her last boyfriend broke up with her, Keisha shrugged it off, "That's his loss." While the rest of us stressed over mid-term exams, Keisha remained unbothered, confident in her intelligence and test taking skills.

I can't even begin to imagine what's keeping her up at night. Could it have something to do with why she was at Mallory's house? Maybe Mallory did something to upset her. If so, why would she keep it from me? We've always told each other everything– or so I thought. It doesn't make any sense.

Before I know it, we're at my front door. Mom waits outside, arms folded across her chest. "Lani!" Red pops out of the car, his arms outstretched.

They embrace, Mom's nightgown billowing in the wind. "I'm going to do whatever I can to help your family," Red says.

"Thank you so much, Red."

"The sun's coming up soon. I must go." Red slides back inside his sports car. The doors lower and snap shut. "I'll be in touch." Red calls out the window. His Ferrari's taillights fade and then disappear down the driveway.

On the front porch, I sit on a wicker rocking chair. A frigid gust whips through my hair, but I barely feel the cold. Adrenaline courses through me, hot in my veins. It's like I'm still out on the dance floor: enraptured by the prismatic lights, hips swaying to the enchanting music, high off the exhilaration surrounding me. It's all so fresh in my mind, and I don't ever want it to fade.

A black cat dives off the porch railing and plops onto my lap. Batman rubs his cheek against me, an affectionate gesture that marks a cat's best friend. If Zoe was home, he'd ignore me and snuggle her. Once she's back, I'll be history. Batman stares up at me, his yellow eyes wide like saucers. He releases a low meow.

"I miss Zoe, too," I say. "Don't worry. She'll be home soon." It's a promise I've made to him every day since I've been home. It's the first time it doesn't feel like a lie.

Mom and I sit in silence, watching the sun rise. Batman purrs against my chest. Birds chirp their morning song. Orange ribbons streak across the sky.

"So," I say, my fingers buried in Batman's silky fur. "Since things worked out so well, I guess I'm not in trouble."

Mom smirks. "Nice try."

Chapter 16

Zoeli

Clack. Clack. Clack. Frederick's footsteps hit the ground, growing closer and closer. Frantic, I search for a hiding place.

A few feet away, a garbage can leans against the wall. My wings flutter, roiling the air beneath me. I ascend, sailing through space and into the trash bin. I don't need to learn how to fly. I already know. It's effortless: as simple as taking a breath.

I feared that this body would feel foreign to me. That couldn't be farther from the truth. I'm not a separate being who's borrowing the body of a crow. I am the crow.

As I plunge into the heap of half-eaten food and dirty napkins, I remember snickering not too long ago when Damian did the same. Karma is a damn bitch.

Frederick's high-pitched whistle moves closer and closer until it's right here. Frederick stands over me, his shadows darkening the cramped space. I remain stock still, praying that I can't be seen amongst the crushed soda cans and spoiled meat.

Frederick never stops whistling as he grips the side of the trash can, tilting it and rolling it along the floor. Inside, I rattle about. A bottle of wine bangs into my beak.

Frederick turns left, then right, then left again. He pushes open a heavy door, pulling the garbage can along with him.

I peer through the pile of waste. Tendrils of orange sunlight stretch across the dawn sky. A gust of fresh air rustles cans and paper plates.

Frederick leaves the garbage pail against a castle wall. He walks away, his footsteps softening in the distance.

I can scarcely believe it.

I'm free.

I wriggle out from in between bottles and soiled paper cups and burst into the sky.

I soar around the palace, admiring the majestic stone towers, weaving through the colorful waves of magic emitted by the Rock of Vitality.

I peer through windows, searching for a very special person.

I find him inside a circular tower. He sits on the edge of a massive bed. He stares at the wall, lost in thought, waiting.

I perch on the edge of his balcony.

Damian's head jerks to the side. His black eyes meet mine.

Chapter 17

The crow balances on the ledge of my balcony. Could this be real? Is it her? My heart hammers in my chest.

I slide open the glass door. I blink fast, praying that she won't vanish. Lack of sleep can drive someone mad, make them hear and see things that aren't there. Or it could just be an ordinary crow, a cruel coincidence that would leave me shattered.

The crow's aquamarine eyes shine, leaving me no doubt. It's her. Even as a crow, Zoe's magnificent. I'm flooded with such intense joy, my knees buckle. I catch myself before I fall, leaning on the balcony railing. "Zoe," I breathe. "It's you. It's really you."

She perches on my hand. Ribbons of blue magic swirl around her, and then she's in my arms. I run my hands through her long black hair, down her back and back up her front. She's so thin. I can feel every bone, every groove, every divot of her rib cage.

She needs food: a real, good meal. I'm going to take care of her, feed her, and make sure that she never wants for anything ever again.

I kiss her. Again and again and again. Every brush of her soft lips sends tingles down my spine. "I love you."

"I love you, Damian." Hearing those words sets me on fire. I lift her up. She wraps her legs around my waist. Groaning, I carry her inside and lower her onto the bed

"Damian." Zoe laughs. "I'm filthy!"

"I don't care," I murmur into her neck. "I need you now."

Zoe presses her hand against my chest. "I haven't had a proper shower in months. I can't even stand to smell myself."

I lift her off the bed, her legs still around me as I kick open the door of my ensuite bathroom. I pass the shower and instead turn the faucet on my jacuzzi. I toss in Epsom salt, essential oils, and bubble bath. As Zoe undresses, I light candles and turn on a romantic playlist. I want everything to be perfect.

I take off my clothes and step inside the jacuzzi. Zoeli climbs onto my lap. I gently wash her hair, caressing her scalp. Then I move onto her body, cleaning her with lavender soap.

I touch every single part of her with every single part of me. Heaven could never compare to this.

A few hours later, we're curled up in my bed, dozing with her head on my chest.

Knock! Knock! Knock! Loud bangs on my door jostle us awake. "Prince Nightingale, I need you to open your door immediately." Elric Hawke's voice booms from the other side.

Zoe's eyes pop open; her lower lip quivers. "It's okay," I say under my breath. "We knew this would happen. Just follow the plan."

Swirls of blue encompass her as she transforms. As a crow, she follows me across my bedroom and into my walk-in closet. I roll her up inside a blue pillowcase. Then, I squeeze her onto a shelf stacked with folded sheets and blankets. "Don't worry," I whisper. "They aren't looking for a bird."

I swing open my bedroom door. Elric peers beyond me, a dozen guards behind him. "Prince Nightingale," Elric drawls. "Where have you been?"

"Sleeping. What the hell's going on?"

He slithers past me, a smug look on his face. I'd like to take his long ponytail and wring it around his neck. "Haven't you heard?" Elric narrows his beady black eyes, studying me, as if he's waiting for a confession.

"I just told you: I was sleeping," I say.

"A prisoner has gone missing. We're searching the entire palace. You don't have a problem with that, do you?" His question feels more like an accusation.

I throw my hands up. "Of course not. Search away."

The guards tear through my room like a tornado. They check under my bed. They move all my furniture. They ransack my closet. Guards toss clothes to the ground. They tear bedding off the shelves. The blue pillow case that contains Zoe is thrown on the floor. I cringe. That must've hurt.

Elric prowls the room, a few steps behind the guards, assessing if anything has been missed.

"No one's here." A guard announces.

"We've checked every nook and cranny." Another guard emerges from the bathroom.

Elric tramps through my closet, scrutinizing every corner. He steps on a hanger, oblivious when it snaps in half. Centimeters away from his boot, inside a rumpled pillowcase, Zoe hides. One step to the right, and Elric will crush her. My breath lodges in my throat. Elric thrusts a coat aside. He nods, seemingly satisfied. "All clear," he says. He turns left and steps out of my closet.

"Should I summon the maid to clean up?" Elric asks.

"I'll handle it," I say. "I'm particular with the way I like my things."

"Hmph," Elric says, dragging his finger across his pointy chin. For a long moment, we stare at each other. Finally, he breaks the silence. "Prince Nightingale, I assume you'll be joining us for the search."

"Of course," I say. "I'll need a few minutes to get dressed."

"Certainly, your majesty." He slams the door on his way out.

I collapse onto my bed and release a long huff of air. I wait until the footsteps are long gone before I check on the crow in my closet.

Chapter 18

Saria

"Miranda Keller's missing," Giselle says. "She disappeared from her bedroom last night."

"I heard," I say. The whole school was buzzing about it all day. Theories ran the gamut from alien abductions to serial killers. One thing's for sure: everyone's shaken up. I wasn't the only one looking over my shoulder today.

"I'm terrified." Penny's lower lip trembles. "We need to be extra careful." Penny's always been scared of her own shadow. She rummages through her backpack and takes out three small plastic containers. She hands one to each of us.

"What's this?" Giselle wrinkles her forehead.

"Pepper spray. Always keep it with you," Penny responds.

"Do you seriously have a stockpile of pepper spray?" Giselle's eyebrows shoot up.

"Do you seriously *not*?" Penny responds. "We have to be vigilant. Do you have a safety whistle on your keychain?"

"Chill with the drama," Giselle says, tossing her pepper spray into her center console. "Miranda probably ran away.

She was kind of weird. A loner. Always kept to herself. Maybe she joined a cult or something."

"I thought she was nice. *Is* nice," I correct myself. I hate how we're talking about her in the past tense already. I slide the pepper spray into my pocket. "Thanks, Penny."

Keisha clutches the bottle in her lap. "Are you okay, Keisha?" I ask. The Keisha who I know and love was always ready with a witty comment. At moments like this, she'd break up the tension with a clever remark. The new Keisha just stares straight ahead, biting her lip. What happened to my best friend? Did Mallory do something to her?

"What?" Keisha startles. "Oh. Yeah. I'm fine."

As we pull in front of my house, Penny continues, "Always be aware of who's around you. Lock your doors. Don't go out alone at night. A lunatic's on the loose."

A shiver runs down my spine. "Be safe, guys." I get out of the car, swinging my backpack over my shoulder. "See you tomorrow." I hop up onto my porch, open the front door and lock it behind me. As I walk through the vestibule, my pink loafers squeak on the tile floor.

When I enter the kitchen, I do a double take. We have visitors. I almost don't recognize King Keifer in his rumpled sweater. Queen Taya wears jeans, her hair tied up in a messy ponytail.

I freeze, ice water shooting through my veins. "W-w-what–" The word catches in my throat. Mom's white knuckles clench the kitchen island. My father stands beside her, biting his lower lip.

"Sit down, Saria," Dad says, nodding towards the kitchen table.

My heart pounds like hooves on a racetrack. What the hell is going on? For the king and queen to come to the human realm, to come to our house… this must be serious.

A terrifying thought crosses my mind: what if they know that I went to see Red? It's illegal for witches to socialize with vampires. King Keifer's final warning in the courtroom echoes in my psyche: *"If you violate any of our conditions, we won't be easy on you next time."*

My hands shake. Even as I shiver, my cheeks heat up, burning like they've caught fire.

"You're going to want to sit down for this," Dad repeats.

With a slick palm, I pull out the chair farthest from the king and queen. My backpack slides off my stiff shoulder and clatters onto the floor.

I sit, staring down at my skinny jeans and pink fingernails. Pretty soon I might have to trade my clean hands and stylish clothes for filthy cuticles and a smelly prison jumpsuit.

I have no doubt that they're here to throw me back in the dungeon.

At least I'll be with Zoeli.

Some part of me is relieved. Maybe this is what I wanted all along. Maybe this is why I sought out Red. Subconsciously, I hoped I'd be caught.

I miss Zoeli so much.

Every day, I grapple with guilt more painful than the guards' strikes. Zoeli doesn't deserve to suffer. It should be me, not her.

My gaze shifts from the king to the queen. They probably expect me to fight and deny their accusation, but I'm ready to surrender.

Zoeli and I will be together again. One day, we'll find a way out. Maybe Red will help us. Either way, Zoeli won't have to spend another night alone.

I clear my throat, my confession on the tip of my tongue.

The king speaks first. "Have you heard or seen from your twin?" King Keifer speaks too loudly for the small space, his voice reverberating in my bones.

"Wha-what do you mean? How could I?"

"Zoeli is missing." Queen Taya wrings her hands. "We thought that she might have reached out to you."

My jaw drops. "Mi-missing?"

"Do you know where she is?" The queen asks.

"No." I shake my head.

"Look at me." King Keifer demands. Reluctantly, I raise my head. His black gaze pierces mine. I swallow.

The king studies my face. Heat moves from my jawline to my cheekbones to the creases on my brow. I feel exposed, like he's seeing parts of me that I didn't give him permission to. I pull my cardigan tighter around my shoulders. "Either she's telling the truth or she's a damn good actress." He turns to my parents. "We're going to search the house."

Dad steps forward. "Is that necessary?"

Mom puts her hand on Dad's shoulder. "It's okay. We have nothing to hide."

King Keifer whistles. Soldiers storm the house, ransacking each room, tossing knick-knacks and figurines in the air. A ceramic angel shatters on the floor, a million pieces that will never fit together again.

I follow the soldiers up the stairs. In my room, they flip my bed upside down. My heart pounds. They hurl my jewelry box against the wall. It flies open, launching jewelry in space. Necklaces ricochet. A friendship bracelet skitters by my feet. It was handcrafted by Zoe when we were kids. The letter-beads stare up at me: Best Sister. Tears well in my eyes.

The soldiers rip my closet door off its hinges. My palms sweat. They fling clothes, hangers, and shoes across the room.

The ringing in my ears grows louder and louder until it's all I hear. I press my fingers in my ear holes. It doesn't help. I can't silence what comes from within.

A soldier knocks down my bedside table. A framed photo of my sister and I plunges to the wood floor. The photo reminds me of a simpler time: Zoe and I posing by our Christmas tree, smiling for the camera, our arms around each other.

The frame cracks in two, separating me and my sister. Spiderweb-like cuts hide my face. Soldiers kick the debris aside. My possessions crunch beneath their boots as they march out of my room.

I sit on the floor, surrounded by the wreckage. Fragments of my life, all of which are meaningless without Zoeli.

I assess the damage: splintered furniture, demolished trophies, fractured mirrors. Broken, like me.

Chapter 19

Zoeli

It's been weeks since I escaped from jail. Now that the initial glow has worn off, I realize that I'm not free. I only moved to another prison.

During the day, Damian goes to school. After school, he often has obligations to fulfill as prince or social plans. He eats every evening in the royal dining room. As for me, I hide in the closet.

On the weekends, Damian hangs out with friends and goes to parties. He claims that he'd rather be with me, but it would arouse suspicion if he declined these invitations to stay home alone. As for me, I hide in the closet.

I must admit that this penitentiary is an upgrade from the last. Compared to the moldy bread thrusted through the dungeon bars, the gourmet meals are heaven. Instead of sleeping on a cold stone floor, I curl up next to Damian, wrapped in downy covers and silky sheets. Oh, and did I mention that my jailer is devastatingly handsome? Every time his lips twist into that lopsided grin, my heart does a flip.

Still, the fact remains. As much as he'll claim that it isn't the case, Damian is my prison warden. He has a life outside these four walls. I do not have a life. I exist. I eat and breathe. I sleep in my jailer's arms inside a glorified jail cell.

Damian doesn't let me fly. He's afraid that someone will realize who I am, and I'll be captured.

After over a week of losing my mind with boredom, I started exploring the castle, navigating the extensive labyrinth of ducts. I peek through the vents, studying rooms and people, admiring lavish furnishings, and eavesdropping on conversations.

A love triangle amongst the servants has been my latest distraction. Even though the maid Daniella and the chef Callum are in a relationship, Daniella's "best friend" Avril hits on him every chance she gets. The last time Avril cornered him in the kitchen, they almost kissed. Callum turned his head at the very last minute, and Avril's lips brushed against his cheek.

Damian doesn't approve of my choice of entertainment, but he knows he can't do a damn thing about it. I'm invested. If Callum doesn't tell Avril to shove it, he'll find a pile of crow poop on his head.

I fly to the top shelf of Damian's closet and squeeze inside the vent. I enter the tunnel, sailing through gaps of darkness. As I glide closer to my destination, slivers of light illuminate the way, shining through the kitchen vents. I peer through the slats. Callum chops vegetables. Daniella wipes down a counter. Avril's nowhere to be found. Maybe she has the day off. After a few minutes of watching the monotonous hack of Callum's knife, I decide to venture onwards.

I've never gone this far out. My feathers brush against the narrow walls of the duct. I move through the maze, right, then left, right and left again, until I'm dizzy and not sure that I'll be able to find my way back.

King Keifer's voice booms through the sheetrock. "We have to find that nimwit!"

I tiptoe to the nearest vent and peek through. King Keifer sits behind an enormous gold desk. An ornate carving of a nightingale decorates the front of the desk. It looks vicious: beak open, eyes narrowed, and nothing like the true appearance of the bird.

Elric sits on the other side of the desk, legs crossed, smoothing his long ponytail. "We've searched high and low."

"Do you think Talon and Licinia have her?"

Elric shakes his head. "Impossible." He flips through some papers. "Our intelligence reports that their militia has grown to over a thousand members. They've adopted the name Descendants of Xaphan, after the demon who's said to be the grandfather of witches. They encourage their members to embrace their demonic side. They claim that Aurelian rules suppress our natural urges. Their primary mission is to take over Aurelia and rewrite our laws, starting with allowing humans to be our slaves."

"Over a thousand members." Keifer bites his lip. "Their numbers are up."

"Yes, their numbers are large, but they pose no real threat to us. They can't get in. They are trying to reverse the spell that protects our borders, which you and I both know is a futile effort."

"That spell is five hundred years old," Keifer says. "Many have tried to reverse it, but none have succeeded."

"The spell was one-of-a-kind, created for the explicit purpose of protecting our homeland. Every record of the spell has been destroyed, aside from the one kept in the Nightingale vault. Even if they manage to coerce seven royal members to participate, the traitors won't know where to begin."

Keifer presses a button on a remote control. Mounted in the corner, a television turns on. A reporter stands amid a raucous crowd. Dressed in a red suit and matching lipstick, she speaks into her microphone. "We're at Lyon Square where many have gathered to protest the Nightingale regime."

Protesters march and chant. "We demand a re-election now!"

Standing beside the reporter, a blonde protestor wears a hat that reads 'Overthrow the Nightingales.'

"This is Holly McCain, one of the organizers of today's protest. What is your purpose here today?" The reporter says.

The blonde woman takes the microphone. "The Nightingales are unfit to rule Aurelia. How can we trust a regime who can't keep track of their violent criminals? With Zoeli Crowe at large, none of us are safe. Not only did Zoeli steal her sister's magic, she has a store of blue magic. She's ruthless, powerful and wants nothing more than to avenge her imprisonment by killing us all!"

I suppress a fit of laughter. The Nightingales painted me as a villain, and now it's come back to bite them in the ass. Watching Keifer and Elric squirm almost makes every tortuous moment in the dungeon worth it. Almost.

Holly McCain isn't done. "With terroristic threats at an all-time high, we need strong leaders who can protect us from evil. Our constitution says that a re-election can be held if the current leaders are not performing their duties up to par. We demand a re-election now!"

Keifer slams his fist on his desk. A glass nightingale topples over the edge, shattering at Elric's feet.

Chapter 20

Saria

"You're going to the club again?" Logan's tone is sharp. He doesn't bother to conceal his annoyance anymore.

"I have the most fun when I'm there," I say.

"Thanks a lot," Logan mumbles.

"I didn't mean…" My voice trails off. I don't want to hurt Logan. The truth is: Red's isn't just a place to dance and laugh with my new friends. It's my refuge.

It's the only time that my anxiety abates. I don't have to look over my shoulder because Red's watching my back. He's not only incredibly powerful, but seems determined to protect me. I'm not sure why. Probably because he was friends with my mom. The bottom line is: no one messes with me when he's nearby. Safe in the smoke, laser lights and heady rhythms, I can lose myself for a little while.

Logan stares down at his chemistry textbook. "You used to think that being with me was fun."

"I still do," I say, but my words feel hollow. It's not that I don't have fun with Logan. It's just exhausting hiding everything from him. I can't tell Logan that Zoe disappeared from a jail in a realm that he doesn't know exists. He still has no idea what I endured during those months that I was missing. When I want to scream and vent about everything I've been through, I call Red.

"Come with me to the club," I say.

Logan gestures to his chemistry textbook. "I have to study. I need to keep my grades up so I can get a scholarship. You used to care about your grades too."

He's right. My grades are slipping and I just can't bring myself to care. Since Zoe's been gone, everything else seems so unimportant. How can I worry about my future when I don't even know if Zoe has one?

"You can study tomorrow," I say. "Come out with me tonight."

"Is it even safe to be going out to New York City? Miranda's still missing. It's been weeks and there's no leads…" His voice trails off. He doesn't want to say Zoeli's name. It hurts.

"Red will make sure that we're safe," I say.

"Red, Red, Red." Logan spits the name like it's a curse.

"Once you meet him, you'll like him." I say, even though I'm not certain.

"Fine." Logan looks up, his hazel eyes meeting mine. "I'll go."

"Really?" I jump up and clap. "I'll text Red to send one of his drivers to pick us up. We're going to have the best night ever."

* * *

A few hours later, the black Rolls Royce parks in front of Red's front door. Logan spent the entire drive pretending not to be impressed by the car, but I saw his fingers graze the smooth leather, his eyes widening when Ezekiel, one of Red's drivers, careened around a curve.

Ezekiel parks, jumps out of the driver's side and darts around to open the back door. "This way, Sari." A line of people hoping to get into Red's stretches down the block. Men and women are dressed to the nines. I follow Ezekiel, passing the blur of sequins, stilettos and red lips. I reach behind me, taking Logan's hand. My boyfriend looks quite dapper himself, dressed in a black collared shirt with white pinstripes and black dress pants. He even used gel to tame his wavy dark-blonde hair.

Ezekiel leads us to the front of the line. "Logan and Sari are Mr. Castigan's special guests this evening."

Luke nods and opens the door behind him. I'm a regular by now.

Logan follows me down the long narrow stairway. The scones flicker, immersing us in intermittent blackness. Logan loops his fingers through mine and squeezes. His palm is slick with sweat.

At the bottom step, I suck in a deep breath. Was it a good idea bringing Logan here? What if he doesn't get along with Red? What if he's scared of my new friends?

Before I grab the knob, the door swings open. Red stands on the other side. He's gorgeous in a tight black t-shirt that emphasizes his sculpted pecs. His eyes are brighter than the neon lasers that shoot across the ceiling.

"Sari!" Red smiles, white teeth gleaming. "I'm glad you made it. And you must be Logan," Red extends his hand.

Logan stares for a moment, then takes it. He keeps his other hand firmly enclosed around mine. "It's a pleasure to meet you." They shake hands. "Sari speaks highly of you."

"Um, thanks," Logan murmurs.

"Sari!" Bea skips over and scoops me up in a hug. Even though she's petite, she has supernatural strength. One of these days she might break my ribs by accident. "And you must be Logan!" She hugs him too, like he's an old friend. "I'm Beatrice, but call me Bea. It's so good to finally meet you. Sari talks about you all the time." She fiddles with the antique locket she always wears. As usual, she's decked out in 1920s attire: beaded cap, sequin dress and fur stole. She's stunning.

Logan visibly relaxes, his shoulders dropping an inch or two. Bea tends to have that effect on people. "I have to mix you a special drink." Bea loves to get behind the bar.

"She makes the most incredible virgin cocktails I've ever tasted," I tell Logan. "Red won't let me have alcohol." I playfully jab Red's side. Logan frowns, his gaze on the place where I touched Red.

"You're underage," Red says. "Besides, when you're at my club, you don't need to be drunk to have fun."

"I know, I know."

Logan and I slide onto bar stools as Bea gets to work. She bobs to the music, pouring ingredients into a silver tumbler. She tosses it into the air, catching it and then spinning it around like a baton.

"Show off," Red teases.

Bea pours our drinks and slides them across the bar. I take a sip: bubbly sweet goodness hits my tongue. "Mmm," I murmur. "So good."

"Delicious," Logan agrees.

"Sari!" Nikita, the lead singer of The Dragon's Psalm, moves through the crowd "What's up?" The other night, Nikki and I chatted for hours. She also lost a sister, albeit many years ago. She understood my pain. I told her about Zoeli's passion for music. She promised that if Zoeli ever comes back, she'll jam with her. Zoeli would die to play with a band like The Dragon's Psalm.

"Hey Nikki. This is my boyfriend, Logan."

"Pleasure to meet you." As she settles on a barstool, Nikki holds her long braids aside to avoid sitting on them.

If Logan notices that my friends are all sipping murky red drinks, he doesn't say. Red slaps Logan on the shoulder. "How about I show you around while the girls catch up?"

Logan shrugs. "Okay." He stands up, wiping his palms on his black pants. As they disappear amongst the crowd, I fight the urge to follow them. This is what I wanted: for Logan and Red to become friends.

"Killer outfit, Bea," Nikki says. "Do a little twirl for me." Bea spins around, smiling ear to ear. "You look hot."

"Where do you buy your vintage clothes?" I ask. "They look straight out of the twenties."

Bea giggles. "That's because they are."

I hit myself on the forehead. "Duh." We burst into laughter.

"I'm sentimental. The twenties were my favorite era. It's also the last time I saw my parents." Bea opens her locket. I lean in, studying the black-and-white photo of a man with Bea's warm smile and a woman with Bea's sculpted cheekbones.

"You look like them," I say.

"Thank you." She wears a wistful expression as the locket clicks shut. "I have a hard time getting rid of anything from my past. My apartment's filled with junk." She chuckles. "I even sleep in the coffin my family buried me in." She shrugs. "It isn't the most comfortable, but it's where they laid me to rest." Her eyes are glassy. "There's things I've held onto for so long, it seems impossible to let them go, even though I know I should."

Logan comes up behind me. His arms slither around my waist as he kisses my cheek. Part of me wondered if Red would be jealous, but he doesn't seem to be.

Red and I are friends, nothing more. He's never tried to make a move on me. Now that I'm thinking about it, he's never even mentioned a love interest. It seems strange. Red could have his pick. Why would he choose to be alone?

A group of partygoers wave and shout. "Hey Red!" A woman in a plaid miniskirt calls out. "It's my birthday!"

"Happy birthday," Red calls back. He gestures to a bartender. "Send a round of free drinks over to that group of ladies."

"Red, come dance with me!" The birthday girl shakes her hips.

Red grins. "I'll be right there." He turns back to us. "Go on and dance, you two. Enjoy your date. If you need anything, give me a holler."

A few minutes later, I bring Logan out onto the dance floor. Without Red leading me, my dance skills fall flat. Unlike Red, Logan doesn't have a hundred years of dance practice under his belt. He doesn't know how to dip or spin me. In fact, he steps on my feet almost as often as he almost trips over his own.

But it doesn't matter. We're clumsy, off-rhythm and awkward, but we're still *us*. Logan's head bobs to the music. His hazel eyes meet mine.

When I look into his eyes, I see more than amber flecks and endless lashes. I see the two of us hiking through the woods, logging every species of bird we saw. I see the young boy who helped me rescue a litter of kittens. I see the two of us dripping with sweat, hauling lumber and drilling boards. Nights later, we laid in our treehouse, studying the stars. I see the boy who grew up and became the young man I fell in love with, the most tender and loyal boyfriend a girl could ever ask for.

Logan's not part of this world. He's a relic from my old life, a gentler existence where my biggest problems were petty arguments and softball scores.

Logan doesn't belong here. He belongs in a place much purer than this.

"I have to go to the bathroom," Logan says. I guide him to an alcove in the corner. He disappears into the men's room.

"Having fun?" Red leans against the wall, a few inches from me.

"Yes. I think Logan's having fun, too."

"Are you happy?"

"You know the answer. As long as Zoe is miss–"

Red cuts me off. "I mean, are you happy with him?"

"Yes."

Red's eyes meet mine. I feel the heat of blue fire. "Good." He nods.

"What about you?" I ask.

"What about me?"

"How come you don't date anyone?"

Red shrugs. "I don't think love is in the cards for me."

"Why's that?" My brow creases.

"Most humans want someone who can give them children, someone to grow old with. I can't do either of those things." Red looks down. "I loathe to admit it, but I used to partake in casual encounters with humans. I even led some on, knowing that it could never work. I broke their hearts. I don't want to cause any more hurt, and the only way to do that is to abstain from romance entirely."

"What if there was a human who would change into a vampire for you?" I ask.

"I could never ask someone to do that," Red says. "Besides, creating a new vampire would break the treaty between vampires and witches. My actions could start another war. At the very least, I'd be sentenced to death."

"It doesn't seem fair. Aren't there any vampires that interest you? What about Bea? She's amazing."

Red chuckles. "And like a sister to me. Not to mention that I don't think that I'm her type." Red nods towards the dance floor. I follow his gaze. Bea dances with a beautiful woman, emerald eyes shining. Bea's ring-clad hand strokes the woman's back. The woman brushes a stray chestnut strand from Bea's cheek. They kiss: mouths open, tongues touching.

"Oh," I say. "I didn't realize. Well, there has to be someone."

"Don't worry about me, Sari. I've accepted my fate."

The bathroom door opens and Logan steps out. Logan's gaze shifts from me to Red, and then back to me. "Do you want to dance?" Logan asks, holding out his hand.

"Yes," I say, taking his palm in mine.

Chapter 21

Zoeli

"I want to get out of here," I say. "I'm sick of being cooped up." I take another bite of the chicken a la royale. After everyone went to bed, Damian snuck downstairs to heat up a plate for me. "Mmm, this is delicious." I saw Callum preparing the sauce earlier today. Avril sidled up and massaged his shoulders while he worked. Callum told her in no uncertain terms to leave him alone. He's avoided a load of crow-poop shampoo–for now. I'll continue to keep an eye out.

"Let's watch a movie." Damian flicks on the television.

"No." I grab the remote and turn off the TV. "I want to go out."

"Zoe, we can't." Damian wraps his arms around me. "What if someone sees us?"

"How will they know who we are? Couldn't we just be two ordinary birds?"

"I don't want to risk it. Your eyes…" His voice trails off.

"If anyone's around, we'll stay far enough away so that they can't see my eyes."

Damian sighs. "It's too dangerous."

"It'll be more dangerous in here when I wallop your ass." I pick up the nightingale-shaped lamp from Damian's nightstand and hold it over my head.

Damian chuckles. I put the lamp down, but I don't join in the laughter. "I'm not happy, Damian."

He rubs my back. "Things will get better."

"When?"

"I don't know. It's not that simple."

"I miss my family: my mom, my dad, my sister. I miss my friends, my band. I should be going to school and practicing for the next battle of the bands." My throat feels thick. I swallow the lump down. "I miss everyone. I miss my mom's cooking and my dad's lame jokes. I miss my cat Batman, his purr, and how he used to greet me with his tail straight up in the air." Biting my lips doesn't stop the tears from falling. "I miss Saria. I miss home."

"I'm sorry." Damian rubs his hands on his thighs.

"I'm going stir crazy. I'm going out tonight, with or without you."

"With me," Damian says. "I'll take you anywhere you want."

"Just not home," I say.

"No, not home. They'll find you there. We'd put your family at risk, too." Damian laces his fingers through mine. "But I'll show you the most amazing places in Aurelia. There are so many incredible sights to see."

"Okay." I stuff the last piece of chicken in my mouth. "Let's go."

A cloud of purple mist and streaks of blue magic intertwine. A nightingale and a crow emerge; the boy and girl seem to vanish.

We soar through the open window and into the night sky. It's exhilarating: the wind blowing back my feathers, sailing up higher and higher. Below me, houses and headlights grow smaller: matchbox villages lit up by fireflies.

Follow me to the Elysian Forest.

We whiz over treetops and rooftops, leaving the city lights far behind us. We fly further out, dancing with the stars. The air is fresher than any I've ever breathed, uncontaminated by the pollution and evil below. I fill my lungs with hope and freedom.

The nightingale begins to descend. I glide downwards, diving into a canopy of lush green. In a meadow of wildflowers, we shift bodies. I have arms, legs and hair again, but I'm not any more me than I was as a crow.

Damian stretches out on the soft grass, lifting his arms overhead. His biceps bulge beneath his white t-shirt. His lips curve into a sexy half-smile. My man is so fine.

"Come," Damian says, rising to his feet. He laces his fingers through mine. Hand in hand, we walk through the meadow. Damian picks a blue flower. "It's tweedia," he says. "Smell it."

I raise it to my nose and breathe deeply, relishing its almond-like fragrance. I slide the stem behind my ear. Damian nods in approval. "It matches your eyes."

I skip over to a patch of oxeye daisies and pick one. I begin to pluck the petals, one by one. "He loves me, he loves me not, he loves me, he loves me not, he loves me, he loves me not…" Beside me, Damian slips his hand over the small of my back. "He loves me…" I pluck the last one. "He loves me not." The final petal falls, somersaulting in the air, twisting and turning before it disappears in the tall grass.

"That's a silly game," Damian says. "Of course I love you. You don't need a daisy to tell you that."

I smile, but my chest feels tight.

"Come this way," Damian says. "There's more to see." I follow him through the field, down a trail and into the woods. Damian leads me through the thicket, climbing over brush and ducking under branches until we reach a river. He steps onto a boulder. "Take a look."

I climb onto the huge rock and look down. Below me, glow-in-the-dark fish light up indigo water. They circle around, every color of the rainbow, creating designs like a kaleidoscope. "That's incredible," I say, mesmerized.

A creature emerges from underwater. It rolls on its back, yellow scales protruding above the water. "What's that?" I whisper.

Damian's eyes widen. "It's a dragoni. They're nearly extinct. We used to hunt them for sport. I've never been this close to one."

The creature floats our way. It climbs onto land and ascends our boulder like a spider. Triangular-shaped eyes stare up at me. Inches from me, it stands on two hind legs and stretches its bat-like wings.

My heart races wildly. The creature is the size of a cat, but looks something like a dragon. I've never seen anything like it.

I hold out my palm. The dragoni sniffs my hand. "Careful," Damian warns. I stroke its head, scales soft beneath my fingertips.

Its mouth stretches wide open, revealing razor-sharp teeth. I pull away, my hand to my lips.

A melody erupts from its throat, raising goosebumps on my skin. I try to decipher the medley of sounds: something like a violin, a harp, a cello and a flute. It's like an entire orchestra lives inside its little body.

"He's singing," Damian whispers. "That means he likes you."

I smile from ear to ear. "Can I keep him?" I ask.

"They aren't pets. They need to be free. If you try to contain one, it'll become vicious," Damian says.

All around me, trees light up. Branches extend, reaching up into the sky. Golden lights flicker, twisting around the boughs. "What's happening?" I whisper.

"They're Whimsy trees," Damian explains. "They pick up on strong emotions. They're expressing your happiness." Damian juts his chin at the dragoni. "And his." Damian runs his finger along my jawline. "And mine."

The trees dance to the dragoni's lullaby. Branches swing, iridescent leaves swaying to the rhythm. "This is spectacular," I say. "I wish Saria could see this." At the mention of my sister, a lump rises in my throat. Tears well in my eyes.

The lights embedded in the bark dissolve. Branches sag. Leaves shrivel up. "Now they feel your sadness," Damian says.

"Oh no," I said. "I don't want to make the trees sad."

"I'll see if I can fix that," Damian says. He kisses behind my ear. Tingles race down my spine. He tangles his fingers in my hair, gently pulling, exposing the crook of my neck. He kisses me there, again and again. Heat rushes through me. His kisses trace my collarbone, then glide down to the space between my breasts.

The dragoni takes off in flight, singing his goodbye, as if he senses our need for privacy. The Whimsies come back to life, red hot fire burning on their branches.

"These trees are on point," I murmur as Damian's tongue moves lower and lower.

Chapter 22

Saria

Everything's falling apart. I thought that Logan and I had a great time at the club, but I was wrong. The next day Logan said that he felt uncomfortable there. He also said that he thinks that my new friends are "creepy," and accused me of having a "thing" for Red. "Do you think I'm blind?" he asked.

Since then, he's been distant. When I call him, he finds an excuse to get off the phone. When I text him, I'm lucky if he responds with one word. In the school hallways, he's brusque, rushing past without a kiss.

It's the weekend again, and I'm all alone. Giselle's busy with some new guy. Logan's all but ignoring me. Keisha still looks like she needs a week in bed. I call her, but she doesn't pick up. I hope she's sleeping, but I doubt it. She still hasn't told me what's wrong or what the deal is with her and Mallory.

Maybe Penny's around. I try her number and get her voicemail. She must be busy, too.

I sigh and shoot another text message to Logan. *I know you're upset. Can we talk?*

A few minutes pass. *Please?*

My phone pings. ***I'm studying.***

I shake my head. This is ridiculous. I pick up the phone and call him.

"Hey," he says.

"We need to talk," I say.

"Are you breaking up with me?" Logan asks.

"What? No."

"You probably should, since you're into another guy."

"I'm not into Red."

"Will you stop going out to his club?"

"What? Why should I?"

"Ah, you're deflecting and not answering my question. Will you stop going there?"

"What? No. You're being ridiculous."

"Ridiculous. Right. So, if I was going out every night to dance with some hot girl, would you be cool with it?"

"I don't go there every night."

"So, you admit that you're dancing with a hot guy?"

"What's your problem? We're just friends."

"Famous last words."

"Logan, in case you forgot, my sister's missing. Why are you being like this? My life is hard enough."

"Go be with Red. He's so amazing. He won't make anything harder for you."

"Are you serious right now?" My heart thumps in my chest. "I feel like I don't even know you anymore."

"The feeling's mutual."

"Are you breaking up with me?"

There's a long pause. My heart beat thrums in my ears, vibrating my eardrum.

"I guess I am."

Something snaps inside me. Another thread comes undone, unspooling, loosening my hold on reality. I'm untethered, floating into nothingness, my sanity drifting further and further from my reach.

Tears slide down my cheeks. I hang up the phone.

My chair seems to rock beneath me. I grip the sides, my knuckles white.

My phone buzzes in my hand. I answer the phone without knowing who it is.

"Hello?"

"Sari! What's going on?"

"Logan broke up with me." I choke on the words.

"I'm sorry, but I can't say I'm surprised."

"What do you mean?"

"I told you that I can sense things. Last week, at the club, I could feel his turmoil. He loves you, but he's intimidated by you. He's deeply insecure. Logan isn't strong enough to be your man."

"That doesn't make it any easier," I say.

"I know, Sari. I'm sorry. It takes time to heal."

"Send a car. I want to go out tonight."

"Are you sure you're up to it?"

"Yes," I say. "Moping around here isn't going to make me feel any better."

"Ezekiel's on his way."

* * *

As Red twirls me around, my skirt flies up around my waist. Good thing I wore spandex shorts underneath.

Red's done everything to show me a good time, but I'm still feeling blue. He says that it will take time, but what I crave right now is a quick fix. In my peripheral vision, a woman sips a glass of champagne.

"I need a drink," I say.

"What do you need? Soda? Water?"

"No, Red. I want a real drink. With alcohol."

"You're underage."

I put my hands on my hips. "How old were you when you changed over?"

"Seventeen."

"I thought so. You're the same age as me."

"I don't drink alcohol."

"That's because you can't." I poke him in the chest. "Are you telling me that you never had an alcoholic drink when you were a human?"

Red sighs. "Touche."

"One glass of champagne?"

Red snaps his fingers. A waiter rushes over. "A glass of Dom Perignon."

"Yes, sir." The waiter darts to the bar.

One glass turns into two turns into three. "One more," I say.

"I think you've had enough," Red says. He spins me around, once, twice, three times, and then steadies me in his arms. I feel like I'm still spinning. His hips move, my body pressed against his. I wrap my arms around his neck, my feet moving effortlessly to the rhythm. "Are you okay?" Red asks.

"I'm good." Is getting drunk a healthy way to get over a breakup? Is flirting with another guy going to help me heal faster? Probably not, but right now, I don't care. I'm weightless. The music is phenomenal. I swing my hips, and I feel like I'm floating away.

The lights are mesmerizing. The band is extraordinary. And the boy I'm dancing with— he's… hot.

Red's gaze is like blue fire. I study his chiseled features: strong jawline, straight nose, full lips, smooth skin. I run my hands along his broad shoulders. I brush one finger on his cheek, just to make sure that he's real. It seems impossible that perfection like this could exist.

Red pulls away. "You're drunk," he says.

"Yeah," I admit. "It's fun. You should try it."

"You know that vampires can't drink alcohol."

"But you can get drunk off blood."

"I like to keep my wits about me," Red says. "I've been known to make poor choices after I've had a few."

I bite my lip. "I'll make sure that you don't make any bad decisions." I cross my fingers behind my back.

"I suppose that one drink won't hurt," Red says. "Let's go downstairs."

In the corner of the club, the guard steps aside. As we walk down the steps to the lower level, the scent of wet dirt tickles my throat.

Hand in hand, we move across the VIP dance floor. A vampire sways back and forth, her drink sloshing over the side of her wine glass. Blood drips down her fingers. Another vampire eyes me like I'm a piece of candy, red droplets on his lips. My heart races. I'm safe, I remind myself. I'm with Red.

Red leans on the bar. "A glass of Type O, Human."

The bartender raises his eyebrows, obviously surprised by the request. "Coming right up, boss."

Drink in hand, Red leads me to the dance floor. He picks me up, swings me around, twirls and dips me. We're both breathing heavy, our chests pressed together. Energy, hot and electric, buzzes between us. Red stands back up and swallows his drink in two gulps.

"You're seventeen years old," I say to Red.

He nods. "Seventeen years, seven months and five days."

"In biology, we were learning about the brain. Scientists have shown that the human brain doesn't fully develop until at least age twenty-five. In some cases, the prefrontal cortex doesn't mature until age thirty. This is why teens are impulsive and prone to bad judgment." I pause. "Your brain stopped aging at age seventeen."

Red smirks. "Now that you've provided a great excuse, I think I'll get another drink." Red downs another drink. We spin. We laugh. He gulps down another.

A crimson color creeps into his irises, like half of a blood moon rising in his eyes. I pump my fist to the electronic beat.

"I need a break," Red says, leading me to the lounge area. We collapse onto a couch. Red puts his feet up on an ottoman.

Gio passes by, his arm around a woman's waist. His nostrils flare when he sees me. Gio still hasn't come around. I can't say that I blame him. Red explained that several of his friends were killed in the Great Witch-Vampire War.

Opposite us, on another couch, a woman straddles a man, his fangs deep in her throat. She moans. "Are they both vampires?" I ask.

"We should move," Red says, looking around for another empty couch.

"Are they both vampires?" I repeat the question.

"No. She's human."

"Is that allowed?"

"As long as he doesn't change her," Red says. "She's a consenting adult. Some vampires choose to take humans as their lovers." Goosebumps rise on my flesh. The human woman moans again.

"It doesn't hurt her," I say. It's more of an observation than a question.

"No," Red says. "Most women enjoy it." He squirms in his seat. "We should find somewhere else to hang out."

I shift closer to him. "What does it feel like?" I ask.

"For a human? I don't know firsthand, but the women I've been with have described it as euphoric."

"And for you?"

"Drinking from a live human?" He shakes his head. "It's been so long."

"What's it like?" My thigh touches his. My hair brushes against his chin.

"It's ecstasy," Red says. He moves over, putting a few inches between us. "Sari, you're too close."

"What's wrong with that?" I move back, closing the gap again. Whoever called alcohol liquid courage wasn't lying.

"It's too hard to resist you," he says.

"So then don't resist." I brush all my hair over one shoulder. I lean forward, my bare neck centimeters from his lips. As much as I've denied it for Logan's sake, I've wanted this. I think I even lied to myself. It took a bottle of champagne to expose the truth: I want this so fucking bad.

His teeth graze my neck. The hairs on the back of my neck stand up.

Red jerks away. He stands, wiping his palms on his pants. Sweat beads along his hairline. "I have to go to my office." We weave our way through the labyrinth of couches. "You can hang out with Bea while I check on a few things."

"Or I can come with you." As much as I love hanging out with Bea, all I want right now is to be alone with Red.

"Sari, you don't know what you're asking for."

"You said it won't hurt."

"I can't promise that." He slides a key into his office door. "Go find Bea." He twists the knob. The college-aged security guard, the one with curly hair and dark bags under his eyes, stands behind Red's desk.

A crease materializes between Red's brows. "Nate, what are you doing in my office?"

Nate shuffles from foot to foot, hands jammed in his pockets. "I, um, had a headache. I was, um, looking for Tylenol. I heard you had some in here."

"How did you get in here?"

"It was unlocked." He glides around the desk and slithers past us, out the door. "Sorry, boss. I'll, um, get back to work."

Red stalks over to his desk, hands clenched at his sides. He flips through stacks of paper, his brow furrowed.

"He's lying," I say. I step inside and close the door behind us. I stumble, almost tripping over the edge of the black-and-white checkered rug. The corner's folded over, probably kicked out of place when Nate raced out of here. I use my foot to smooth it back out.

"Bea must've left the door unlocked." Red leans back in his desk chair. "I'll talk to her about being more careful. As for Nate, the kid has a drug problem. He was probably using in here." His forehead creases. "I'll talk to him in private. Offer to pay for rehab if he can't afford it."

I eye a paper on Red's desk. "Commercial real estate listings in London? Are you planning to buy another bar?" I ask.

"I need to move before people realize that I don't age. I love New York, but I've already stayed longer than I should."

"So, you're moving to London?" I say. It's like a gut punch, but I don't know why. I've only known Red for a month, but it feels like so much longer. I don't want to lose him.

"Don't worry," Red says, misreading my expression. "I'm not leaving until I find your sister. I gave you my word." He stands. "Let's go back to the club."

"I thought you had work to do." I lean against his desk, tossing my hair behind my shoulders.

"Sari, you don't understand what you do to me."

"Then tell me about it."

"It isn't a good idea for us to be alone."

"Why? Do you think you'll lose control and kill me?"

"No, of course not." Red bites his lip. "I already told you why. You and me–" His finger wags back and forth between us. "We could never be together. It's impossible."

"I understand that," I say. "No relationship. No expectations. No strings attached."

"I can't do that. You're not some random hookup, Sari. You're my friend."

"Haven't you ever heard of friends with benefits?"

"It's a bad idea."

"Okay." I shrug. "Let's go back out into the club."

Red doesn't move towards the door. Half-red, half-blue eyes are glued on me. "You're gorgeous," he says, taking a step closer. Electricity crackles between us. He leans even closer. "Can I blame my underdeveloped brain?" Our lips are millimeters apart.

"Bad brain," I murmur.

Our lips touch. It's like an explosion. Shivers race through me. Sparks ignite beneath my skin. Damn. He hasn't even bit me yet.

Red lowers me down on his desk and climbs on top of me. Papers are brushed aside and fall to the floor. His lips never leave mine. We kiss, again and again, but none of the kisses are the same. Some are soft and delicate, sensual and slow. Others are deeper, frantic, tongues thrashing against each other.

His hands are in my hair. I arch my back against him. My fingers run down his chest, tracing his defined pecs and traveling down his washboard abs.

He moves lower, his lips against my neck. My jugular pulses against his teeth. He groans. He bites.

I gasp as his teeth puncture my skin. One flash of pain followed by pure unadulterated pleasure. Every cell in my body comes undone: splitting open and overflowing with bliss.

Red pulls away. His gaze meets mine. His eyes are saturated with red. Even the whites have disappeared. "You taste incredible." He slurs the words. A dopey grin spreads across his face. He's high as hell– off me. Knowing that I did that to him gives me another rush.

"Do it again," I demand.

He complies.

The rest of the world drifts away. It's only the two of us. My heart pumps blood into his veins.

Ecstasy doesn't even cover it. There are no words that could do justice to this sensation.

Euphoria. Utopia. Paradise. Rapture.

All of those words are hollow compared to what Red does to me.

Chapter 23

Zoeli

Where are we going tonight? I float along the breeze, feathers rustling with the wind.

To the Azula Sea. I'll show you the mermaids.

Mermaids?

Damian perches up on the highest bough of a Redwood. I land beside him. **Look over there.**

I peer through the leaves. Below us, the full moon reflects on a large body of water. A pelican dives, disappearing into the water, and then re-emerging, a fluorescent fish flopping in its beak. A pink frog hops between lily pads.

Over there. Damian points with his claw. There's a woman in the water. Neck deep, long white hair splays around her. She lowers herself, vanishing into the sea. Minutes pass.

Is she okay?

She's fine.

No one can hold their breath for that long.

Mermaids can. He turns his head. **Look. Right there.**

She reappears, close now, only a few hundred feet away. Her purple eyes glitter like amethysts. Wet hair clings to her copper skin. She squirms up onto a boulder, biceps flexing as she pulls up her body weight. Just like the mermaids in the movies, she's human from the waist up, and a fish from the waist down. She lays on her stomach, flipping her tail.

I had no idea that mermaids existed. Why didn't you ever tell me about them?

It isn't a nice story.

A merman hoists himself up onto the rock. He looks similar to the woman: copper skin, purple eyes, white hair, strikingly beautiful.

I want to hear it.

I don't remember all of the details. History wasn't my best subject, but I know that our kinds do not get along. Centuries ago, there was a conflict. The Wolfes were the leaders of Aurelia at the time. The curse was determined necessary for the safety of our people.

What kind of curse?

Merkind used to be able to transform their tails to legs. They divided their time between the earth and the sea. The curse prevents that.

If this happened hundreds of years ago, these merkind weren't even alive when the punishment was instated. What did they do to deserve this?

I don't make the rules.

But you will.

I will.

When you're king, can you break this curse? It doesn't seem right that they should suffer for the sins of their ancestors—if the punishment was even fair to begin with.

I'll look into it.

I swallow hard, staring at the beautiful creatures who've suffered a fate similar to my own family. Deemed enemies from birth, a part of their identity was stolen. Instead of being exiled to the human realm, they were banished to the sea.

It's criminal. As far as I can tell, since its beginnings, Aurelia has been ruled by bigots and tyrants. When Damian becomes king, he'll finally straighten out this crooked empire. It's my only hope that one day all of the unjust curses will be broken, and everyone— half-breeds, humans, duds and merman— will be treated as equals.

Do you think that my mom and sister can shift now?

Yes. The curse was imposed on your entire family. Once broken, you all were freed.

I envision my mom and Saria, swooping across the moon, cawing at the stars. Even though I wish I could fly with them, imagining their joy gives me some comfort.

Come. There's another stop on our field trip.

We fly over the Azula Sea and into a thick patch of woods. We twist our way through the tangle of branches and brush. Out here there is dead silence. There isn't another bird or creature in sight. The light flutter of our wings feels loud in the quiet.

A cackle breaks through the silence. Below us, a witch dances beneath the full moon, her wrinkled hands stretching up to the sky.

Who's that?

Edith's a notorious recluse. She exiled herself years ago, choosing to live alone in the wilderness. Some call her a genius. They travel all the way out here and pay a bundle for her advice. She claims that she can see the future, but I think she's just a crazy old hag.

Damian and I rest on a branch, watching as Edith sways beside a tiny cottage that I presume is her home. A fire glows beneath a cauldron, red flames licking its cast iron bottom. Edith tosses some herbs in. The cauldron crackles. Edith cackles maniacally. There's an explosion of green smoke, casting an eerie jade glow over the scene.

A visceral fear that I've never known before drills my bones. My heart pounds: a freight train clanging against a broken track. A wave of nausea washes over me. It feels like a premonition: an omen of evil to come.

I think we should get out of here.

But I can't move my wings. I'm frozen in this spot.

Edith jerks her chin up. She looks around. Her gaze moves slowly, inch by inch, and then stops on me. We're cloaked by foliage, deep within the snarl of branches and twigs.

Can she see us up here? It seems impossible.

"I know who you are, little bird." Edith calls in a sing-songy voice. "I know all of your secrets." She howls like a rabid animal. "Come to me, little crow."

I shiver. My claws slice the branch I perch on, bark crumbling between my talons.

"The end is coming soon!" Edith cries out. "You're all fools!"

Let's go!

My wings are my own again. Damian and I take off into flight. Wings beating, I soar away as fast as I can.

Edith's cackles echo in my mind, haunting me long after she's out of sight.

Chapter 24

Saria

I squint at the sunlight shining through my bedroom window and pull the covers over my head. I feel like shit.

There's a knock on my bedroom door. "Go away," I say. I have no idea if it's 6am or 11am. Probably the latter. If Mom thinks I'm going to be useful today, she's got another thing coming. The door squeaks open. "Leave me alone, Mom." I whine, still hiding under my blanket.

"Saria." Logan's voice makes me jump. I peer out from beneath the blanket, revealing only my eyes. Logan stands in my bedroom doorway. He holds a bouquet of autumn flowers: precisely arranged orange roses, yellow pansies and burgundy mums. My stomach turns. "I came to apologize." Logan sits on the edge of my bed and runs his fingers through his messy dirty-blonde waves. "I'm a jealous idiot. I was so convinced that you were going to break up with me for Red that I sabotaged myself." His big hazel eyes are round with hope and regret. He looks so young. "I love you. I've loved you my whole life. All I've ever wanted is to be with you and now I've gone and screwed it up." His bottom lip quivers. "I'm so sorry,

Saria. I love you so much. I don't want to break up with you. I want to be with you forever."

I sit up, keeping the blankets by my chin. "Logan," I start. My stomach flip flops. Bile rises in my throat. "Oh my God, I'm going to be sick." I dart into the adjoining bathroom and vomit. I hover over the toilet, my stomach lurching. I speak loud enough for Logan to hear me through the closed door. "I'm sorry. I'm sick."

"Do you need anything?" Logan asks from the other side.

After several more rounds of emptying my guts into the porcelain bowl, my stomach feels a little better. My head still feels like it's being stabbed by a thousand ice picks. I stagger to my feet, steadying myself on the wall as I open my bedroom door.

Logan waits on my bed. "Are you okay?"

"I'm hungover."

Logan's eyes narrow. "What the hell happened to your neck?"

My hands fly up to my throat. "Logan, I, um—"

"You hooked up with Red last night, didn't you?" Logan asks, fists clenched at his sides.

"You broke up with me," I say weakly.

"I can't believe this." Logan paces back and forth. "While I was crying in my room, you were—" He shakes his head. "I can't even think about it."

"I was hurting too. I didn't know how to cope, and they say the best way to get over someone is to get under someone else."

"You had SEX with him?"

"No." *Not because I didn't want to. Red was the one who showed restraint.* Logan doesn't need to know all the details.

"But you kissed him? And he did—" Logan points, at a loss for words, "*that* to your neck."

"Yes," I admit. *Among other things.*

Logan throws the bouquet on the floor. "We were broken up for a few hours, Saria."

"I'm sorry."

I watch as the pain seeps in. It starts in his forehead, creases etching his brow, then moves lower, his lips twisting into a grimace. "You lied to me." Agony contorts his features. His whole face squishes up. "You told me that you didn't want him." Logan squeezes his eyes shut. He covers his face with his hands, but there's no hiding from this. "So, I guess it's really over." Logan drops his hands. Tears slide down his face.

I reach out to him. "Logan, please." I want to hold him. I want to tell him that it's going to be okay. That we're going to be okay. The words stick in my throat because I know they're lies. We're broken beyond repair, but I don't want him to go. Not like this.

Logan holds his arm out, keeping me away. He doesn't want my comfort. I can't say that I blame him.

Happy memories race by in reverse: two kids trekking through the woods, carving our names in a treehouse, climbing up trees and swinging from their branches, our first kiss, his trepidation to reveal his feelings for me, the wonder in his eyes when I told him that I felt the same.

All those moments will be forever tainted by this one. Even if we recall the joy, the times when we delighted in each other, it will slip away in a flash, overshadowed by the anguish and misery of how it ended.

This moment can never be undone. It's one that leaves a mark on your soul—forever.

Logan leaves. The door clicks shut behind him. His footsteps disappear down the stairs. The front door slams.

I sink to the floor and cry like a baby.

Chapter 25

Zoeli

I wait patiently for Damian to get home from school, like a puppy dog waiting for her owner. At 3:40pm, the door creaks open. I pounce and kiss him on the lips. "I want to go out tonight."

Damian grins, brushing his black hair out of his eyes. "Good afternoon, beautiful."

"I want to go out," I repeat. "When night falls."

Damian tosses his backpack on the floor. "Not tonight."

I throw my hands up. "You've been saying that for weeks. Ever since Edith shouted at us, you haven't let me out of this room."

"It's not safe, Zoe. She recognized you."

"We don't know that. She never even said my name. You told me that she's a looney who yells crazy nonsense. Who knows what she was talking about?"

Damian sighs. "I need to keep you safe."

"If it means keeping me locked up in your bedroom, I don't want safety." I put my hands on his shoulders and meet his eyes. "I'm losing my damn mind."

Damian averts his gaze. "I can't tonight. It's Cali's birthday."

"Oh." I drop my hands. "What are you doing for her birthday?"

"There's a little party downstairs." Damian hangs up his coat. "I have to get ready." In the adjoining bathroom, Damian turns on the shower. "Want to join me?"

Damian's shirtless in the bathroom doorway, his sculpted abs on display. He looks like a dark angel, white steam clouding around him.

I shake my head. "Not right now." I climb back onto the bed and pick up Damian's *History of Aurelia* textbook. Even though I'm not in school, I've been studying more than Damian. The more I read, the more I'm convinced that his textbooks are biased. In every conflict, Aurelians are depicted as the righteous, while vampires, humans and merman are framed as evil scoundrels.

Damian returns to the bedroom, shaking out his wet hair. A towel is wrapped around his waist. He enters his walk-in closet. A few minutes later, he re-emerges, wearing fitted black dress pants, a white button-down shirt, and a royal blue tie. He looks gorgeous.

"I didn't realize it was a formal event."

"My family uses any excuse to get all decked out." I can tell that he's trying to downplay it for my benefit. As though that might lessen the sting of my lover leaving me to parade around with his beautiful fiancé.

"Right." I fold my arms across my chest.

"What's wrong?"

As if he needs to ask. "Don't you think this charade has gone on long enough?"

"Zoe, it isn't that simple. I'm trying my best."

"Are you?" I raise my eyebrows.

Damian shrugs on his suit jacket. "I'm sorry. As soon as the party is over, I'll be right up. I'll bring you a big plate of food."

"Oh, your majesty, how will I ever repay you for your charity?" I curtsy. "Dear great ruler, I'm eternally grateful."

"Zoe, stop it," Damian says. "You know I don't want it to be this way." He kisses me on the lips. I'm not sure he even notices that I don't kiss him back. Damian checks his watch, wiping off the dust until the diamonds sparkle. "I have to go. I'll see you in a few hours."

Once he's gone, I pick up the textbook, *Spells and Rituals*, and collapse into bed. After an hour of studying the properties of crystal and potions, my mind drifts to the party. What's Caliah wearing? I'm sure she looks gorgeous. Does Damian look at her the way he looks at me?

I have to know. I shift into a crow and shimmy inside the ducts. A few minutes later, I'm peeking through the ballroom vents. The "little party" has over a hundred guests dressed in black tie attire. A ten-piece band plays on the stage. Waiters bustle about handing out glasses of champagne. Daniella balances a tray of hors d'oeuvres: bacon wrapped scallops, stuffed mushrooms, and lamb medallions.

The dance floor is packed. Teens and adults shimmy and shake, their hands in the air. I find Damian and Caliah in the middle of the crowd. My heart drops.

Caliah's stunning. Strawberry blonde curls cascade down her back. Her royal blue satin gown is both elegant and sexy, clinging to her modelesque figure. Damian and Caliah dance close together, his hand on her back. He whispers in her ear. She throws her head back with laughter.

I feel sick. Damian tells me that their relationship is just for show. He swears that Cali knows that he isn't in love with her. He says that it's nothing but a political move for the both of them. Either they're phenomenal actors or Damian is a goddamn liar.

King Keifer clears his throat in a microphone. All eyes turn to the stage. "I hope everyone is enjoying the party." He wears a royal blue cloak over his black suit. "Tonight, we celebrate the birth of Caliah Crowe, a magnificent young woman who will soon be my daughter-in-law." Everyone bursts into applause. Cali glows with happiness, pearly white teeth framed by smiling red lips. "Let us all sing to Aurelia's future queen."

Two busboys wheel in the birthday cake on a circular table. It's enormous: five tiers, elaborately decorated with fondant roses and scrollwork.

The singer's sequin gown glitters under the spotlight. As she belts out the lyrics, the whole room joins in. Caliah poses beside her mother, my Aunt Gwenna, for a photo with the cake.

I've seen enough. I fly back to Damian's bedroom, my mind on overdrive. It's Caliah's seventeenth birthday. In one year, she'll be eighteen. Legally an adult and ready for marriage. Secure the bag, as Aunt Gwenna would phrase it.

What will I do then? Does Damian expect me to hide in the closet and cover my ears while they consummate their marriage?

I curl up under the covers, wrapping myself in a velvety cocoon. I should be grateful to have a warm place to sleep. Instead, I find myself wondering if I was better off in the dank cold of Nightingale dungeon. At least I had Saria, and then Rosa, to hang out with. Now, I spend most of my time alone.

More than that, I miss having hope that my situation would improve. When I was in the dungeon, Damian was determined to help me escape, my heart and head full of his promises for a better future to come. Now, misery stretches endlessly in front of me, and Damian seems content for things to go on as they are.

"Hey." Damian's voice startles me. I was so engrossed in my own thoughts that I didn't even hear him come in. "What are you doing?"

"Oh, you know, living the dream," I mutter. He slides a plate in front of me. "I'm not hungry."

Damian slices the prime rib with a serrated knife. Red juices escape, circling the edge of the plate. He stabs a piece with his fork and holds it to my lips. "I know you're upset, but going on a hunger strike isn't going to help the situation."

I keep my mouth sealed in protest. All Damian does is spoon feed me lies and facades. I've lost my appetite.

Damian's phone rings inside his pocket. He puts the fork down, and digs around to find it. "Hello?"

"Hey, babe. Where'd you go?" I hear Caliah on the other end. "I'm with Jas, Layal, and Austin. We just picked up a mini keg. It's time for the afterparty."

"Um, Cali, I'm not—"

"Go," I say, waving my hand. I don't want to be around him anyways.

"Who's that?" Caliah's voice is loud enough for me to make out every word.

"Um, Zoeli just stopped by."

Apparently Cali has no idea that I live in Damian's room. Another lie.

"Oh." There's a short pause before Cali's voice booms through the speaker. "Tell her to come out!"

"It isn't safe."

"We'll meet deep in the woods. It's cold, but nothing a campfire and a few drinks can't fix."

"Someone might see her."

"It's just us. No one else will be around," Caliah says.

"I'm not comfortable with this," Damian responds

"Why not?" I fold my arms across my chest.

"Um—" Damian starts.

I don't let him finish his sentence. I snatch his phone. "Happy birthday, Caliah. I'd love to come out. Thank you for the invite."

"Yay!" Cali squeals. "I'm so excited to see you, cousin."

I disconnect the call. Damian paces back and forth across his bedroom. "This is a very bad idea." Damian tugs the ends of his black hair

"Why?" I raise my brows. "You don't want your mistress to see you romancing your fiancé?" I smirk. "It's too late for that. I was watching you through the ballroom vent tonight."

Damian stops short. "What did you see?"

"Enough," I mutter.

"You know that's all for show," Damian says. "You're the one I love." He resumes pacing. "It's too cold. You don't have a coat."

"I'll survive." I lift my chin.

Damian gestures to my clothing. "You don't have anything to wear." He's pulling out all the excuses now.

I look down; I'm drowning in Damian's t-shirt and sweatpants. "I didn't realize there's a dress code."

"I'll tell Cali that we can't make it. We'll fly together instead— wherever you like. We can go to the Elysian Forest and visit the Whimsy trees. Maybe we'll even see your dragoni friend again."

I shake my head. "You're not talking me out of this. I'm going to the afterparty." I pull Damian's old shirt away from my chest. "You're right about my wardrobe, though. This won't do." I grin. "Luckily, I know a remedy." I wink. "Sit tight. I'll be back in a few minutes." Blue swirls snake up my legs and twine around my waist.

"Zoe, what the hell are you doing?"

His voice fades away as I wriggle inside the vent. I zoom through the ductwork, navigating through the intricate maze. When I was spying on Caliah's birthday party, I saw Fallon wrapped up in some guy's arms. They looked really into each other. If I'm right, she's still off making out with him somewhere.

I twist the screws with my beak until they loosen. I squirm through the vent and into Fallon's bedroom. I shift into human form effortlessly.

A dome-shaped canopy swallows her king-sized bed. I walk past the red lace curtains that sheath her crown-shaped headboard, admiring the intricate gold curlicues and black crystals embedded in the furniture.

I peek through the beaded curtains that separate her bedroom and dressing room. Her walk-in closet could be a small clothing boutique. She won't notice if I borrow something to wear tonight.

I brush the black crystals strands aside and enter the closet. I walk up and down the aisle, fingering the luxurious fabrics: velvet, silk, satin, and cashmere. I breeze past shelves of loungewear. I flick through a row of conservative choices. This isn't right for the occasion. Tonight, I'm dressing for revenge.

I pull hangers out, one by one, analyzing and then discarding each option. I catch sight of a black leather outfit: skin-tight pants and midriff-baring cold-shoulder top.

I have to jump to get the pants over my butt. I pull the shirt over my head. The outfit fits my body like a glove. I twirl around in front of the full-length mirror. I look like a bad-ass superhero witch. It's perfect.

I paint on a touch of blush and lip gloss. I tug on black leather boots. I run a comb through my dark hair, leaving it long and loose. I'm ready.

I shape-shift and jet back through the ducts to Damian's room. He waits on the bed, his suit jacket lying beside him. His hair is mussed: black waves tumble over his forehead, covering one of his eyes. His tie hangs loose, the top buttons of his collared shirt undone. In a word, he's irresistible.

But I will resist. Blue ribbons swirl around me as I return to human form. "I'm back."

Damian's eyebrows shoot up. His gaze moves up and down my body, his lips curling into a seductive smile. "Damn," he says under his breath. "You look amazing." He reaches out, grabs my hips and pulls me hard against him. His fingers run up and down my sides. "I think we should cancel and stay in."

I push him away. "Not so fast, buddy." I spin around. "Let's go." I don't give him a chance to refuse. I walk to the balcony, thrust open the doors, shape-shift, and take off into flight.

Damian flies ahead of me, leading the way. We soar over trees. Stars seem to zip by, leaving trails of glitter in my wake. I'm lighter than air, sailing through the night.

A half hour later, Damian dips lower. I follow him between trees, descending into darkness. My claws graze the dirt. I flap along the ground, a few paces behind Damian.

Blue beams of light swirl around the purple haze. Cells burst and rearrange; tissues and tendons meld together. My boots dig in the dirt. Damian's breath is white. Through the trees, a fire dances. I hear Caliah's laughter, light and warm, like a familiar song.

Here goes nothing.

I duck under a branch and step into the clearing. Four pairs of eyes land on me. I lift my chin, wind blowing my dark hair back.

"Zoe!" Caliah jumps off the rock she was sitting on and cheers. "It's so good to see you!" She skips over and sweeps me up into a hug. "I'm so glad you're here."

"Happy birthday," I say, as sweetly as I can muster. As much as I want to hate Caliah, none of this is her fault.

"Thank you. I'm so excited for you to meet my friends."

"I'm Jasleidy." The brunette offers her hand. She smells like pine trees and honey. "It's so great to finally meet you." Her clear blue eyes twinkle against her tan skin.

"I'm Layal." The redhead slinks up, sizing me up with narrowed green eyes. Even though she didn't say her last name, I can tell that she's a fox. She touches my hair, like I'm some kind of alien specimen. "Holy shit, we did it," she breathes.

I recoil, pushing her hand away. "I did my own hair, thank you very much."

"Layal, that's rude," Caliah says. "I'm sorry. She's just happy to meet you." She claps her hands together. "Let's go sit around the campfire."

"Kumbaya," Layal's drawl drips with sarcasm. She tilts her head back and takes a long slurp of her drink.

Chair-sized boulders surround the fire pit. A boy with spiky hair and Mediterranean features stands up. "I'm Austin Deere," he says.

"I'm Zoe." I sit on a rock. "I've heard a lot about you." Late at night, curled up in Damian's arms, we talk about everything: hopes, dreams, family, and our childhoods. Damian's two best friends, Austin and Colson, are fixtures in his stories. From crazy dares to botched spells, their antics never fail to amuse me.

"Likewise." Austin presses the tap of the mini-keg. He fills a plastic cup and hands it to me. I take a sip, frothy goodness sliding down my throat.

Flames leap against the wind: their heat singeing my cheeks. Austin and Damian sit on either side of me. Even though there's plenty more seats, Caliah plops on Damian's lap. She giggles and runs her fingers through his hair. I stifle a gag.

I did this to myself. I chose this. We could've been tangled up in his covers right now, telling stories and jokes, kissing and laughing. I could pretend that everything is okay: remain blissfully ignorant.

Except that's not my style. I can only bury my head in the sand for so long before I'll suffocate.

"Ow, my knee is killing me," Damian says, lifting Caliah off his lap.

"What's wrong? Do you need me to heal it?" Caliah kneels in front of him, caressing his kneecaps. I'm not sure how much more I can take before I smack a bitch. I suck in a deep breath. It's not her fault, I remind myself. I shoot Damian an icy glare. It's his.

"I'm okay, Cali," he says.

"Oh good." She jumps right back into his lap.

She isn't very good at taking hints, is she?

Zoe, I told you this wasn't a good idea.

Why? So you could continue to lie to me? You said she knows that you aren't in love with her.

I never said 'I love you' to her. I promise you.

That isn't the same as telling her that you don't.

"Your outfit's hot," Layal says, her gaze flitting from my bare midriff to my exposed shoulders.

I feel another set of eyes on me. Goosebumps sprout on the side of my neck. I turn and catch Austin staring, his mouth half-open. "I'm sorry." He shakes his head. "I still can't believe that we actually did it."

"Right here," Caliah says, intertwining her fingers with Damian's. "This is the place where magic came undone."

I study the way her fingers wrap around his, her thumb lightly caressing his palm. "I can see that," I say. Another form of magic comes undone: the magic I felt when Damian put his hand in mine, the rush I felt when his lips touched mine, the trust I had in him. Even when my instincts warned me to stay away, the magic kept pulling me back in. I'm a fool.

"It scares me." Jasleidy wrinkles her brow. "I mean, if we were able to pull it off, who says that DOX can't undo the spell that secures Aurelia?"

"DOX?" I ask.

"The Descendants of Xaphan," Austin responds. "Talon and Licinia's crew. Rumor is they're trying to break the spell that protects the portal."

"Before the spell was enacted, our borders were open," Jasleidy explains. "Anyone who knew where to find the portal could get in. For a while, our ancestors hid the portal with big rocks and other barricades, but when intruders that meant us harm found their way in, we had to develop a security spell. Dozens of scholars came together to write the spell. It was a very comprehensive and elaborately designed spell, intended to last for eternity. Once completed, seven witches were selected to execute the spell, one from each royal family."

"And one of those seven was Eleanor Fox," Layal jumps in. "Of whom I am a direct descendant."

Jasleidy rubs her chin. "Didn't Eleanor Fox disappear? She just vanished, and no one ever saw her again."

"That's true," Layal agrees. "But she left behind a young son, Benjamin Fox, who later married Pearl Rehn. They went on to have two children, Cordelia and Henry Fox, who each went on to have two children, and on and on. I won't bore you with the details, but I can assure you that the Foxes carefully track their family tree. I am indeed a direct descendant of Eleanor Fox."

Jasleidy shrugs. "What's your point?"

Layal's green eyes glow in the firelight. "Maybe I'll help DOX reverse the spell."

Caliah and Jasleidy burst into laughter. My jaw drops. Caliah puts her hand on my shoulder. "Don't worry, Zoe. Layal says absurd things for shock value. She's not serious."

"Or am I?" Layal's eyes meet mine, gauging my reaction. I stare right back. If she thinks she's going to intimidate me, she's wrong. Layal waves her hand, blood-red nails sailing above the flames. "Our current leadership is garbage. I don't see how Talon and Licinia could be much worse."

"Layal," Damian's voice has a warning edge.

"Babe, relax. She's trying to get a rise out of you," Caliah says.

"And it's working." Austin observes.

Layal shrugs. "Your father's administration is laden with scandals and corruption. Don't blame me for speaking the truth."

"I know there's some…" Caliah pauses, choosing her words carefully, "problems that need to be addressed." She raises her chin, strawberry blonde curls dancing in the breeze. "When I'm queen, everyone is going to have equal rights in Aurelia: half-breeds, duds and even humans."

"What about merkind?" I cut in.

"Merkind?" Jasleidy wrinkles her nose. "They want us dead."

"Are you sure about that?" I ask. "I've been doing research. Some reports say that witches were the aggressors, and the merkind were only defending themselves. Just because they're different, the witches didn't trust them. The fear was that they'd grow in number and become a threat, so we got them out of the way."

Austin shakes his head. "Those are crazy conspiracy theories. If we set the merkind free, all hell will break loose."

Layal's lips curve into a grin. "I like the sound of that."

Jasleidy's mouth presses into a firm line. "I love the idea of equal rights, but merkind are our enemy. We have to put our own first."

"Under the Crowe regime, everyone will be treated fairly. That includes merkind," Caliah says.

Damian clears his throat. "You mean the Nightingale regime."

Caliah's head whips around. "My family's waited decades for the throne to be rightfully returned to us."

Layal cackles, her head tossed back. "I can't believe you two haven't discussed who's changing their name."

"Well, isn't it obvious?" Damian says. "The woman takes the man's name."

"Not royal women," Layal retorts.

My brow creases. "In Aurelian marriages, is it customary for the husband to take their wife's last name?"

"For royals, yes," Jasleidy says. "My husband will become a Wolfe."

"The royal name usurps the patriarchy," Layal explains. "Since interspecies marriages are traditionally condemned, this issue hasn't come up before."

"My mom wouldn't give up her name," I say, another piece of the puzzle clicking into place. My mom stayed true to her culture. "She compromised with a hyphenated last name."

"That's an option," Caliah agrees.

"No, it's not," Damian grunts. "But we don't need to talk about this. It's a long way in the future."

Caliah folds her arms across her chest. "I just turned seventeen. I'll be eighteen in one year. A year goes fast."

"I can't wait to go dress shopping." Jasleidy squeezes Caliah's hand. "You're going to be the most beautiful bride."

"Our constitution states that the king and queen can't take the throne until they're both twenty-five. There's no need to rush a wedding," Damian says.

"But we agreed." Caliah taps her foot on the ground.

"We'll discuss this later," Damian says. "Now isn't a good time."

Even though the temperatures are frigid, my boiling blood keeps me warm. Damian uses the same avoid-and-delay tactics with Caliah that he uses with me.

"I have to pee." Caliah puts her cup down on an empty rock. "I'll be right back." She disappears into the woods.

Do you want to go home?

I'm not going anywhere with you.

Zoe, I'm going to fix everything. I just need more time.

"Zoe, how do you like Aurelia?" Jasleidy asks.

I shrug. "I've mostly been in hiding."

"Have you been out at all?" Austin asks.

"I visited the Elysian Forest," I say. "I saw the Whimsy trees. Oh! A dragoni let me pet him. That was sweet."

"A dragoni?" Jasleidy's blue eyes widen.

"You're a liar." The bonfire reflects in Layal's eyes, raging red flames. There's no hint of joking in them.

"Excuse me?" I gulp my drink.

"Dragonis are so rare that even the scientists who study them barely get a glimpse." Layal raises her brows. "Even if you managed to see a dragoni, an event that's less likely than getting struck by lightning," Layal's voice drips with sarcasm. "You're lying about petting it. Dragonis aren't pets and they don't snuggle. They're vicious."

"I'm not lying." I fold my arms across my chest.

"Did you take a picture?"

"Um, no, but–" I catch Damian's eye, waiting for him to jump to my defense. He was there. He knows that I'm not lying.

Damian looks away. He stares into the fire, elbows propped on his knees. Of course. I should've known. He's not going to admit that we spend time together. It might upset his fake fiancé. I clench my fists at my sides.

"Damian?" On the border of the clearing, Caliah peeks between leaves. "I thought I heard something."

Damian jerks upright. "What did you hear?"

"I thought I heard footsteps. It could've been an animal, but I'm not sure. Can you come look?"

"Maybe we should just go home."

"Someone might've seen us," Caliah says. "We need to check it out."

Standing up, Damian addresses the group. "Stay right here. No one move. I'll be back." He steps into the thicket, glancing back once before he disappears.

"How sweet," Layal drawls. "Our dear prince steps onto the path of great danger to protect his future princess."

Austin barks out a laugh. "It's probably a rodent."

"You have to admit it, though, they are meant for each other." Layal's green eyes probe mine. "Don't you think so, Zoe?"

I look down. "Sure."

"They're the perfect match," Jasleidy agrees. "Barbie and Ken: The Witch Edition."

Layal purses her ruby red lips and takes another sip. "I've never seen a couple more in love. They can't keep their hands off each other."

I tip my glass and chug. Beer spills over the sides, dripping down my chin. Is Layal doing this on purpose? Is she trying to rile me up? But that would mean that she knows…

"They're obsessed with each other," Layal continues in her taunting drawl. "Cali calls me every day to gush about Damian. He treats her like a queen—"

"I have to go to the bathroom." I can't take another moment of this. I half-walk, half-run into the woods.

"Zoe, come back. Damian told us to wait here." Austin's voice fades as I curve around the brush, twigs snapping beneath my boots. They might follow Damian's commands, but not me. Not anymore.

I duck under branches. The forest is all around me, thick and closing in. Thorn branches puncture my palms and scratch my cheeks. Leaves crunch under my feet. The white puffs of my breath are the only color in the blackness.

I hear a male voice in the distance. I pause. A female voice follows. It's Caliah and Damian, but I can't make out what they're saying. Their words are muffled, the sounds absorbed by the blankets of leaves and gnarls of branches between us.

I suck in a deep breath and access my blue power. It comes so easily now, it's hard to remember when I used to struggle to find it. Blue energy flows into my ears, opening up my cochlea, allowing for supernatural hearing.

"I don't see anyone," Damian says. "Just a few rabbits and a snake. Are you sure that you heard footsteps?"

"It really turns me on when you try to protect me." Cali giggles.

"Huh?"

"I didn't hear anything, silly. I just wanted to get you alone. Now you're all mine."

"Cali, this isn't the time or place."

"It's my birthday," Cali says. Her lips make a smacking noise as they kiss some part of my boyfriend. I cringe and cover my ears, but it's no use. Everything is magnified. I can hear the thrashing of tongues, the slosh of shared saliva, the nibble of lips.

I was looking for Damian to say goodbye.

Now I know that he doesn't deserve that courtesy.

I transform and take off in flight. The woods shrink beneath me; the castle fades into the distance.

I'm gone, like a ghost.

Chapter 26

Saria

The last sliver of sunlight slides below the horizon. My phone rings. "Hello?"

"Hey, it's me," Red says.

"Hey." I swallow. My throat's sore from crying. "What's up?"

"Um, I thought we should talk. Last night…" His voice trails off. "We got a little carried away."

"Yeah," I say, my voice scratchy.

"It was fun."

"Yeah." I still haven't sorted it all out. On one hand, I experienced a euphoria that I never knew existed. On the other hand, I destroyed my relationship with Logan. My feelings are all tangled up: a knot of passion, desire and regret.

"But it can never happen again."

The knot drops into my stomach like a ball of lead.

"I'm sorry, Saria. We made a mistake."

"A mistake?" I croak out. Part of me knows that he's right, but it still hurts to hear it.

"You know what I mean. You're a human. I'm a vampire. It just won't work. We should end this now before anyone gets hurt."

It's too late for that. My mouth opens and shuts, but no words come out.

"I'm a man of my word. I promised you that I'd help you find your sister. I have a few leads that I'm looking into. I'll be in touch."

"I appreciate that."

"We'll talk soon."

I disconnect the call.

* * *

One Month Later

They say time heals all wounds, but I don't believe that. It's been months since I left Aurelia. Yet, in the dead of the night, I wake up screaming, tangled in blankets, disoriented and confused to find a warm pillow under my cheek rather than the cold dungeon floor. I blink until my bedroom comes into focus. Reality floods back in, and I wish that I stayed asleep. Even my nightmares are a respite from the hell I'm living.

Zoeli's still gone. No one knows where she is. I don't even know if she's alive. I miss her so much. Old memories rise to the surface, climbing up from the recesses of my mind. The other day, I remembered that silly board game we used to play, the one that looks like a mall. We'd roll the dice and move our game pieces from store to store, searching for articles of clothing to create the perfect ensemble. The pink skirt was my favorite. Whenever Zoe drew that card, she'd give it to me, even if it meant that she lost the game. That stupid memory was enough to send me spiraling— my knees buckled and I collapsed onto the kitchen floor, crying my damn eyes out until I had no tears left.

They say that you don't know what you've got until it's gone. They may be right on that one. Every day, I miss Logan more. He was more than my boyfriend. He was my best friend. A carousel of memories circle around me: Logan and I climbing a tree, Logan and I building a fort, Logan and I dancing in the kitchen—

Someone snaps their fingers in front of my face. "Earth to Saria. Anyone home?"

The world materializes around me. I'm in the school hallway, staring into my open locker. Penny waves her hand in front of my eyes. "Saria, are you with me?"

"Hey, Penny." I reach into my locker and grab my history textbook.

"Are you okay? You scared me. You were staring into space like a zombie."

Lately I float around in a haze, memories appear and moments disappear, living in the past and the present at once. "I'm fine."

I shut my locker and walk beside Penny, bumping against hips and shoulders in the crowded hallway. "I know what'll cheer you up: a sleepover at my place. We'll do face masks and foot baths. Once we're exfoliated, we can eat ice cream and watch rom coms all night." Penny smiles up at me, brushing red bangs out of her hazel eyes.

"I'm so lucky to have you as a friend." I sling my arm over her shoulder. We walk down the hallway, our steps in sync, sneakers squeaking in unison on the linoleum.

A few paces ahead, I see the back of Keisha's head, her black curls tied up in a sleek ponytail. Mallory walks in the opposite direction, a folded white paper pinched between her fingers. As she passes, Mallory slips the note to Keisha. They never stop moving. It happens so fast. If I blinked, I would've missed it.

I press my lips together, my gaze glued on Keisha's hand. She drops the note in her tote bag and walks into history class.

"See you later, Penny." I follow Keisha into class.

"Text me later. We'll plan that sleepover." Penny calls after me.

I slide into the desk next to Keisha, staring at her canvas tote bag. It lays open on the floor next to her chair, inches away from me. "Hey Sar," Keisha says. "How are you?" Her big brown eyes are brighter than they've been in a long time. At least one of us has been sleeping better.

I shrug. "I'm alright."

I must look like hell because Keisha reaches out and puts her hand on my shoulder. "I know this breakup has been really hard on you."

I try to swallow and choke on the lump in my throat. I gag, tears welling in my eyes. I bite my lip, silently begging myself not to cry. I used to have it all together. Now I'm on the verge of bawling all over my history homework. I'm pathetic.

"Oh, Sar." Keisha's gaze lands on a tissue box across the room. "I'll be right back."

Her back is to me as she makes her way to Ms. Sander's desk. It's my chance. I reach into her bag, pushing folders and notebooks aside, searching for the slip of paper. My finger grazes a sharp edge. Ouch! I grab the note. Blood oozes from my papercut.

On the other side of the room, Keisha grabs a wad of tissues. I unfold the note and read three short lines.

Saturday 5:30 am
13 Gallow Road
SLAY

Chapter 27

Zoeli

For a long time, I was a prisoner. First, I belonged to Nightingale Dungeon. Then, I belonged to Damian. Now, I belong to the sky, the wind, the open air. I am a free bird.

Little by little, my old self fades away. The ropes that tethered me to my home, my friends, my family, have come undone. I built walls thick enough to block out Damian's calls. I belong to no one but myself now.

I fly with the crows. I survive off nightshade berries, turtle eggs and beetles (which taste much better than I expected). Sometimes, the other crows give me funny looks. Their gaze lingers on my blue eyes. They know I'm different. Still, they accept me. They invite me to roost with them. They share their food. I often wonder why we assume that animals are intellectually inferior. There's a lot that we could learn from the crows.

Most days, I fly aimlessly, drifting wherever the breeze takes me. I fantasize about going home: bursting through the front door and launching into my parent's arms. I'd cherish every moment with my sister. I'd never take another second with them for granted again.

I caw at the stars, offering to bargain with Gods, Goddesses, even demons, but no one answers my calls. I guess I'm on my own.

I devise schemes to get home: hiding inside someone's luggage who's crossing the portal, or casting a sleep spell on the portal guards. The problem is: everyone's on high alert. There are backups upon backups. Every item that crosses the portal is triple checked. For the time being, I'm stuck here in Aurelia.

Sometimes, I spend hours watching for merkind, fascinated by the enigmatic creatures. When I spot a tail skimming the lake's surface, I follow overhead, hoping to catch a glimpse of the mysterious world below.

Today, I wake with a purpose. Last night, I dreamt of Rosa. I soar against the wind, flapping furiously against gusts that threaten to propel me the other way.

I sail over Nightingale Palace. Magic blazes from the Rock of Vitality, filling the sky with ribbons of color. I glide over a sparkling indigo stripe, passing over the stone bridge beneath me. I surge past Nightingale city, leaving its skyscrapers and jeweled roads in my wake. I slide down a red beam, zooming over the Elysian Forest. Ruby sparks shoot from my feathers, ricocheting off the leaves of the Whimsy trees.

As I coast away from the Rock of Vitality, its magic dims. Even further out, the brilliant colors dissolve into a gravel gray sky. Bejeweled roads are replaced by pothole-ridden paths. Out here, far from the Rock of Vitality, the outskirts are inhabited by duds and outcasts.

The outskirt dwellers are denied the benefits provided by proximity to the Rock of Vitality. Aside from missing out on the aesthetic pleasure of a shimmering rainbow sky and the burst of energy that accompanies breathing magically-infused air (better than a strong coffee), the Rock of Vitality provides fuel for all of Aurelia. On particularly cold days, when resources are stretched to their limits, the outskirts are cut off from heat and electricity. As more energy-guzzling skyscrapers are built in the city, the outskirts' power shuts off more frequently.

When she was my roommate, Rosa shared stories about the hardships they endured. Two winters ago, the outskirts were without heat for almost three weeks. Rosa's daughter, Ivy, was only six weeks old. Temperatures dropped below zero. Rosa, her husband Theo, and their infant daughter huddled together under piles of blankets, teeth chattering, praying that Ivy wouldn't succumb to hypothermia.

Another time, King Keifer threw a lavish rally at the stadium. Thousands gathered to celebrate the Nightingale regime. The party was replete with extraordinary music, gourmet food, acrobats, and dancers. Fireworks lit up the night. Ribbons of magic stretched and curved across the sky, creating awe-inspiring depictions of the Nightingale family.

King Keifer knew that the elaborate displays would tap out their energy source. To ensure that his festivities wouldn't be disrupted, he shut off the electricity to the outskirts. Every home and building, including the outskirt's tiny hospital, went black. A dozen patients who required electricity to run their life-sustaining equipment died. One of those deaths was Rosa's neighbor's eight-year-old son. He was in critical condition after a car accident. Prior to the electricity being shut off, the doctors were hopeful that he'd have a full recovery.

I float over dilapidated cottages and worn-out roofs, searching for Rosa's artwork. Rosa told me that when she wasn't scrubbing Adelyn Nightingale's floors or caring for her daughter, she loved to paint. In an effort to brighten up her depressed neighborhood, Rosa painted an enormous sunflower on her front door.

I weave through the streets. Children play tag, smiling despite their holey shoes and concave bellies.

At the end of Blue Fig Road, a cheerful yellow flower adorns an old wooden door. As I move closer, I admire the intricacy of her work: a network of veins running through the green leaves, a brush stroke for each individual seed that composes the sunflower's center.

With its thatched roof and arched shutters, Rosa's cottage has an old-world charm. I perch on a windowsill, peeking inside through a gap between the curtains. A woman paces in the kitchen, holding a toddler on her hip and a phone by her ear. "What do you mean he isn't on the list? The Nightingales promised to provide healing services for my brother. Queen Taya said it herself." The woman pauses, presumably listening to someone on the other end. She paces faster, the child jostling against her gray sweatshirt. "Obviously I'm aware that there's a hospital for the duds. Are you aware that the medicine my brother requires isn't available in the outskirts because it's too expensive? The dud doctor, as you so kindly referred to him, said that the medicine can only slow down the progression of symptoms. Given that Theo's condition is already severe, the medication would have little effect on his quality of life. The doctor also said that one good healing session could have my brother back on his feet for at least six months. He can't care for his two-year-old daught—"

The woman's face reddens. "Hello? Hello?" She throws her phone down on the counter. "Heartless assholes." She storms out of the room.

I flutter alongside the tiny house, peering through blind slats into a bedroom. Rosa's husband, Theo, lays in bed. "That scumbag hung up on me!" Theo's sister rants. "I'm going to that castle–"

"Don't." Theo holds up a shaky hand. "They'll imprison you, too. You'll be locked up. Just like Rosa." He chokes on his wife's name.

"It isn't fair."

"Don't do anything crazy, Phoebe. You're all I've got," Theo says. Ivy wriggles in Phoebe's arms, reaching for her father. Phoebe places her on the bed, and Ivy curls up in her father's arms, her light brown ringlets splayed across his chest.

Phoebe sits on the edge of the bed, raking her fingers through her curly brown hair. "What are you going to do, Theo? You can't walk a few steps without falling over. You can't work and you're out of money. You can't care for the child. There's barely any food in your fridge. What are you going to feed her?"

"I don't know," Theo says.

"I have four children of my own to feed." Phoebe shakes her head. "I wish we could help. Healers charge by the hour, and their rates are tremendous."

"I know, Pheebs. I appreciate everything you've been doing for us."

"Ivy can stay with me while we sort this out. I'll keep trying to find a healer I can afford."

"Thank you, Pheebs."

Phoebe checks her watch. "I have to go home and cook dinner. Let's go, Ivy." She reaches for the little girl.

"No!" Ivy shouts. "I stay with Dada." Ivy clings to her dad, arms tight around his neck, little fingers gripping his shirt.

"It's okay, sweetie. Go with Auntie Phoebe."

"No!" Ivy wails as Phoebe wrestles her away from her father. Tears streak down her cherubic cheeks, her red lips wide open as she wails.

"It's okay, Ivy." Phoebe soothes her niece even as the child's fists slam into her chest. "We'll see Dada tomorrow."

I watch from the roof as Phoebe loads Ivy into her car seat. "Dada!" The child's voice echoes as Phoebe's sedan clunks away, easing around potholes and out of sight.

When I was sequestered to Damian's bedroom, I read Healing-101 from cover to cover. I learned that not all witches possess healing powers, but that it usually runs in families. Since my mom and aunt are healers, there's a good chance that I'm one too.

It takes years of practice to become an adept healer. I've never done it before. Heck, there's a first time for everything. It looks like tonight's my night. Let's see what I've got.

The sun goes down. I wait until every light in the neighborhood turns off. I can't risk being seen. I've heard that there's a huge price on my head. I wouldn't even blame any of these poor duds for reporting me.

On the front steps, I transform. It's been a while since I've had arms and legs. I stretch out my stiff muscles. As I roll my neck, it cracks a few times. I wrap my fingers around the doorknob. A tendril of blue power slips inside the keyhole and *click*. It unlocks easily.

I shut the door behind me. Inside, it's pitch black. I feel my way through the kitchen, hands bumping into walls and objects as I tiptoe down the hallway and into the bedroom. Theo snores softly, his breath wheezing on the way out.

I follow the instructions from the textbook. I start at his feet, palms hovering over him, feeling through his skin. As my hands graze his body, evaluating ligaments, tendons, nerves, and muscles, my throat tightens. His condition is worse than I imagined. The disease has wreaked havoc on his entire body.

I pour magic into each disease-ridden sight, loosening his stiff muscles. I work slowly and precisely, undoing tight and intricate knots, pulling them apart, setting them free. I roll him over. His breath quickens for a moment before it reverts to its slow, steady rhythm. I massage his back, fingers digging into rigid cords and tissue, healing them one by one.

If I'd grown up in Aurelia, they would've called me a dud. Blue magic is the hardest to access, but the most powerful of all. As I study Theo's body, I search for untapped magic, but find nothing. Maybe my theory that other duds are like me is wrong.

Hours later, I walk my fingers up his scalp, identifying the source of his disease. I sink healing energy inside his brain. I open up blockages between neurotransmitters. I mend their broken connections.

When I'm done, I collapse on the floor, covered in sweat. I hope I didn't overdo it. MOSS, or Magic Overuse Shock Syndrome, can be deadly.

My tongue sticks to the roof of my mouth. I stumble to the kitchen. Aside from a half-used quart of orange juice, the refrigerator is empty. I guzzle the juice and drop the empty carton in the trash can.

As hard as I tried, I don't know how much I helped him. It was my first time. Even if he's feeling better, Theo will need food to regain his strength. But how can I help? I've been living off the land, eating as a crow.

I suppose that I could play Robin Hood: break into rich people's homes and steal their food. But I'd risk getting caught and sent back to the dungeon—or worse.

As a carousel of ideas spin through my mind, one image stands out above the others: Nightingale kitchen, its pantry overflowing with freshly baked bread and muffins, its freezers stacked with meat and produce.

Hey. I reach out even though I doubt that Damian will respond right away. It's the middle of the night—

Zoe? Thank God. I've been trying to reach you.

I need a favor.

Anything.

Bring food to Rosa's husband, Theo Halliwell. Not just one meal either. Fill up his fridge and pantry with groceries.

Okay. I'll ask my servant to—

Do not tell anyone. You need to do this yourself. I don't trust anyone in that corrupt castle.

Does that mean you trust me?

I sigh. This isn't about you. Theo needs help.

I want you to come home.

Nightingale Palace is not my home.

Can we meet up? We need to talk.

Are you going to do this or not?

Yes, but—

I have to go. Thank you, Damian.

I stagger out the front door. I use my last drops of energy to shift into a crow. I fly into a canopy of trees and settle on a bough. Shrouded by burnt orange leaves, I drift into a deep dreamless sleep.

Chapter 28

Even before my alarm goes off at the ungodly hour of 4:40am, I'm awake. I can't stop thinking about Red. He says that we can still be friends. He assured me that I'm still welcome to come down to the club anytime I like.

Even if he rolled out a red carpet for me, I'd never go there again. I can't even hear his voice on the phone without reliving the sting of rejection.

Every time I replay him saying, 'It's complicated,' in my mind, it sounds more and more like a lame excuse. Maybe the truth is that he just doesn't want me.

I roll out of bed and stretch my arms overhead. I tie my hair up in a messy bun. Dressed in black jeans and an oversized black hoodie, I tiptoe down the stairs. By the front door, I slip car keys off the hook in the hallway.

"Where are you going at this hour?"

Startled, I spin around. Dad stands on the stairs, arms folded across his pajama shirt. "I'm going to meet up with Keisha." Keisha may not know it, but it isn't a lie.

"At five in the morning on a Saturday?" Dad creases his brow in disbelief.

"We're both going through a lot and having trouble sleeping." It still isn't a lie. "We're going to sip coffee and watch the sunrise." At least I hope that's what this event entails. "Can I take your car?"

Dad's expression softens. "Okay. I was going to make pancakes for breakfast, but I guess they can wait for dinner."

"Pancakes for dinner." My lips curve into a smile. "With whipped cream and strawberries?"

"Is there any other way?"

I wave on my way out the door. Late November in New Jersey means it's still dark outside. A gust of cold hits me in the face, drawing tears into my eyes. I shiver, pulling the hoodie over my bun.

My dad's engine squeals, sputters and then comes to life. Hopefully I don't break down on the way there.

I enter the address, 13 Gallow Road, into Google Maps. The computerized voice directs me to take a left at the end of my driveway.

Even as I drive, my mind wanders, images whipping round and round. Red's bright blue eyes and red-stained teeth. Logan's hazel ones, tears sticking to his long black lashes. Red in his crisp shirt and black slacks, twirling me around the dance floor. Logan's goofy smile, holding out a handful of stolen pink tulips.

As impossible as it seems, I'm in love with two boys. And now I've lost them both.

"Make a left on Tristars Road."

Logan: hammer in hand, beaming proudly as he nails the last board in place, completing our treehouse. Red: coming to my rescue, tossing the creep aside, flicking him away like a speck of dirt.

"Make a right onto Gallow Road. You've arrived at your destination." I shake my head, warding off the memories.

I pull into the parking lot of what looks like an abandoned warehouse. Even though the windows are boarded up and the street lights are dark, the parking lot is full of cars. I drive up and down the rows, searching for an empty spot. In the very back, I find one.

What are all these cars doing here on a Saturday night? I pull into the spot and shut my headlights. Darkness, thick and black, besieges me. I clench the steering wheel, my knuckles white. My heart pounds in my ears. Why would Keisha meet Mallory in a place like this?

I check the time. 5:15 am. Five more minutes until God knows what. Headlights slice through the darkness. A red coupe drives past and parks a few spaces from me. A young woman steps out of the car. She strides to the building, her blonde ponytail swinging. She hops up onto the sidewalk, opens the warehouse door and disappears inside.

I suck in a deep breath, a cold sweat beading along my hairline. I fumble with the handle several times before I manage to open the car door. My sneakers hit the pavement, my legs wobbly beneath me. As I walk towards the warehouse, a wave of dizziness has the parking lot spinning around me. The buzzing in my ears intensifies: a shrill ring that vibrates in my bones.

I suck in a mouthful of air and fling the warehouse door open before I can chicken out. A man in a black trench coat stands on the other side. He strokes his goatee. "Password?" He asks, his voice gruff.

My mind races. I don't know the password. Then, an image of the note flickers in my mind. "Slay." My voice trembles.

For the longest second in history, the man stares at me, his dark eyes boring into mine. Then, he waves his hand. "End of the hallway."

I swallow. "Thank you." An emergency light flickers in the dark hallway. A generator produces a racket that rattles my teeth. I walk forward, my heart knocking against my ribcage.

Inside a cavernous room, metal folding chairs are lined up in rows. In the front, a projector shines on a wall, exposing cracks and chipped paint. A man I recognize stands at the podium. Mallory's dad wears a white polo shirt, his bald head gleaming under the fluorescent lights. What the hell is going on? He speaks into a microphone. "Everyone please take a seat. We're about to get started."

I choose a seat in the very back and pull my hoodie down over my eyes. I scan the room for Keisha. My gaze moves up and down the rows until I recognize her spiral curls and puffy red coat. In the front row, Mallory sits beside her, auburn hair fastened in a high ponytail. I keep my head down, hoping not to be recognized.

"Wow, what a turn out." The microphone emits a high-pitched squeal. Mallory's dad adjusts a knob and taps on the microphone, testing the sound. "Sorry about that." He chuckles. "I see that we have a lot of newbies tonight, so I'll start with introducing myself. I'm Dustin Fawley, the fifth generation in a long line of vampire and witch hunters. As a family, the Fawleys are dedicated to keeping humans safe from supernatural threats. I've passed my mission and expertise down to my teenage children, Mallory and Derrick, who are both heavily involved in the business. We're one of several witch-hunting agencies who work directly for the government." Mr. Fawley pauses, his hands spread wide on the podium. "Over the past hundred or so years, witches and vampires have gotten better at hiding among us. Out in California, we went through a dry spell. For several years, our team didn't identify one witch or vampire.

"I heard rumors about a possible supernatural presence in Mountainside, New Jersey. A couple of years ago, I relocated my family over three thousand miles. My daughter, Mallory, befriended a girl who we suspected was a witch. After a year of investigating her and her family, it turned out to be a dead end."

My hands shake in my lap. When Mallory first moved to town, she showered me with compliments. She even bought me concert tickets to see Taylor Swift, my favorite pop star. I never imagined that she had an ulterior motive. Looking back, I can recall moments when I caught her lurking around my house, probably searching for clues. Hindsight is always twenty-twenty.

Another thought strikes me. Did she seduce Chad to try to pull information from him? Maybe it was a test to find out if he was bewitched. Or perhaps she was trying to provoke me into using magic against her. After she succeeded in stealing my boyfriend without consequence, she proved that I wasn't a witch. Or so she thought.

"Just when we started wondering if we moved across the country for nothing, something very strange started happening. You see, my wife Nancy and my daughter Mallory run our website, a forum where we recruit members and communicate with other witch-hunting groups. Out of nowhere, our forums became inundated with young people plagued by unusual dreams. Even more bizarre, many of these young men and women come from right here in Mountainside. My daughter's friend, Keisha, suffers from these recurring nightmares. Keisha, if you don't mind sharing your story, I think it will resonate with many of our attendees."

Mr. Fawley steps aside as Keisha, my best friend since preschool, hops up, chin high, confident as always as she takes the podium. Her black curls are a glorious frame for her beautiful face. "Hi everyone. I know from experience how overwhelmed and scared you may feel, so I'm happy to try to help you through this process. A few months ago, I started having nightmares. Every night, it was the same: witches and vampires killing innocent people. It was a bloodbath: violent and gory and—" Keisha swallows. "I barely slept for weeks. Even when I was awake, I could hear voices whispering, 'You must save them.' I searched the internet for answers. On the Fawley Agency website, they had information about slayers: people who are chosen to protect humans from supernatural threats. It said that one of the most common ways that a slayer is called to service is through dreams.

"When I emailed The Fawley Agency, Mallory responded. She invited me to meet up with her family and their team. I told them what was happening to me, and they said that I'm a slayer." Keisha smirks. "I'll be honest. At first, I thought they were out of their damn minds. I never imagined that vampires or witches were real, let alone that I'd be capable of fighting them." Keisha leans into the microphone. "Still, the urge got stronger and stronger. It was like an itch I couldn't scratch. Bloody hallucinations followed me everywhere, even during the day." Keisha takes a deep breath. "Mr. Fawley told me that the visions would continue until I accepted who I am. Even though I tried to fight it, I realized that he was right. I needed to face reality and prepare for battle." Every attendee sits on the edge of their seats, eyes fixated on Keisha, hanging on her every word.

"I trained with The Fawley Agency. They taught me the skills, but I still doubted myself. How could a one-hundred-fifteen-pound teenager defeat supernatural creatures? Mr. Fawley assured me that as a chosen slayer, I'd acquire superhuman strength as soon as I engaged in combat with an enemy. I was still scared. Before my first encounter with a vampire, I texted my mama and my brother that I love them, just in case." Keisha shakes her head, a faraway look in her eyes. "As soon as I threw the first punch, I knew that I had nothing to worry about. Power surged through me with an intensity that I never could've imagined."

"Don't be shy, Keisha. Go ahead and brag about your first kill, or I'll do it for you." Mr. Fawley calls out.

Keisha grins. "I kicked his ass." My pulse thrums in my ears. "There's a bar in Manhattan that we've been investigating. A few blocks away, I cornered a vampire in an alleyway. He was one of those pretty boys: well dressed with nice eyes. Probably used his looks to lure victims." My heart throbs in my throat. I slide my phone out of my pocket and click on Red's name. What can I say? Are you alive? Did my best friend kill you?

"It only took one punch to knock him down. I drove the stake into his heart, and poof!" Keisha flicks her hands open. "He was a pile of ash, just like in the movies. By killing him, I know that I saved countless women's lives. Once I started hunting and killing them, the nightmares and visions stopped. I sleep like a log, better than ever before. Now I know that being chosen isn't a curse, but an honor. I've been chosen to protect humankind."

The audience bursts into applause. My fingers tremble as I type out a text message: *How are you?* I stare at the screen, willing Red to respond.

Mr. Fawley puts his hand on Keisha's shoulder. "Thank you so much. You are a very talented slayer. We're so happy to have you on our team, Keisha." Keisha steps down, smiling as she returns to her seat. Mr. Fawley leans on the podium, his biceps flexing beneath his polo shirt. "In less than six months, we've had over one hundred new slayers reach out to us. The sudden uptick in slayers begs the question: why? The answer is clear: something big is coming."

My phone lights up in my clenched fist. *Hi Sari. I'm okay. How are you?* My shoulders drop as relief flows through me. Red is okay.

Mr. Fawley presses a button on a remote control. The projector displays a picture on the wall: an enormous farmhouse surrounded by military-style obstacle courses where crops should've been. He clicks through more photos: white siding, wrap-around porch, large windows covered by black-out curtains. "This old farmhouse is located about an hour from here at 22 Shadowbrook Road in Shamong, New Jersey. We believe it's the headquarters for a military operation run by both vampires and witches. In all our years of studying super-naturals, this is the first time that we've seen vampires and witches working together. It seems that they've teamed up to attack a common enemy, more than likely, us." Mr. Fawley's lips stretch into a long thin line. "We believe that the two missing girls, Zoeli McKinney-Crowe and Miranda Keller, are prisoners in this farmhouse. More than likely, they've been victims of the most heinous torture imaginable, if they're even still alive." Two photographs appear on the screen, side by side. On the right, Miranda wears a yellow bikini, exposing her pencil-thin legs and gangly arms. Her toes dig into the sand: horn-rimmed glasses perched on her nose, dirty-blonde hair blowing in the wind, blue waves cresting in the background.

On the left, Zoeli commands the stage at The Battle of the Bands, looking hot as hell in a black leather mini-dress and purple boots. Her aquamarine eyes shine as she strums her guitar. I swallow hard. Despite my best efforts, a tear rolls down my cheek. I wipe it away before anyone sees. That photo was taken right before Zoeli and I were captured. Watching her that night, my heart swelled with pride. My sister was a goddamn rockstar. Now, I wonder if I'll ever have the chance to see her perform again.

"For weeks now, we've been watching the farmhouse. It's obvious that they're preparing for war. This supernatural militia calls itself Descendants of Xaphan, or DOX, for short. At least two hundred DOX soldiers train at this facility, and we have reason to believe that this is one of many factions." Mr. Fawley shakes his head, his mouth set in a grim line. "We've never seen anything of this magnitude before. If we don't stop them, all of humankind will be killed off or enslaved." A chorus of gasps ricochet on the peeling walls. "Expert military analysts are helping us develop a strategy. Since we're dealing with an immensely powerful enemy, we need to catch them off guard and be precise. We also need to keep in mind that there may be two or more human prisoners inside the facility. We must do everything we can to preserve their lives."

For the first time since Mr. Fawley took the stage, I wonder if this slayer agency could be a good thing. Maybe we could band together to fight a common enemy. Maybe Keisha and I could rescue Zoeli, side by side.

Mr. Fawley presses the remote. A new image appears on the wall: a sketch of a five-pointed crown. My heart drops into my stomach. "The evilest witches are marked by the crown. If you see a mark like this one, don't hesitate and don't ask questions. Attack and kill. Rip their eyes out of their skulls and their hearts out of their chests. Rid the world of these monsters."

So much for working together. The skin on the back of my neck burns. My pulse hammers in my ears. I tug on the strings of my hoodie, tightening it around my face. If my hood slips off, everyone will see the crown on the nape of my neck. I'll be ravaged and slaughtered while the crowd cheers. Ding-dong, the witch is dead.

Like all Crowes, I'm marked by a three-pointed crown. The five-pointed crown projected on the wall looks like the one on Damian's chest, the mark of the Nightingales.

"If you're interested in joining the fight against DOX, you'll need to attend training sessions. Please see me after the presentation for more information." Mr. Fawley flips over a note card. "Next, I'd like to introduce another slayer who has been instrumental in our efforts. Nathan Fogarty, come on up."

My jaw drops as the tired-looking security guard from Red's club steps up to the podium. "Hi, um, hi, everyone." He brushes a stray curl off his forehead. "So, um, I guess, I'll start at the beginning. A few years ago, I started having nightmares, like the ones that Keisha described. Psychiatrists couldn't understand what was wrong with me. The medications they prescribed only made me worse." Nate's eyes dart back and forth. "When I stopped sleeping, the gory images followed me around all day. I'd see blood dripping down the walls at school. I had visions of people being killed, tortured, chained up, their necks broken, organs ripped out of their bodies. I couldn't escape it. I dropped out of high school and started doing drugs to cope." Nate is talking too fast. Some of his words are garbled and difficult to understand. I wonder if he's nervous or high. Maybe both. "Red seemed like a nice guy. At first, I was thankful that he offered me a job at the club. I'm not exactly security material." He pulls on his wrinkly t-shirt, drawing attention to his skinny frame. "The visions and dreams became more and more violent. I went weeks without a moment of sleep. I was up searching for the truth when I found the Fawley Agency website. About a month ago, I met Mr. Fawley and found out that I'm a slayer and my boss is a blood-sucking vampire." The pitch of his voice rises, excitement evident in his tone. "Since then, I've made copies of Red's keys." He lifts his fingers. Two keys jangle on a silver ring. "With help from Mr. Fawley's contacts, I hacked into Red's security system and uncovered his passwords. We have access to the entire club, including the secret crypt where Red and his vampire friends sleep." Wild laughter escapes from Nate's throat. The crowd erupts in whistles and applause.

Cold sweat slips down my back. I have to warn Red.

Nate steps aside as Mr. Fawley returns to the podium. "Time is of the essence. We need to strike before Red realizes that someone's been messing with his security system. Some of you may be wondering why we met at this ridiculously early hour. The reason is: we're going to attack this morning. We'll kill those evil vampires in their sleep!" Mr. Fawley pumps his fist in the air. The audience bursts into applause. "Who wants to join?" Dozens of hands fly up. "If you're able to join today's mission, stick around. I'm going to pick up some bagels and coffees. We'll discuss the details over breakfast. For the rest of you, we'll see you at the next meeting." As the crowd disperses, I race out the back door, head down. My boots thwack on the pavement as I sprint across the parking lot. With shaking hands, I open my car door and slide into the driver's seat. The sky is already brightening. Several long rays of light stretch above the horizon into pink clouds.

I pick up my phone and dial Red. Please be awake. It rings once. Please be awake. It rings twice. Please, Red, be awake. It rings again.

Chapter 29

Damian

I jerk up in bed, rubbing my eyes. I was sound asleep when Zoeli interrupted my dreams. Her presence, even telepathically, sent electricity coursing through my bones, filling me with a tingly warmth, buzzing with life. Now that she's gone, I'm cold and empty, an open grave.

I try to reach her again, but my words ricochet off her icy walls, leaving me covered in frost. She's still mad at me. I know that I deserve every ounce of her anger. If she gives me the chance, I'll do whatever it takes to earn her forgiveness.

I'll start by delivering food to Theo Halliwell. It's the wee hours of the morning. The castle is dead quiet. No one is awake.

I tiptoe down the stairs and into the kitchen. I stuff an assortment of items into brown paper bags: milk, meats, yogurt, bread, fish, pasta, and cereals. I make several trips back and forth to my car, filling my trunk with a dozen bags.

Two young women in staff uniforms arrive for their morning shift, chattering to each other. Their eyes widen when they spot me kneeling beside the pantry, loading a grocery bag with cookies and juice.

"Good morning, Prince Nightingale." One of the women scurries over. "Do you need help with anything, your majesty?" She curtsies before me, dipping her head low.

"No, thank you." I grab the bag and move towards the exit. The other servant holds the door open. I nod as I pass by, moving swiftly down the hall and towards the garage. I need to get out of here before anyone else sees me. If someone asks what I'm doing, I don't even have a cover story.

I race down the concrete steps, my breath white puffs as I enter the cold garage. My SUV is parked amongst a fleet of luxury vehicles. I toss the last grocery bag on the empty passenger's seat and hit the gas.

Thirty minutes later, I swerve around potholes in the outskirts, the sky a dull hazy purple. Out here, the sunrise pales in comparison to the vibrant hues by the palace.

I park in front of the Halliwell's cottage. My headlights shine on an exquisite sunflower painted on the front door. I pull my baseball hat low over my brow, hoping that no early risers peek through their windows and recognize me. Grocery bags draped over my arms, I easily unlock the front door with a short blast of magic.

Zoeli's scent lingers in the air: a sweet mixture of mint and sandalwood. My heart bangs against my chest, longing for her.

The kitchen is smaller than my closet. The floor is so worn that in some places, I can see the earth beneath. The wooden counter is dotted with stains, chips and burns. Thin, fraying curtains do nothing to block the frigid draft. I almost can't believe that people live like this.

I peek around the cottage: a cramped living room with a ragged old couch, a tiny bathroom with a rusting tub, and a child's bedroom, so narrow that I'm not sure how one would squeeze past the twin bed. Behind a closed door, I hear the steady breaths of deep sleep.

I return to the kitchen. Shelf by shelf, I fill up the refrigerator. Next, I move on to the pantry. When there's no more space, I stack the remaining items on the counter, table and chairs.

Before I leave, I take another look around, struck by the vast difference between my living space and theirs. I could fit their entire house inside my bedroom suite.

Dad would say that they don't deserve what we have. He would say that duds are simpletons who are satisfied with less and wouldn't know what to do with more.

I used to believe him. Now, I wonder if it's just another sorry excuse for our greed. Head hung, I'm overwhelmed by a myriad of emotions. Everything I used to be proud of now brings me shame. What I thought makes me a man is what makes me a boy.

I'm also overcome with admiration for Zoeli: her natural kindness and compassion. I yearn to feel her in my arms, and yet I know that I don't deserve her. Even when I'm not with her, she finds ways to make me a better man. Maybe, if I work hard at it, I'll be good enough for her. Even good enough to rule Aurelia beside her.

Zoeli would be the most incredible queen. She wouldn't judge anyone's worth based on their family status or magical ranking. I can imagine it now: Zoeli and I on the bejeweled thrones, golden crowns atop our heads, moonlight sparkling in her eyes. She'd treat everyone with fairness and dignity. I only wish it could exist outside of my wildest dreams.

If I'm being honest, Caliah would make a great queen too. With her intelligence, grace, and progressive thinking, she could turn this whole kingdom around.

Together, Zoeli and Caliah would be an unstoppable force. They'd go down in the history books as the greatest rulers ever. Yet, it will never happen. Everyone would scoff at the idea of two queens. They'd say that women are too emotional and fragile to lead.

And so, our world will never know its true potential.

When a king presents a radical plan, he's praised for thinking outside the box. Even those who don't support his ideologies will respect his boldness. On the other hand, a progressive queen is mocked, and often dismissed as silly and unreasonable. It could be the same exact proposal, word for word.

Over the years, how many men have taken credit for ideas thought up by their wives? How many wives sat by quietly and watched their husbands accept accolades that they deserved?

I've watched it happen to my own mother, time and time again.

When I'm king, it won't be like that.

Zoeli will be my queen.

If the bigots don't like bowing to a half-breed, they can kiss my royal ass. If anyone disrespects my queen, they can get the hell out of Aurelia.

Zoeli will be given the credit and praise that she deserves.

I'll even take her last name.

Maybe. At least I'll think about it.

Chapter 30

Saria

"Sari, what's up? It's time for me to sleep."

"Red! You're in danger. Nate's a vampire slayer. He's coming to kill you."

"My security guard? Sari, if Nate was a slayer, I would know. Slayers emit a very specific energy that's unlike any other. I would recognize it right away."

I press the pedal to the floor. "Well, if he isn't a slayer, he damn sure believes he is. He's even got the Fawley Agency convinced that he's one."

"The Fawley Agency?" For the first time since our conversation began, Red sounds nervous. "What do they have to do with this?"

I speed out of the parking lot. "Nate's working with them. They're planning to attack today while you're sleeping. They have your keys and your passwords."

"Impossible. No one knows my passwords."

"Do you remember that night in your office?" My heart rate picks up. It's hard to think about that night without remembering Red's teeth on my neck while his fingers traced my hips and thighs. Oh Lord. I suck in a deep breath. "Nate was snooping around in your office. He had access to your computer. The Fawley Agency works with the government. They can probably hack into anything."

"I change my passwords frequently."

"Have you changed them since that night?"

There's a pause. "I don't think so."

"You need to change them right now. Before Fawley and his crew get there."

"Sari, I can't—"

"You have to!"

"I physically can't. I'm inside my coffin right now. As the sun rises, my body shuts down. My muscles are paralyzed. My voice is the last to go, and it's already getting harder to speak."

"I'm coming. I'm going to get you out of there."

"Sari, don't. Don't put yourself in danger."

"I'm already on my way."

"In case I never see you again, Sari," Red's voice dissolves into a cracked whisper. "I want to tell you that—" And then he's gone.

"Red!" I shout. But I know it's no use. He's out cold. Dead until he rises again tonight. Unless Keisha stakes him in the heart. Then, he'll be gone forever.

I need to get him to safety. But how? I may be a witch by blood, but all my magic has been taken from me. For a moment, I allow myself to be angry with Zoeli again. If I had my power back, I might be able to break in and save him.

As I fly around a sharp turn, I grab my phone. My wheels screech as I dial someone who I can count on no matter what. The phone rings.

Another right and I'm on the highway, barreling towards New York City. Cars honk as I cut them off, weaving through the lanes. I gag, burning rubber searing my lungs.

"Saria? Is everything okay?"

"Mom, I need your help."

* * *

Forty minutes later, I'm posted up outside Red's bar. True to its reputation, New York City never sleeps. A few minutes ago, the sun crept over the horizon. Cars honk. Sirens wail. A jogger belts out a song, his footsteps a steady clap on the sidewalk.

In New York, everyone is the star of their own show. Caught up in their own worlds, no one seems to notice me shoving a bobby pin into a lock. I pull the handle, but the door doesn't budge. Another minute ticks by. I jiggle the bobby pin, hoping to hear the click that always happens in the movies. It doesn't work. Another sixty seconds closer to Red's demise. I wish I knew what to do. I wildly jab the bobby pin into the keyhole. At least I'm trying.

The U-Haul screeches to a stop, double parking in front of Red's bar. Mom jumps out of the passenger side. Dad rushes around the other side, laptop balanced on his open palm.

"You got here fast," I say. Hope hammers in my heart. Maybe there's still a chance that we can save Red.

"All the lights turned green the moment we drove up." Mom winks. She looks more alive than I've seen her in months. "I guess it was our lucky day." She plucks the bobby pin out of the lock. "Allow me." Mom rests her hand on the lock. She closes her eyes, dark eyelashes fluttering against her cheeks. I hold my breath, waiting. A moment later: click. Mom wipes her palms on her jeans. "It's been a while, but I still got it."

Dad swings the door open. The alarm blares. My parents are already at work: Dad tapping away on his laptop, Mom's hand hovering over the alarm control pattern. A few seconds later, the siren stops. "I win," Mom says.

"I'll get the next one." Dad huffs. A playful smile touches his lips.

My brows move together. "I didn't know that picking locks and disabling alarms was that easy."

"Ha!" Mom guffaws, descending the stairs two at a time. "It's certainly not. Breaking and entering is a very specialized skill set that takes both natural talent and years of practice to master."

"Years of practice?" I repeat.

"Before you were born, your father and I had our vigilante era."

"Your what?" My jaw drops. Aside from my mom's supernatural abilities, my parents have always been as ordinary as they come. At her weekly grocery store jaunt, Mom peruses produce in high-waist jeans and cardigans. To my horror, Dad would show up to my softball games wearing ill-fitting shorts with long socks. My parents have a recurrent debate over how to load the dishwasher to prevent crusted-on food bits. Can these be the same people who were into vigilante shit? I'm blown away.

"I'll save the stories for another time," Mom says. "Where to next?"

We step inside the main area of the club. Dad flicks on the lights. Without the hypnotic music, lively partygoers, and laser lights, it's just a tremendous room with scuffed floors. Above the mahogany bar, drink specials are scribbled on chalkboards. "This way." I lead my parents across the dance floor to the far corner. We forge ahead: into the alcove and down the sloping hallway into the VIP area.

Because of its exclusive nature, the VIP room has seen less wear and tear. The marble bar shines beneath cast-iron torch-like sconces. The soles of my sneakers squeak on the freshly polished ceramic floor. I guide my parents along the perimeter of the room, stopping at Red's office door. As expected, it's locked.

Mom wraps her fingers around the knob. Her thumb circles the keyhole as she bites her lip in concentration. Her eyes open, a satisfied smirk on her lips. "Like riding a bike." She twists the knob and pushes the door open.

I step onto the black-and-white checkered area rug. Inside Red's office, flashbacks accost me. I'm back in that moment, the last night that we were together: papers fluttering to the ground, my back against the glossy desk. Red climbs on top of me, his words slurred. I taste my blood on his lips. He's high on me. I'm drunk on champagne and his teeth. His fingers twist in my hair, caress my neck and shoulders, move down to my thighs.

I remember it all too well.

I drag my palms along the walls, searching for a secret panel or hidden latch. I rip artwork off the walls. I shove bookshelves to the side. Books clatter on the floor: pages bent, spines broken. "It has to be around here somewhere," I say. My foot catches on the edge of the area rug. On the night when Nate was snooping around, I remember that the corner of the rug was folded up.

I crouch and grab the edge of the rug. It's a lot heavier than I expected. I grunt and pull, but it only moves a few centimeters. Mom tosses it aside like a feather.

I release a trapped breath. Underneath the rug, there's a heavy-duty lock, a screen, and a hatch door. Dad's fingers flutter on his keyboard. Mom hovers over the security system, tracing the letter buttons.

Minutes pass. Five, then ten. The clock tick, tick, ticks. My heart slams into my ribs. Any second now, The Fawley Agency could burst in. I stare, helpless. Twenty minutes. Then thirty. I lean against the wall, trying not to lose hope.

Pop! The hatch slides open, revealing a gaping black hole. "I win, again." Mom dusts off her hands. "Never underestimate a skilled witch." Dad shines a flashlight into the pitch dark.

I follow the beam of light down a short staircase. Three coffins rest in the dirt, side by side. On the right, I immediately identify Bea's coffin. Stained and beat up, it's marred by chips, scuffs and scratches. On the left is a much newer cherry wood coffin. It boasts raised decorative carvings and ornate gold handles.

In the middle lies the largest coffin: a dark walnut hexagon with a high gloss finish. Classic with a modern touch. Sleek, yet sturdy and solid. I don't have to open it to know that Red's inside.

I grip the brass handle and pull with all my might. It doesn't budge. Who am I kidding? I couldn't even pick up a goddamn rug.

Mom lifts one side of the coffin with ease. My dad groans as he hoists up the other. I grab the middle handle, determined to be helpful, however little it may be.

We climb the stairs, Dad grunting on each step. We work our way across the VIP room, up the long hallway, through the main room, and up the final stairway. Out on the sidewalk, we slide the coffin into the back of the U-Haul.

Dad hunches over, hands on his knees, huffing. "We don't have time to waste. Let's go." Mom says, lightly slapping Dad on the back.

Dad raises his chin, face bright red. "I'm only human. I'm going to break my back, woman."

"If you do, I'll heal it," Mom promises. "Saria, stay here. Watch the truck and keep a lookout. If you see anyone, holler."

As Dad follows Mom to the front door, I sit on the tailgate. A woman passes by, her gaze glued to her phone. A man stalks past. He checks his watch, his trench coat blowing open. He nearly knocks over an elderly woman as he lurches ahead, oblivious to everyone's existence but his own.

Mom and Dad reemerge, carrying Beatrice's timeworn coffin. If anyone notices, no one stops to question them. New York City is a place where you're never alone and always alone. Around here, people mind their own business. Wrapped up in the hustle and bustle, chasing their dreams, they don't have time and don't want trouble.

Once Beatrice is safely on the truck, my parents race back inside. Seconds feel like hours. Sweat drips down my back. Any minute now, The Fawley Agency could arrive. If they catch my parents hauling the last coffin, the battle will be ugly. I could lose one of my parents, or my best friend.

Mom and Dad reappear. As the last coffin slides in, I roll down the door and click the lock into place. I exhale. Fawley and his crew aren't here yet. Red's safe.

"I'll lock up," Dad says.

"Hurry." As Dad runs back, Mom touches my arm. "We need to talk. Red's password is BEAUTIFUL CROW." Mom says under her breath.

I forget to breathe. The city street tilts under my feet.

"I don't think he was talking about me," Mom whispers.

I study a long crack on the sidewalk. It splinters into several directions, zig-zagging like a jagged cut that would take forever to heal.

"You're lucky that I didn't tell your father. He'd lose his mind. And even though I love Red, I don't approve of this relationship. He's too old for you, Saria."

"Technically, he's seventeen," I protest.

Mom folds her arms across her chest and gives me *that* look.

I give it right back. "How old was Amos when you dated him?"

"Touche." Mom drops her arms. "As you know, that didn't turn out well. I don't want you to get hurt."

"It's too late for that," I mutter. Mom's expression softens. "Red ended it before it started."

"I'm sorry," Mom says. "But it's for the best."

I swallow hard and change the subject. "Why didn't you just change the password? It seems a lot easier than all this." I gesture to the moving truck.

"Red has safeguards to ensure that only he can change the password. I could've cracked them, but it would've taken more time. We don't have that luxury." Mom shakes her head. "Besides, if the Fawley Agency is determined to get in, they'll find a way. They have skilled hackers on their team. I couldn't leave Red in there."

Dad sprints across the sidewalk and opens the driver's side door. His hair is damp with sweat. "Let's go." Mom jumps into the passenger seat.

"I'll see you at home," I say. Since we came separately, I'll have to drive myself home. My parents wait until I'm inside the car and lock the door. Then, they peel out of there. The truck disappears around the corner.

I take a few deep breaths, trying to steady my shaking hands. A black van pulls up in my rear-view mirror. Mr. Fawley is at the wheel, half of his face darkened by shadow. On the other half, his greasy skin glistens in the sun.

In the passenger seat, Keisha stares straight ahead, her lips a straight determined line.

I pull my hoodie over my eyebrows. Head low, I drive out of the parking spot and away from Red's bar.

As my car blends with city traffic, the black van pulls in front of Red's bar. I hold my breath until they're out of sight.

Chapter 31

Zoeli

As the sun lowers in the sky, I weave through turquoise clouds, avoiding the Elysian Forest. During my last visit, the Whimsy trees shriveled up, branches collapsing on each other, sap dripping down their trunks like teardrops. I don't need another reminder of how sad and lonely I am.

Soon, I'll get out of this godforsaken country. In a few weeks, they'll assume I'm dead or already gone. As soon as security at the portal border lightens up, I'm out of here.

I sail over the Azula Sea, admiring the sleek silhouettes of the mermaids far below the surface. The last rays of sunlight glitter on its smooth surface.

As darkness descents, I soar further out, deeper into the wilderness. It's quiet out here: only the flutter of my wings on the breeze. I close my eyes, basking in the serenity.

A shriek-like cackle cuts the silence like a knife. My eardrums might bleed from its force. My eyes fly open. Edith's outside again: frolicking in her backyard, shouting to the moon.

Puffs of smoke escape from her cottage's chimney. Purple mist swirls out of her cauldron, stretching up into the trees. I draw closer, unable to look away. The lavender haze creeps all around me.

I perch on a bough, high in the tallest tree, concealed by a labyrinth of branches. Below, Edith's gray curls blow in the wind. She reaches up, a gnarled finger pointed at me. "Hello, little crow." She rasps. "I see you, Zoeli Crowe."

I feel like someone smacked me in the chest. How does she know? I'm not surprised that she recognized a supernatural being nearby; many witches have that ability. But this is Aurelia: the land of witches. I could've been anyone. Even if she managed to see a crow, I could've been any Crowe. I'm not even sure how she saw me at all, given that I'm hidden amongst the brush and bark.

"Don't be shy, Miss Zoeli." Edith's green eyes glow in the moonlight. "You know what? I'm feeling generous tonight. Come on down and I'll give you a free session. Folks pay a pretty penny for my readings. You're not in a position to pass up on this offer now, are you? You're alone and on the run. Don't you think that you could use some guidance?" Edith cackles. Her lips peel back, revealing horse-like teeth. "What's the matter? Are you scared, little crow?" She sprinkles stardust into her cauldron. Sparks shoot into the sky.

I'm not afraid of anyone, especially not this crazy hag. With my reserves of blue power, I'll blast her into the grave if need be. She better not try to mess with me.

"Come to me, little crow."

If this withered crone keeps calling me little, I'll have to go down there to set her straight. Yes, I'm small, but I'm tough. Her tone reminds me of a trapper coaxing a mouse. If that's what she thinks of me, she has the wrong number.

"Zoeli. Oh, Zoeli." Edith calls in a sing-song voice. I look left and right, fury rising within me. What's wrong with this woman? There's a price on my head. If anyone's around, they'll do their best to haul me back to the dungeon. If King Keifer has his way, I'll be beheaded on the guillotine. "Zoooo-elllll-iiiii!" Edith taunts.

I've had enough. I'm going to tape her damn mouth shut. I dive to the ground, blue swirls rushing around me. I transform as soon as I hit the ground. I clamp my hand over her mouth. "You idiot! Are you trying to get me killed?"

Beneath my palm, Edith's lips curve into a grin. Her eyes crinkle. "Of course not, my dear." Her horse teeth graze my hand. I pull away.

"How did you see me?" I ask.

"Vision extends far beyond our eyes, little bird." Edith says. There she goes with that little shit again. I swallow down some nasty words. My mom taught me not to disrespect my elders. "Come with me, Miss Zoeli." Edith gestures towards her cottage.

"I think I'll pass." Coming down here was a bad idea in the first place. Anyone could be lurking nearby, ready to strike.

"You have somewhere better to be?" An eerie cackle escapes her lips, an unsettling sound that could only be produced by a madwoman. I'm getting the hell out of here. I turn to go. "What's the matter? Are you afraid?"

Hell no. I spin back around. "What do you want from me?"

"Only to give you a reading, my dear." Her tattered housedress hangs on her pear-shaped frame, swaying as she moves towards the door. "Come, my dear. Unless you're scared, of course."

I sigh. I'm damn well not afraid of an eccentric grandma who forgot her psychiatric medication. Also, I have to admit, my curiosity is piqued. Witches pay top dollar to hear this woman's rambling. At the very least, it must be entertaining. And as Edith so flagrantly pointed out, I don't have anything better to do. "Alright," I mutter.

The cottage door creaks as Edith tugs it open. Compared to Edith's unkempt appearance, the cottage is surprisingly tidy. Inside, flowered wallpaper adorns the kitchen's walls. A dish towel embroidered with roses hangs over the oven's handle. Past the kitchen, a blue loveseat with white polka dots faces an antique television.

I follow Edith through the living room. A black Persian cat lifts his head from a throw pillow to hiss at me. "Edgar, where are your manners?" Edith scolds. "Don't mind him. He's just an old grouch." She scratches his head. Edgar's golden eyes close as he resumes his nap. It must be nice to be a cat. "This way." Edith waves her arm. She leads me to a space separated from the living room by a beaded curtain. She holds the curtain aside as I step inside.

My jaw hangs open. There was a time when I thought that my mom's magical supply was extensive. Not anymore. Edith's shelves are stocked with every ingredient, herb and crystal imaginable. Thousands of tiny jars are lined up in rows. Along another wall, a library of books stretches from floor to ceiling, organized by categorical tabs.

Most fascinating of all is the object in the center of the room. Atop a glass table is a sphere-like crystal sculpture the size of a basketball. It appears that dozens of crystals were welded together to create the piece. I recognize several varieties: agate, bloodstone, amethyst, chalcedony, and moonstone, to name a few.

The power that radiates from it thickens the air. It's palpable with every breath, tingling in my lungs.

"Welcome to my office," Edith says. "Have a seat." A crooked finger points to a wicker chair. As I sit, Edith pulls out a chair on the other side of the table. The crystal is inches away.

Despite her gnarled hands, Edith expertly shuffles a deck of black cards. "Ask a question, my dear."

I think it over. "I'm not sure what to ask. I don't believe that the future is fixed. I believe that our choices are what determines the future."

"There's truth to that, my dear. Many times, the choices we make can change our course, for better or for worse. However, certain things are written in the stars and cannot be changed, no matter how hard one may try." She rests the deck on the table.

I grimace, remembering when Damian and I swam in the waterfall called Clarity. The breeze whispered that Damian was made for me. It even said that a love like ours only comes along once in a lifetime. What a load of bullshit.

"Not for me," I say. "I'll make my own decisions." I prefer to have an internal locus of control. If I never find love again, I'll love myself, my family and my friends. I'm not settling for a lying asshole because destiny tells me that I should.

"Not everyone asks about their futures. Many seek advice or information about the present. Perhaps you long to know the true intentions of a friend or lover. For example, I've had women ask if their partner has been unfaithful."

"I figured that one out on my own, too," I mutter. "Although I'll admit that it took too long. I should've come here a few months ago."

"Maybe there's someone that you haven't seen in a while, someone you've lost touch with. You think of them often and you want to know how they're doing."

Saria. I swallow a lump in my throat. I miss her so damn much. "My sister," I say.

"Yes," Edith says, her eyes crinkling.

"How is she?" I ask.

"Don't ask me." Edith tilts her head towards the crystal. "Ask her. Tell her why you need to know. Tell her your story. The more information you provide, the more emotion you convey, the more accurate your answer will be."

I resist the urge to roll my eyes. This woman is certifiable.

"I call her Betty," Edith continues.

I don't know much about naming crystals, but if you call her Betty, I'm going to call you batty. I bite my tongue, remembering that this old woman lives all alone in the wilderness. Maybe Edith's Betty is like Tom Hank's Wilson in the movie Cast Away. A pang of sympathy hits me in the chest. "Um, okay." I clear my throat. "Betty, from the moment we were born, Saria and I were inseparable. As toddlers, we waddled around, playing with dolls and unicorn figurines. As we grew older, our witchy roots became apparent in our shared love for nature. We hiked and climbed, learning every tree and rock in the forest. At night, we studied the sky, counting constellations and searching for shooting stars." I swallow hard, tears welling in my eyes. "Twins have a special bond that I can't even put into words. It's almost like we're two halves of the same soul. Even when I hated her, I still loved her. I'd still put my life on the line for her." I take a deep breath. "I'm not sure when or how, but we drifted apart. She hurt me, but I held onto a grudge for far too long. We should've sat down and talked it out. So much time was wasted" I shake my head. "The only good part about us being captured is that we got to be together. Even though we were frozen and starving, we rebuilt our bond. It was never really broken to begin with." My hands clench together. "Now here I am, a fugitive hiding in the supernatural realm. And she's over in the human realm. We haven't spoken in months. I don't know if we'll ever see each other again." My voice cracks. "I just want to know how she's doing, if she's okay, if she's happy."

"That was beautiful. She heard you and she has your answer." Edith taps the deck of cards against the tabletop three times. Then, she separates it into three stacks. Starting on the left, she flips the top card. Face-up on the table, a drawing of an embracing couple looks like it was scrawled by a grade schooler. Beneath the picture, in shaky handwriting, THE LOVERS.

Edith turns another card over, this one from the middle stack. It's another poorly drawn figure: a man in a dracula-esque coat with long fangs protruding from his mouth. Below him, a scribbled descriptor: THE VAMPIRE.

Okay, that's weird. Edith flips over a card from the final deck. A heart sliced in half by a medieval sword. The words beneath: THE HEARTBROKEN. Edith lines the cards up next to each other.

I crease my forehead, waiting for an explanation.

"Your sister fell in love with a vampire," Edith says. "And he broke her heart."

I suppress the urge to double over with laughter. It's not only unbelievable, it's absurd. Saria loves Logan. Even in the unlikely circumstance that they broke up, my sister wouldn't go near a vampire. I can't believe that people actually pay this imposter. I'll give her a few points for creativity, but I didn't come here for fiction. If I wanted a vampire love story, I'd pull out my old copy of Twilight.

"I'm sorry that it wasn't better news," Edith says. "But the good news is that she's alive. She'll get over the heartbreak. We all do."

"Sure," I mutter, tapping my foot. I've had about enough of this nonsense. "I think it's time for me to go."

"You don't have another question?" Edith taps on the deck.

"I think I'm good. Thanks for your time."

"Stay." Edith puts her wrinkled hand on mine. "Watch me ask the question I ask every night. I always get the same answer." Edith raises her hands towards the ceiling. "What will cause the demise of Aurelia?" Edith whacks the deck onto the table and separates it into three piles. "The fox!" Edith yells it out before she turns the card over. The animal is so poorly drawn that if it wasn't for the label, I wouldn't be sure if it was a fox, cat or racoon.

"The vampire." Edith slams the next card on the table. It's the same one that appeared in the last round.

"Magic coming undone." The final card depicts a magic wand, arrows pointing at the wand, indicating magic returning to it, rather than radiating outwards from it.

I don't know what any of it means. "I have to go," I repeat.

Edith stands abruptly, knocking over her chair behind her. "Watch out, little bird. The end is near. Only a few of us will make it out alive."

She leads me through the beaded curtain and into her living room. Edgar hisses. As I pass, he swipes me with his claws. "Naughty cat," Edith scolds. I can't wait to get the hell out of here. I quicken my pace through the kitchen and fling open the front door.

"Thanks a lot," I say, stepping out into the cool air.

"Goodbye, little crow. Be careful out there." She cackles wildly.

I shift into a crow and take off in flight. As I zoom above the trees, Edith's scream echoes on the wind. "The end is near! We're all doomed!"

Chapter 32

Saria

If it wasn't for the three coffins lined up in the center of our living room, we might look like an ordinary family watching the evening news. Outside, the sky has taken on an orange hue. Inside, crimson flames and black smoke fill the television screen.

We watch and wait as the sky changes colors: amber, burnt orange, crimson, and finally, indigo blue.

The lid of Bea's coffin rattles. She pops up, emerald eyes wide as she looks around. "What the—"

Gio rises next. He looks back and forth between my parents before his eyes narrow on me. His nostrils flare as he dives at me. If it didn't happen so fast, I would've tried to explain. His fingers clamp around my throat, sucking all the air from my lungs. My mother screams. Gio slams my head into the wall. "You little witch. Red should've known better." Crack! My head hits the sheetrock again. Agony blasts through me. I'm pretty sure my skull shattered into a million pieces. Blood shoots out of my ear.

"Get off of her!" Red tackles Gio from behind and throws him across the room. Gio crashes into the opposite wall. Shelves rattle. Trinkets clatter to the floor.

Gio opens his mouth to speak. Before he gets a word out, Red socks him in the face. Gio's neck snaps back. Blood sprays from his nose, splattering on our family portrait and television.

I fall to the floor, my head searing with pain. Mom kneels by my side.

"What the hell, man?" Gio growls. "They kidnapped us."

"They saved us, you idiot! Look at the TV." Red says.

A reporter's voice comes from the television. "New York City firefighters continue to fight the blaze at Red's, a popular downtown nightclub. The trendy night spot has been reduced to a pile of charred rubble. No injuries have been reported at this time."

"You idiot!" Red repeats. He slides by my side. "Sari, stay with us." His fingers lace through mine.

I'm being sucked down a dark tunnel. The world moves farther and farther away. Black spots cloud my vision. My ears buzz like my head's stuck in a hornet's nest.

Mom's fingers thread through my hair, drawing warm circles on my scalp.

The buzz quiets, and then my hearing is gone. My vision goes next, soft black edges closing in until I'm floating in total darkness.

That's when I realize that I've lost my sense of touch. I can't feel the floor beneath my back or the air moving in and out of my lungs. I can't tell if I'm breathing at all.

Then, I'm gone.

Chapter 33

"What's up, man?" I lean back on my couch, phone to my ear.

"I was in Nightingale City today. I saw all the protestors. It was wild, man. They're demanding that the Nightingales be dethroned," Colson says.

"They're the least of my concerns," I say. I'm worried about a lot of things: Zoeli, Caliah, the Descendants of Xaphan. The protestors don't even make the list.

"I don't know, man. I've never seen a turnout like this. They're calling for a revolution."

"They'll get over it," I say. "My father and his PR team are working around the clock. In a few weeks, it'll be old news."

"I hope so," Colson says. "Austin and I are heading to the gym in an hour. You want to come?"

"I don't know, man. I'm kind of tired."

"Dame, you know moping around about that girl isn't going to bring her back, right?"

I sigh. Colson's never been in love. He doesn't understand how bad it hurts. It feels like my heart was ripped out of my rib cage. I'm half-alive: a gaping hole in my chest, blood stagnant in my body. And worst of all, it's my own damn fault. At least he called her a girl and not a nimwit.

"Come hang out, man," Colson says.

"I'll let you know if I'm up to it." I disconnect the call and shrink back into my pillows. Frigid air blows in through my open window. I shiver and pull a fur blanket over me.

Someone knocks on my door. "Who's there?" I bellow.

The door inches open. Cali pops her head in: big turquoise eyes and long strawberry curls. She's undeniably gorgeous. "Is it okay if I come in?"

"Yeah, sure," I say.

She steps inside and closes the door behind her. A form-fitting royal blue sweater dress accentuates her lean, lithe body. Her eyes widen when she sees me curled under the blanket. "Are you sick?" She strides over to me. "It's so cold in here." She wraps her arms around herself, looking around. When she spots the open window, she walks over and slams it shut. "That's better."

Even as the temperatures drop, I keep my window open for Zoe. If she decides to visit, I don't want any barriers in her way. I sleep under multiple comforters, hoping that I'll wake up with Zoe next to me. My only solace is when she appears in my dreams.

Cali snuggles next to me. "I'll warm you up." She leans in for a kiss. Her lips are soft against mine. I turn away. "What's the matter?" Sadness sweeps over her delicate features.

I shrug. "Nothing. Just not feeling great."

"I'll make you feel better," Cali licks her lips. She leans in again, her tongue sliding between her lips and into my mouth. Why shouldn't I let her make me feel better? I've been so depressed, and Zoe isn't even speaking to me.

Cali deepens the kiss, her fingers in my hair. I kiss her back. She presses her body against mine. It feels so… wrong. I pull away.

Cali studies me, her brow furrowed. "What's wrong with you?"

"I told you. I'm not feeling well."

Cali's cheeks redden. "You're lying."

I avert my eyes. "Why would you say that?"

"You're in love with her, aren't you?" Tears well in her eyes.

I play dumb. "With who?"

"I'm not stupid, Damian." Cali folds her arms across her chest. "Ever since she disappeared, you've been miserable."

I shrug. "I'm just worried about her. That's all."

"Stop lying to me!" Cali stands up, fists clenched at her sides. "I deserve the truth, Damian."

I take a deep breath, preparing my next lie. "I, I…" And then I stop. Because she's right. She deserves the truth. "I, I, I'm sorry, Cali."

Something snaps in her. Her eyes darken. "You led me on. You lied to me. You snuck around with Zoeli behind my back." She lists my sins like a rap sheet. I don't have a defense.

She points at me. "You're going to pay for this, Prince Damian Nightingale. I'm going to tell everyone what you've done."

"Cali, please, don't. I'm sorry."

Tears stream from her eyes. Strawberry curls stick to her wet cheeks. "I'll ruin you. You'll never see the throne. You're going to spend the rest of your life locked in the dungeon." Her cupid-bow mouth twists into a scowl. "I'll make sure of it." She storms out, slamming the door in her wake.

As soon as she leaves, I crack the window open. I collapse back on the couch, head in my hands. For the first time, sweet talk isn't going to get me out of this mess. I thought I was immune to consequences, but I was wrong.

If I was a better man, I'd let Zoeli find someone who deserves her. But selfish as I am, I still want her.

I'd cheat, lie and steal to get her back. I guess I haven't really changed at all.

Chapter 34

Saria

Everything is a blur aside from him. I study his face: thick black hair, blazing blue eyes, skin that hasn't seen the sun in a hundred years. "Red," I murmur through parched lips. "What happened?"

"You died, and then I turned you into a vampire."

My eyes fly open. "What?"

Red grins. "That woke you up quick."

"Are you serious?" I sit up, my bedroom walls spinning around me. Somehow, I wound up in my bed. "Am I really a vampire?" I don't feel like a vampire, but then again, how would I know what a vampire feels like? My stomach growls. I would kill for a burger and fries right now. Aren't vampires supposed to crave blood? I like my burgers rare, but still…

"I'm kidding." Red chuckles. "You're not a vampire. Your mom healed you."

The door creaks open. Mom, Dad and Bea enter my room. "Is she awake?" Mom asks.

"Yes," Red says. "You gave us quite the scare. We thought we lost you."

"We almost did," Mom says. "You had a fractured cranium and several brain bleeds. Without immediate intervention, you wouldn't have survived."

"But I'm not a vampire," I say.

"No, you're still human," Red assures me. I should be overcome with relief, so why is part of me disappointed? Drinking blood is gross. I can't imagine life without chocolate and pasta. In the summer, I love laying out in the sun. I plan to finish high school and go away to college. And one day, I want to have a family of my own. I wouldn't want to give all of that up. Right?

Bea perches on the edge of my bed. "Thank you, Sari, for saving my life." She looks over at my mom and dad. "Thank you all."

Gio pops his head in the doorway. "Is Sari okay?"

"Yes, she's awake," Bea answers.

Gio steps inside, holding a bloody rag against his nose. "Thank you for saving us," he says. "I guess not all witches are bad."

"You're an asshole," Red growls. "You almost killed Sari."

"I fucked up." Gio says. "I thought she kidnapped us. I was wrong. I'm sorry."

"It's okay," I say. "I understand."

"You're more forgiving than me." Red mutters.

Bea holds up a glass. "I fixed you a beverage." Fresh raspberries and mint leaves float in sparkling water. I take it from her and drink greedily.

"Delicious." I raise the drink. "Cheers." I still feel woozy, like there's more than fresh fruit and seltzer in the glass.

"How can I ever repay you?" Red asks, his gaze shifting from me to my parents. "Name your price. Do you want money, cars or real estate? I'll sign everything I own over to your names."

"Don't be ridiculous," Dad says. "We don't want a thing."

Red is already shuffling through his wallet. He pulls out a wad of hundred-dollar bills.

"Don't you dare." Mom holds up her palm. "If you hand over that money, I'll smack you with it."

"We'll work this out later," Red grumbles and turns to me. "How are you feeling?"

"I'm okay. Just tired and hungry."

"Stay in bed. You need your rest," Mom says. "I'll bring dinner up to you."

Red's phone rings. "I have about a thousand missed calls from friends, neighbors and insurance companies. I should take this." He glances back before he leaves the room. "Are you sure you're okay?"

I nod. "I'm just sleepy." The words come out slurred, my eyelids heavy.

"We'll let you rest," Dad says, as the rest of the group shuffles out the door.

"Thank you, Sari," Gio says again on his way out. "I'll never forget what you did for us."

Mom clicks off the light. Moonlight filters through my window. My eyes shut.

* * *

I only know that time passed from the position of the moon. I sit up in bed and rub my eyes. I hear muffled voices downstairs, coming from the kitchen.

I stagger into the hallway. As I walk downstairs, I grip the handrail like a lifeline. Red and my parents sit around the kitchen table. Red smiles when he sees me. "Hey, sleepyhead. That was a long nap. How are you feeling?"

I collapse into a kitchen chair. "I'm okay. Where'd everyone go?"

"Bea and Gio went to get something to eat. I stayed around to wait for you to wake up." Red glances at my mom. "Even though Lani assured me that you'd be okay, I needed to see for myself." He looks me over, his blue gaze piercing my skin. "You've got the pink back in your cheeks. That's a good sign."

"You need to eat," Dad says, sliding his chair back as he stands up. "I'll heat up leftovers from dinner." Dad shuffles around in the refrigerator.

I peek through the archway into the living room. "The coffins are gone," I observe. The microwave beeps as Dad presses its buttons.

"I had them delivered to another one of my properties," Red says. "My workers came and left while you slept."

The mention of his properties reminds me of his nightclub. "Oh, Red," I say. "I'm so sorry about your bar." I wonder if the building is salvageable. Based on the news report, my favorite hangout is a mound of ashes and debris.

Red shrugs. "It doesn't matter. I was planning on moving anyway. All that matters is that no one was hurt. Thanks to you."

Dad slides a plate of spaghetti in front of me. I dig in, grateful that I'm not a vampire. "So, you'll be heading to London, then?" I try to keep my voice as casual as possible. It shouldn't matter to me if Red moves to the other side of the ocean. It *doesn't* matter to me.

"Yes," Red nods. "I closed on the property over there." I pretend that doesn't hurt more than Gio bashing my head into the sheetrock. "But first, I'm going to find your sister. I already promised you, and tonight I promised your parents. I'm not going anywhere until Zoeli is safe at home." Tears well in Mom's eyes. Dad reaches over and puts a hand on my shoulder. I swallow hard. My parents almost lost another daughter today.

Dad yawns. His eyes are bloodshot. "It's been quite the day. I'm exhausted."

Red checks his watch. "It's almost midnight." He stands up. "Forgive me for staying so late. I'll go so you can get some sleep."

"I'll walk you out," I say. Red says goodbye to my parents and follows me to the front door. Behind us, the stairs creak as my parents head upstairs.

Outside on the front porch, the cold stings my cheeks. White puffs escape my mouth with each breath. Red and I stand face to face, my chin lifted to meet his eyes.

I thought I knew exactly what I'd say, but now I forget everything. All I want is to melt into his arms. I'd move closer if I didn't think he'd push me away.

"Thank you, Sari," Red says. "You saved my life. You risked your own to save mine. I'll never forget that." Despite the cold, he keeps his black leather jacket unzipped. I can make out the shape of his defined chest and six-pack abs beneath his white t-shirt. It takes all my restraint not to touch him.

"It was nothing," I say, even though it was everything. We're getting used to lying to each other about things like that. "We need to check 22 Shadowbrook Road in Shamong. Mr. Fawley thinks that Zoeli might be a prisoner there."

Red nods. "I'll take care of it."

"The slayers are planning an attack. If Zoe's there and they see her crown mark, they'll kill her too." My lips quiver. "This can't wait. We have to go tonight."

Red rests his palms on my shoulders. "I promise you that I'm going to do everything I can to find Zoeli. But you need to go back to bed and rest, safe and sound. I almost lost you once tonight, and I'm damn sure not putting you in harm's way again."

I lift my chin higher. "I want to go."

"It isn't safe, Sari. There might be hundreds of powerful witches and vampires stationed there. Their leader, Talon, has a personal vendetta against your family. You can't go there."

I suppose he has a point. I don't remember moving, but somehow, we're closer together. His lips are inches from mine. Electricity courses through my veins. Red bites his bottom lip. I don't feel the cold. Every spot his teeth pierced last time tingles, hot as fire. My body remembers.

I can't resist. I move even closer. If I just lean in another inch, I'll close the gap…

Clack! Red and I spring apart. "What was that?" Red asks. Clink! The sound rings out again. "Someone's out there."

My heart races. Who's lurking around my house at this hour? I check my watch. It's almost one a.m. Clack! "It's coming from that side of the house," Red whispers. On tiptoes, we slink alongside the house, ducked down in the hedges.

Around the corner, Logan bends over, his fingers digging in the dirt. The puffy coat on his lanky frame reminds me of a marshmallow on a stick. Logan and I have always loved roasting s'mores. I can see us now: laughing around the campfire, piling marshmallows, chocolate bars and graham crackers, competing over who can fit the largest stack in their mouth. Lord, I miss those days.

In an alternate, much simpler reality, Logan and I roast s'mores together tonight, our greatest worry a blackened marshmallow. Years later, we'd continue the tradition with our kids: a little boy and girl with wavy blonde hair and sticky marshmallow goo on their lips. Tears of what might have been well in my eyes. When did everything get so damn complicated?

Instead of pursuing a hot vampire, I should be begging Logan for forgiveness. What's wrong with me? I'm so damn confused.

Logan turns and launches one pebble at my bedroom window, and then another. Clink! Clack!

"Logan?" I say. "What are you doing?"

"Saria?" He spins around. Bulky glasses slide down his nose. "Is that you?" He squints.

"It's me," I say. Dewy grass squishes under my sneakers as I step forward. "What are you doing here?"

"I, um, I, I guess…" His voice trails off. "I miss you," he blurts out.

"Oh, um," I stumble on my words. Red is right behind me and I'm not sure what to say.

Logan walks towards me, his arms out in front of him. He stops. His eyes widen as he seems to see Red for the first time. His arms drop. "I'm such an idiot." Logan winces, pain sweeping from his glassy eyes to his trembling lips.

He takes off and runs, footsteps pounding on the dirt.

"Logan!" I call after him, but he's gone. "Logan!"

Red stands stiffly, his hands stuffed in his pockets. "I'm sorry about that."

I spin around. "No, there's nothing to be sorry about," I say. Did I hurt Red too, shouting after Logan like that? God, I'm such a mess.

Red looks away. "Let's get you inside." We walk to the porch in silence.

"I had no idea that Logan was coming by," I say. "I haven't even talked to him in over a month." I'm rambling now, but I need Red to know that Logan and I are over. But are we? Although I can't deny my attraction to Red, I still love Logan. I'm a freaking mess.

"Goodnight, Sari," Red says. "I'll wait until you're inside and lock the door." I look up at him. He won't meet my eye.

I go inside. As soon as the lock clicks shut, he's gone. Above the trees, a bat fades into the black sky.

Chapter 35

Zoeli

I know the Aurelian landscape like the back of my claw now. Late at night I drift through the stars, taking it all in.

Tonight, I draw loops around Mount Zamus, Aurelia's only volcano, admiring its beauty. Sparks shoot from its opening, bursting open in the night sky. Mount Zamus never fails to put on a fantastic fireworks show.

Out here, close to the Rock of Vitality, bold ribbons of magic dance across the sky. I zig-zag through orange swirls, and then slide down a beam of blue. Mount Zamus spits out a comet-like sphere. The fireball shoots across the sky, purple glitter in its wake. Everything is magic here.

I meander over to Enchantments Academy, the school that rejected me because of my human blood. Its diamond-like bricks glimmer in the moonlight. It stands at an impossible angle. Even though it looks like it might topple over at any moment, a powerful spell makes it one of the sturdiest buildings in Aurelia.

Next, I sail over to another of my favorite places, the Azula Sea. Moonlight glistens on its placid surface. A rainbow-feathered duck and its ducklings swim around metallic rocks. Even in the winter, pink and orange flowers bloom from lily pads. It's idyllic.

At first glance, no one would guess that a prison lies underneath. Like most of Aurelia, cruel secrets are hidden just below the surface. Only a thin veil of beauty masks the horror, but most choose not to look too closely. Ignorance is bliss, I suppose. But not all of us have that luxury.

It's time for me to visit a friend. I soar over the sea and into the forest. When I hear the rushing river, I dive through the trees. On the ground, I perch on a smooth rock, checking to make sure I'm alone. Once I'm sure, I shift into my human form.

I tap my fingers against the boulder, calling for my little friend. Leaves rustle. Triangular eyes peer through a honeysuckle bush. The dragoni leaps out. He lands on my lap and nuzzles against my belly.

"Hey Moz," I murmur, stroking his black fur. I named him Mozart after his musical talent. When he makes music, I forget that I'm a fugitive on the run. For a moment in time, I'm at peace.

Lonely as I am, this little creature has become my best friend. He reminds me of Batman, my cat back home. I hope that Saria is giving him extra hugs and attention.

Moz sings to me. Tonight's symphony raises goosebumps on my flesh. Moz stands up on his hind legs, bat-like wings spread open as the melody reaches a crescendo.

If I had a phone, I'd take a picture and send it to Layal. She had some nerve calling me a liar. If Layal saw me and my dragoni snuggled up like this, it'd wipe the sly smile right off her foxlike face.

Edith said that a fox would doom us all. At the disastrous afterparty, I heard Layal joke about reversing the spell that secures the portal. Is Layal a threat to Aurelia? For a few moments, I wonder if I should keep an eye on her.

Then I remember that Edith also said that Saria had her heart broken by a vampire. The hag is bat-shit crazy.

Moz rubs his cheek against mine, singing directly into my ear. The tune is calmer now, soft and serene, lulling me to sleep.

It isn't safe to fall asleep out here. A hiker or hunter could pass by. It wouldn't take long for them to confirm my identity. My photograph is posted on every street lamp.

Yet, I feel my eyelids growing heavy.

In my dreams, two realms collide. I'm under a spotlight, guitar strapped over my shoulder. My band, The Exiled Crows, rocks the stage at a packed arena. Yazmin belts out the lyrics, her powerful voice rising over the cheering crowd. Scott strikes the drum, his fists a blur as he keeps the fast beat, sweat dripping down his skinny arms and freckled nose. Even the most vigorous head thrashing doesn't disturb Justin's blue mohawk. His turquoise nail polish matches his electric guitar.

We even have an additional band member tonight. Moz is perched on my shoulder. Beautiful music emanates from his throat, in perfect harmony with the rest of us.

In the front row, Saria, Mom and Dad dance, their hands in the air. Beside them, Damian flashes his signature lopsided grin. As his big black eyes meet mine, he mouths, "I love you, Zoe."

"Wake up," a male voice interrupts my dream. Is it my dad? Am I late for school? Someone shakes my shoulder. "Wake up," the voice repeats.

As I drift towards consciousness, I become aware of the hard rock beneath me, the gurgle of a river rolling over rocks. That's when I realize my fatal mistake. I fell asleep in the woods, and now I've been found. I'm a fool.

I jump to my feet. Moz falls out of my lap. Mid-air, he startles, eyes flying open. In the nick of time, he twists his body and lands on his feet, claw marks in the dirt. I raise my fists, poised to fight.

My opponent puts his palms up. "I'm not going to hurt you."

I recognize his strange eyes: irises so pale they almost blend into the whites. "Kian?" I barely recognize him out of his guard's uniform. In baggy jeans and a rumpled sweatshirt, he looks like he should sit next to me in biology, not patrol dungeon hallways.

"It's me." Kian's handsome in his own peculiar way: silky blonde hair tapered on the sides and longer on top, a scar that slashes through his eyebrow, the slightest gap between his two front teeth. Moz pads over to Kian. He rubs his chin on Kian's leg.

"Traitor," I mutter.

Kian scratches behind Moz's ears. "I see we have a mutual friend. You should be careful about falling asleep out here. Someone else could've come along."

I furrow my brow. "So, you're not going to turn me in?"

"No, of course not," Kian says. "I tried to tell you, Zoe. I don't like how the Nightingales govern."

"Why do you work for them?"

Kian shrugs. "It's a job. I'm on my own and I have bills to pay." He flashes a devious smile. "Haven't you heard the expression: keep your friends close and your enemies closer? When we rise up, I'll be in a unique position to help from the inside. We're planning a revolution."

"I've heard," I mutter. "Protestors blame the king for my escape. The Nightingales failed at keeping Aurelia safe from villains like me. They march through the cities, demanding that the Lyons take over the throne."

Kian shakes his head. "I'm not a part of that. In my opinion, the Lyons are worse than the Nightingales. What I want is to dismantle the entire system. Overthrow the dictatorship and establish a democracy. I've been researching governments in the human realm, like the United States, for example, as a template."

"I'm from the U.S.," I say. "Our government is far from perfect. There's corruption and racism and economic disparities—"

"It's a hell of a lot better than what we have over here."

I can't argue that. Behind me, leaves rustle. I spin around, fists raised and clenched. A white bunny darts out of a bush. It hops down the trail, puff-tail bouncing. I release my breath. "I should go," I say.

"We meet at my house at seven p.m. on the first and third Sunday of each month. Would you like to join?"

"Who's 'we'?"

"The Resistance. Unoriginal, I know." Kian shrugs. "We're having trouble agreeing on a name."

"I can't go. I have to stay hidden. There's a huge price on my head." I step back, pressing my back against a tree trunk, hoping it provides some coverage.

"That's no way to live," Kian says. "If we overthrow the Nightingales, you'll be free. You can go anywhere you want."

I shrug. All I want is to go home. Every day, that seems more and more impossible.

"I think you'd be a great asset to our team, Zoe. You're tough and clever. I still haven't figured out how you managed to escape." Before Damian broke my heart, I was a fighter. Lately, I've been wasting time, wallowing in my heartbreak. But that's not who I am. I'm not a quitter. I'm a warrior. "I'm lucky that you didn't break out on my shift," Kian continues. "All of the guards who were on duty were interrogated and fired."

I remember that night, hitching a ride in a dumpster, Frederick's whistle grating my ears. I can't help my smug smile as I imagine Frederick getting fired. After all the times he spit on me, I guess karma paid him a visit.

"I'll let you go, Zoeli. If you change your mind, my address is 13 Opal Moon Road."

"Thanks, Kian," I say. "And thanks for waking me."

He raises his hand in a military salute. "If you need anything, you know where to find me." He walks away, acorns crunching beneath his sneakers.

Something moves in a nearby shrub. I spin around, ready to defend myself. A squirrel prances towards the river. It takes a pit stop to munch an acorn.

When I turn back, Kian's gone, swallowed up by the thicket.

Chapter 36

Saria

Someone taps on my bedroom door. I push my chemistry homework aside. It's not like I was getting any closer to the answers anyway. "Come in."

My dad steps in. "How are you feeling?" Dad looks like he's seen better days. Dark half-moons hang beneath his brown eyes. I guess having one missing daughter and almost losing the other takes a toll.

"I'm fine." I force a smile. Physically, I feel brand new. If any doctor examined me, they wouldn't believe that yesterday I suffered a cranial fracture and multiple brain bleeds.

Mentally, I'm on the struggle bus. I've lost almost everyone closest to me: Zoeli, Logan, Red, and now Keisha. How am I supposed to look her in the eyes and pretend that everything is okay when she tried to kill my friends? When I know she'd kill me if she knew my true identity.

Dad pulls the enertron out of his jean's pocket, looping its black plastic band around his finger. "For months now, I haven't been able to figure out what's wrong with this thing. Today I finally figured it out. When the error message came up, were you with Keisha?"

"Yes." I remember that morning: Keisha in the front seat, a smile that didn't quite meet her tired eyes. I thought we were best friends, but she didn't confide in me. She suffered through nightmares and visions alone. But can I blame her? She knew that I was going through hell. She probably didn't want to worry me.

"That's it!" Dad raises his finger. "Slayers emit a unique supernatural energy: markedly different from a witch, vampire or demon. The enertron detected a magical force, but couldn't figure out what it was."

"That makes sense," I say.

"I'm going to reprogram it to recognize slayers." Dad reminds me of a mad scientist today: uncombed hair sticking out in every direction, bloodshot eyes, a wild grin as he describes his latest invention. "I'm going to increase the enertron's sensitivity so it will not only detect supernatural energy, but also identify the source, whether it be a slayer, vampire, witch or demon. You'll know exactly who and what you're dealing with."

"That's awesome, Dad."

"I'm also going to make the new model sleeker and more, um, trendy," Dad says.

I grin. My dad wears socks with sandals. Most of his t-shirts are from the nineties and should've stayed there. He doesn't know a thing about fashion, but it's sweet that he's going to try for me. "Thanks, Dad. I appreciate that."

Dad rubs his hands together. "I'm going to get back to work. I'll keep you updated on my progress." He practically skips out of the room.

"See you later." I turn back to my chemistry homework. Why are chemical equations so damn confusing?

My phone ringing is a welcome distraction. "Hey, Penny," I answer the call.

"Hey!" Penny says. "What are you up to?"

"Homework." I sigh.

"Screw the homework. Let's go shopping," Penny says.

Shopping with my bestie sure sounds tempting. I still have birthday money that I never spent. "I need to finish my work." I grimace at my homework. "If I don't bring up my grades, I'm going to fail."

"Are you mad at me or something? I called you last night to come over for a sleepover, but you never called me back. I feel like you're blowing me off."

"No, last night, I, I…" My voice trails off. I wish I could tell Penny the truth, but it violates supernatural laws. The last time I told a human my secret, I put myself and Logan in jeopardy. "I had a headache."

"You've had such a rough year. First, Chad and Mallory went behind your back. Then Zoe disappeared to God knows where and Keisha became all secretive and distant. I know you loved Logan, and breaking up hurts. I want you to know that I'm always here for you. Even as your other relationships grow or fall apart, I'll be by your side."

I swallow hard, fighting back tears. It isn't easy to find a friend like Penny.

"I've been thinking a lot about the old days. Do you remember how me, you, and Giselle used to coordinate our outfits in junior high school? We'd spend hours searching for the perfect clothes, not matching but complementing, like we were a nineties girl group or something. We'd shop until we dropped," Penny says.

My lips turn up at the memory. The three of us would quite literally shop until we collapsed of sheer exhaustion.

"Sometimes we dragged Keisha and Zoe along, but they'd get bored after an hour."

"They weren't down with the marathon shopping sesh," Penny giggles.

I close my chemistry textbook. "You know what? I'll finish my homework later. Let's go shopping."

"Eee!" Penny squeals. "I'm so excited. I'll call Giselle. We'll even try on matching fits, just like old times."

* * *

A half hour later, Penny rolls up my driveway in her mom's sedan. I slide into the passenger seat. "Where's Giselle?" I ask.

"She couldn't make it." Penny reaches into her cup holder. "Peach iced tea." Penny hands me the plastic bottle. "Your favorite."

I smile. "You're so thoughtful." I unscrew the lid and take a sip. "Delicious."

"To the mall!" Penny says. She turns on our favorite Taylor Swift playlist. We both sing Bad Blood at the top of our lungs. I take another gulp of my drink.

A few songs later, the car tilts on the road. I grip my seat, fingernails piercing the gray upholstery. The world comes untethered from its axis. The landscape teeters. Trees bend. The sky crumbles to the ground.

I try to cry out, but my lips won't cooperate. It feels like marshmallows are jammed down my throat, blocking my vocal chords and airways. What the hell is happening to me? Am I losing my mind again?

I'm still wondering if I'm insane as the world turns dark and silent.

Chapter 37

My eyes are open, but I'm blind: trapped in endless space, darker than the blackest night. I'm not sure if I'm awake or asleep.

Slowly, I regain sensation: a hard surface beneath my backside, stiff and aching muscles. Something squeezes the back of my head, like a tight band around my skull. I try to lift my hand, an attempt to remove it, but I can't move. Rope burns my wrists. I want to scream, but my lips are frozen.

My heart wallops against my ribcage. I thrash, my ankles stinging against their restraints. The chair I'm strapped to rocks, its feet rattling against the floor.

I flail harder, using all my force. It's useless. I'm not strong enough.

"Lookie what the wolf dragged in." The smooth female voice comes out of nowhere. My instincts scream at me to run or fight, but I can't. Instead, I freeze: a deer in headlights, a duck playing dead.

Someone rips the blindfold off my eyes. I squint, my vision adjusting to the light. A single spotlight dangles from a chain overhead. A petite woman wears a skintight black catsuit, accentuating her hourglass figure. Long, platinum blonde hair cascades to her waist. Her eyes are as scarlet as the liquid in her glass.

She's a daydream and a nightmare in one. She leans forward and rips the duct tape off my mouth. Black nails slice my cheek like knives. "Licinia," I say.

"Filthy nimwit," Licinia replies. "We meet again."

"This is the nimwit that everyone's been talking about?" Another woman watches me with almond-shaped green eyes. "What's so special about her?" Her red-streaked brown hair is tied up in a ponytail, revealing the crown mark just behind her ear. Whoever this woman is, she's a royal.

"Her mother and the queen were childhood best friends. We think we could use her as a bargaining chip. Keifer always caves to his wife. That's why the little nimwit was released in the first place."

The door opens, a triangle of light beams in from the hallway. Two shadows obstruct the light: one bulky and masculine, the other small and slight.

Uncle Talon enters the room, his lips curling into a smug smile. He's dressed in formal wear: black slacks, black vest, white button-down shirt. His thick gray hair is brushed back from his face. "Well, well, well," he muses. "My grandniece has come to pay me a visit."

Penny steps beside him, her slim stature dwarfed by my great uncle's hulky frame. My heart smacks into my breast bone. "Oh, Penny, I'm so sorry that I dragged you into this mess," I choke out.

Licinia embraces Penny, her sharp black nails running along the back of Penny's sweatshirt. "Penelope, my dear great-great-great niece, you've done a wonderful job." My heart dives into my stomach, leaving a hollow space in my chest. Niece? What the hell is she talking about? Penny leans into Licinia's hug, resting her head on Licinia's shoulder for a moment before they separate. My mouth hangs open. I'm too stunned to speak.

"Some nieces understand the meaning of loyalty," Talon says, his gaze fixed on Penny and Licinia. He turns back to me. "My own niece, your mother, didn't know the first thing about it." Talon shakes his head, his mouth set in a firm line. "When Alaina was a little girl, she was my favorite. When my brother and his wife were busy with their royal duties, who do you think watched little Gwenna and Alaina? I was like a second father to those girls." Talon's brown eyes narrow. "I bought them ice cream and cookies, for God's sake. And this is how your mother repays me? By disgracing the entire Crowe family and forcing us off the throne?"

If Zoeli was here, she'd have a sarcastic quip about how awful our mother was for falling in love. She'd definitely have a witty comeback about the sweet treats. Because I mean, come on, ice cream is a big deal. How could she be so ungrateful to marry the man that she loves?

Zoeli would probably point out that my mother's choice of husband was only considered a "disgrace" because of the twisted philosophies of hateful witches like Talon himself. My mother didn't force Talon or any of the Crowe's out of the palace. The Crowe's were kicked out by a royal vote and the Nightingale regime when they moved in. But I'm not Zoeli, so I just stare, dumbfounded, my tongue glued inside my mouth. Besides, there's no rationalizing with a madman.

Talon wears a ruby snake ring on his pointer finger, and a silver skull on his ring finger. "The Descendants of Xaphan will take our rightful place as the rulers of Aurelia." Talon stands over me, his claw-like fingers reaching into my hair. His nails scrape my scalp. My heart races like a jackhammer. I squirm against my restraints, but they don't budge. "Don't test me, Saria. I could kill you right now if I chose to. You see, I don't actually need you. While you may prove useful at some point to sway Queen Taya, I'll accomplish my goal with or without you." Talon twists my hair into a rope, ripping strands from my scalp. I suppress a yelp. "With you, Saria, it's more personal than it is business. My niece deserves to pay for what she did. You see, when I found out about her little love affair, I warned her to end it. I told her what the consequences would be, not only for her but for the rest of us. But did that selfish wench care? No, she went ahead and destroyed all our lives." Talon's lips curve into a maniacal grin. "So now I'll ruin hers. And what better way than to make her precious daughter my own personal slave?"

Licinia flicks open a switchblade. She slices my restraints, releasing my ankles and wrists. Talon coils my hair around his fist and jerks me to my feet. "Let's go, slave." He drags me out of the room, pain searing from my skull down to my sore ankles.

I cry out, eyes wide as I instinctively reach towards Penny. I trusted her. She was my best friend. I still haven't processed her betrayal. Part of me hasn't faced the truth. Part of me still believes that this is all a sick joke, and any second now, Penny's going to jump on Talon's back and beat him over the head.

But there's only coldness in her green eyes.

Licinia and Penny follow us into the living room. A maid uses a feather duster to clean the television. Bent over in stilettos and a tiny black dress, it's a miracle that her ass isn't exposed. The maid turns, wiping off her lacy white apron.

My jaw drops. It's Miranda Keller, her dark blonde hair pulled back in a severe bun. When she sees Talon, she curtsies, "How may I serve you, Master Talon?" At the same moment my eyes bulge with recognition, hers do the same.

"I want you on your hands and knees, scrubbing the wood until it shines."

Miranda smiles. "As you wish, sir." She drops to all fours, sheer white underwear peeking out from beneath her microscopic dress.

Uncle Talon leers at her behind. "Scrub harder," he demands.

Miranda cleans vigorously, her hips gyrating with the motion.

"Good girl," Talon says. He tugs my hair. "Now let's go upstairs. You're going to scrub my bathroom."

"I won't!" Even though my hands are free, I haven't used them. I've been almost paralyzed: shell-shocked into submission.

Fighting back is probably useless. I won't win. Still, my fists ball up, itching to get a shot in. If Zoe was here, there's no doubt that she'd punch Talon in the face.

I do it in Zoe's honor. I swing. Crack! My fist slams into Talon's jaw.

"Don't do it, Saria!" Miranda shouts. "Don't fight back! It'll only make it worse."

"Who gave you permission to speak, vermin?" Licinia asks.

"I'm sorry, I-I-I," Miranda stutters.

Licinia holds up her palm.

"Please, p-p-please, don't—" Miranda begs.

Licinia flicks her fingers. Miranda rocks like she's having a seizure. Her neck lurches back at an unnatural angle. She wails in agony.

Licinia giggles. "It's too easy."

Talon rams me into the wall. "I could use magic, but it's more fun the old-fashioned way." He knees me in the stomach, over and over again.

The pain is unbearable. I lose my breath, the wind knocked out of me.

"Are you ready to scrub my toilet now, nimwit?" Talon breathes in my ear.

I could say no and take a further beating, but what would be the use? "Yes," I say.

Talon yanks me by my ear. "Let's go."

Every single fiber in my body hurts, but looking over at Penny, seeing her delight in my pain, what hurts most is my heart.

Chapter 38

Saria

One Week Later

My new prison makes Nightingale Dungeon look like a luxury resort. Miranda and I work around the clock. As we cook, clean, fold laundry and otherwise wait on our captors, they shoot insults at us.

Tonight, Miranda and I hustle to prepare dinner: sauteed mixed vegetables, duchess potatoes and rosemary-garlic leg of lamb. Since we spent most of the evening ironing DOX patches on hundreds of black army jackets, we're behind schedule. If dinner is late or the meat isn't perfectly cooked, we'll get lashed to a bloody pulp.

We aren't allowed to eat the food that we prepare. Once per day, Talon gives us food: usually some combination of stale bread, slimy mystery meat, and spoiled vegetables. It always stinks. To get it down, I have to hold my breath. Talon watches as we eat, snickering until we finish our last bite.

From the crack of dawn, soldiers are in and out of the farmhouse. They train from dawn until mid-day: practicing magic, physical endurance and military skills. Both spellcasting and assault rifles are their weapons of choice.

On most nights, the top military officials are invited in for dinner. Tonight, there's a different crew. As I chop vegetables, I stare out the kitchen window. Six witches, including Licinia and Talon, encircle a steaming cauldron. Licinia tosses a handful of herbs into the pot. The spellcasters hold hands and sway, chanting in an unfamiliar language.

"What do you think they're doing?" I ask Miranda under my breath.

She doesn't respond. I can't say that I blame her. We aren't allowed to speak to each other. If Talon finds out, we'll face consequences.

Miranda walks to the dining room table, her stilettos clicking on the tiles. These damn shoes are the worst part of our ridiculous "uniforms." I'd sell a kidney for a pair of sneakers.

Miranda and I set the table for six, careful to fold the napkins and place the silverware according to Talon's requirements. I fill two wine glasses with human blood, the rest with red wine. From a distance, it's hard to tell the difference.

As the guests shuffle in, Miranda and I light candelabras on either end of the table. Talon enters the dining room, studying the table, searching for a mistake to chastise us for. "Saria."

I jump at his voice. "Yes, Master Talon. How may I serve you?"

Talon thrusts a fork in my face. "This silverware is dirty. What's wrong with you, nimwit?"

"I'm sorry, Master."

Talon cocks his hand back. I brace myself. I know what's coming. Crack! He slaps me in the face. My neck jerks to the side. My cheek stings in the shape of a handprint. I lift my chin, trying to stop my lower lip from trembling.

Licinia curls her lip. "Nimwits are such filthy, disgusting creatures."

A man with salt-and-pepper hair slides into his chair. "Not everyone can be as marvelous as you ladies. There's a reason we call them nimwits, after all."

Nellie, the woman with the red-streaked hair and almond-shaped green eyes, giggles as she lifts her glass of blood.

"Clean this, now," Talon demands.

"Yes, Master." I scurry into the kitchen, fork clasped in my fist. In front of the sink, I analyze the fork. I can't find a speck of dirt. Anger boils inside me.

I look over my shoulder. I'm alone in the kitchen. There's a guard just outside the door, but he can't see what I'm about to do.

I spit on the fork and wipe it off with a dishrag. Looks clean to me.

I return to the dining room and place the fork in front of Talon. Miranda serves the first course, beet and carrot salad with citrus-scallion dressing. Talon twirls the fork in the candlelight, nods his approval, and then pierces a carrot.

I step aside, out of the way but close enough to promptly respond to any requests, just as Talon trained me.

"Overall, the rehearsal went well today." Licinia says. "But there's still a few areas that need improvement. Vaeda, you need to work on your pronunciation."

A woman with a blonde pixie cut looks up from her salad. "Speaking backwards is a challenge for me."

"Practice, practice, practice!" Licina taps her dagger-shaped nails on the table. "We gave you a recording of the entire spell. It's your job to study it. There's no room for error."

"I understand." The oversized neckline of Vaeda's pink blouse reveals a crown mark on her left shoulder.

"Gabriel, you need to work on your timing. Your hand motions were a second late. Remember, if we want this to work, everything has to be perfect," Licinia says.

"Got it." Gabriel's massive diamond-encrusted chains probably cost more than my family's entire net worth. He leans back in his chair and takes a drag of a cigarette.

"Caleb, you missed your cue to toss the obsidian shard into the cauldron."

"Noted." The man with the salt-and-pepper hair says. "I can assure you that on the night that counts, my performance will be impeccable. I didn't build a billion-dollar empire with lack of attention to detail." As Caleb raises his fork to his mouth, I notice the crown mark on his middle finger. "However, I must voice my concerns that we don't have a Nightingale rehearsing with us. What's the probability of success if we don't have representation from all of the royal families?"

"As you can imagine, being that the Nightingales are the reigning family, we've faced some difficulty finding a Nightingale willing to join our endeavor," Talon says.

Licinia raises a slender hand, long black nails like knives flickering in the candlelight. "I have it covered."

Talon raises his brow. "You've recruited a Nightingale?"

"If a spellcaster is unable to attend on the night of, they may perform the spell in advance while they bleed into a glass vessel. When the ritual commences, their blood may be added to the cauldron in lieu of their presence."

Talon nods. "I'm aware of that option. Is there a Nightingale willing to contribute their blood?"

Licinia's crimson lips curve into a smile. "Indeed, there is. This individual is not willing to join in person, as their actions would be deemed treasonous and they would prefer to remain anonymous. However, they've completed the ritual and I've made arrangements to retrieve their blood."

Talon lifts his glass. "Excellent work, my dear. Although I never had children of my own, you're like a daughter to me. Licinia, I am so very proud of you."

"While I appreciate the sentiment, you must not forget that I'm older than you, Talon." Licinia taps her glass against Talon's. "Cheers." She tilts her glass back, blood plunging down her throat. "Ahhh." Licinia licks her blood-stained lips. "Refill," she orders. As Miranda races to the kitchen with Licinia's empty glass, I collect the salad plates. It's time to serve the main course.

In the kitchen, Miranda and I work at a frantic pace, preparing each dinner plate. We return to the dining room, main dishes balanced on our palms.

"I'd like to burn the Aurelian constitution and piss on its ashes," Gabriel says. "Their unreasonable laws are the reason I joined DOX. The laws about human slavery need to change. My humans are happy to serve me. It's a *privilege* to serve me." Gabriel takes a big bite of meat. "The human police are all up in my business, but that's nothing I can't handle. Why should I have to worry about prosecution from the Nightingales? Who are they to tell me that I can't keep slaves?"

Vaeda clears her throat. "I'm not a fan of the Nightingales, but they didn't write the constitution. The laws are ancient."

Gabriel shrugs. "I failed history. I wasn't interested in any of that bullshit. I dropped out of school, moved to the human realm and joined the mafia. My choices served me well. I'm doing better than all the fools with their fancy degrees."

"I can sense your disdain for academia, but I thought you'd be interested in the origin of the law you hate."

Gabriel grunts. "Enlighten me."

"Historians believe that the human rights section was written by Aurelia, the mother of witches," Vaeda explains.

"Why were human rights so important to her?" Gabriel grimaces.

"Because she was one," Vaeda replies.

Caleb waves his hand. "That myth is pure nonsense. There's no filthy vermin blood in my veins."

"I agree. It's rubbish," Talon says. I follow my great uncle's gaze out the window. A crescent moon glints in the night sky. "In just a few nights, we'll reverse the spell that secures the portal." Talon's eyes glow like a demon's, iridescent red flecks in his brown irises. "Aurelia will be mine."

Chapter 39

Saria

My back cracks as I stretch out on the cement floor. I'm alone in pitch blackness. Each day, I'm on break for a few short hours. Most of the time, fatigued and aching, I pass out, tumbling into a deep and dreamless sleep.

Other times, like now, my mind races. I've lost track of how many days I've been here. I can't even imagine what my parents are going through. I hope that my mom hasn't returned to her catatonic state, but I fear that she has. I need to get out of here. I need to go home.

Yet, I struggle to come up with a cohesive escape plan. Exhausted and hungry, I can't seem to piece together anything that wouldn't result in an immediate capture and a severe beating.

My only glimmer of hope is Red. I gave him the address of the farmhouse. Why hasn't he come looking for me?

The door bursts open. Licinia smirks. "Break's over, nimwit. I need my nails done."

* * *

I hate to admit it, but Licinia looks gorgeous in a form fitting black lace catsuit. Pale blonde hair, almost silver, falls in beachy waves to her waist. "My new boy toy should be here soon," Licinia says. "He's hot as hell and he's all mine. Eat your heart out, nimwit." Licinia winks at me.

I struggle to keep a neutral expression when all I want to do is scrunch my face up in disgust. What kind of repulsive demon would entertain this evil fiend? And for her to insinuate that I'd be jealous? Even if he's the sexiest man walking the earth, if he likes Licinia, he's not for me.

I dip the nail brush into the jar of red polish. I focus on painting Licinia's nails: black with red French tips.

Beside me, Miranda is on her knees, giving Nellie a pedicure. "Tonight's the big night." Nellie watches out the window. "The buses are here." I follow her gaze. At least a dozen charter buses park in front of the farmhouse. Doors open, and soldiers pour out. They're clad in full tactical gear: black and gray camouflage pants, battle helmets, and jackets adorned with a DOX patch. Crystal wands dangle from their utility belts. Assault rifles and ammunition belts crisscross their chests.

"Do you think it'll work?" Nellie asks. "I know the theory, but is it really possible to undo magic?"

Vaeda applies pink lip gloss in the mirror. "It's definitely possible. I've done it myself." She sweeps mascara over her black lashes.

"You did?" Nellie's eyes widen. "When?"

"When I was eighteen, the Nightingales charged me with casting love spells. They said that I used my magic to manipulate and take advantage of others, but I was just a kid having fun." Vaeda says.

Nellie nods. "Love spells are forbidden."

"King Keifer acted like he was doing me a favor by excusing me from jail time, but his punishment, in my opinion, was much worse. He put a curse on me that made me look hideous to any potential love interest. The curse was meant to last for twenty years." Vaeda scrunches up her face. "It was awful. Guys would gag at the sight of me. I was so depressed that I contemplated suicide." Vaeda slides brass knuckles on her hands. "My best friend told me that I didn't have to go on like this. At the time, she worked for the Nightingales doing administrative work. She made a copy of the curse. I practiced until I was blue in the face. When the moon was just right, I freed myself."

"That's impossible," Licinia says. I finish the last stroke of top coat. Licinia slides her hands under the nail dryer.

"You can't deny living proof," Vaeda says. "We were out at a nightclub with your new boyfriend last night. Did men keel over and vomit in my presence? Not one. Quite the contrary, in fact." Vaeda's lips curl into a satisfied grin.

Licinia looks unconvinced. "I'm not sure how you pulled it off, but you can't undo your own curse. Every reputable source says that you need the original participants or their descendants to reverse a spell."

"You're wrong," Vaeda insists. "Our leaders don't want us to know how much power we actually have. That's how they keep us in line."

"So, you're trying to say that anyone who's been cursed can just undo it?" Licinia scoffs.

"Not anyone." Vaeda laces up her black boots. "The reversal ritual invokes a battle of wills. My desire to be free of the curse was stronger than Keifer's desire to curse me. I won."

She slides a DOX hat over her pixie cut. "It also wouldn't have worked if my curse was justified. My victory proves that King Keifer's punishment was harsh and ruthless. My best friend advised me: don't get mad, get even. So here I am. I can't wait to see him shaking in his tacky fur-lined boots."

Flanked by DOX soldiers, Talon appears in the doorway "It's almost showtime," he says.

"We're ready." Licinia blows on her nails.

"Lock that one inside her cell." Talon points to Miranda. "Saria's going with us." Talon nods in my direction. "Igor, take her outside. You're in charge of her until I tell you otherwise. Do not let go of her."

"Yes, sir." Igor grabs my arm and jerks me out of my chair. Jeez. He could've just asked me to stand up. He almost pulled my arm out of its socket.

Igor drags me down the stairs in a similar fashion, his fingers a vise on my upper arm. He forces me through the vestibule and out the front door. A gust of cold wind hits me in the face. It's my first taste of fresh air in weeks. I suck it in, shivering as frost coats my lungs.

Hundreds in black coats and shiny helmets move about the backyard, like a swarm of angry black bees. I'm freezing in my ridiculous outfit: tiny black dress, lacey white apron, fishnet stockings, and black stilettos. As always, my hair is tied up in a severe bun. If any of my filthy human hair tainted the gourmet food, there would be consequences. Now, as frigid gales blow, I wish my hair was long and loose, providing some protection for my neck and shoulders. I shiver, goosebumps sprouting on my skin.

Rows of chairs are lined up in front of a wooden stage, like an outdoor theater. As guests make their way to their seats, Igor and I stand to the side, his nails piercing my flesh.

A familiar figure makes his way across the field. Even from this distance, I recognize him: broad shoulders, long stride, angular jawline, black hair blowing in the wind. "Redvers Castigan." I whisper his full name like a prayer.

It takes a moment for me to register that he's wearing a DOX jacket, one that I ironed the logo patch on. In another split second, there's a blur of white blonde hair. Licinia runs and leaps. Her legs wrap around Red's waist as she kisses him.

I'm not cold anymore. Heat surges through my veins. Tears burn the corners of my eyes. First Penny, and now Red. Somehow, this hurts so much more. I was close with Penny, but I bared my soul (and most of my body) to Red.

During our hours on the phone, I shared every detail of my imprisonment with Red. I went back even further and told him about the person I used to be: vapid, shallow, and status seeking. He knows all my regrets: how I betrayed Zoe, how I agonized over it every day and night. He knows me. He knows my pain.

And I thought that I knew him. I'm a damn fool.

I can't believe that I trusted him, that I saved his life. I should've let him burn.

Talon steps on stage. A half-moon shines above him. He lifts the microphone. "Good evening." Everyone settles in their chairs. "Thank you for coming out this evening. Whether you're a vampire or a witch, your presence here tonight tells me that you believe in embracing your true nature. All of us, vampires and witches alike, are descendants of the demon Xaphan. The same demon who's believed to be the grandfather of witches also created the first vampire. He's an integral part of us, a part that must not be denied or suppressed.

"The current laws imposed on us by the Aurelian regime are not only unrealistic, but counterproductive to our progress. Denying reality doesn't erase facts, and the fact is that witches and vampires are superior beings." The audience bursts into applause. "As harsh as it may seem, the truth is that humans, and by humans I mean anyone with one drop of human blood, are simply beneath us."

"Yeah!" Someone in the crowd hollers. A howl slices the night.

Talon continues. "It doesn't make sense for us to drain our precious magical energy performing menial tasks. Our energy should be reserved for more important matters. However, the current constitution forbids us from using humans as our slaves."

A chorus of boos comes from the audience.

"Our demon instincts tell us that humans should serve us. Instead, we deny our inherent rights in favor of empathy and compassion, traits that are unnatural for demons. It's time that the laws are amended to reflect our goals and values."

The audience is thundering now: hooting, whistling, boots stomping on the ground.

"For years, we've dreamed about breaking the spell that secures the portal to Aurelia and bombarding their streets. We've been told that our venture is impossible. They insisted that every record of the spell had been destroyed. They were correct in that assertion, but there was one factor that they didn't anticipate. More than one hundred years later, one of the original spellcasters is alive." A murmur passes through the crowd. "When Eleanor Fox was a young woman, she seemed to vanish into thin air. As years passed without any clues about her whereabouts, she was assumed dead. No one guessed that

Eleanor, better known to her friends as Nellie, craved power and eternal life. She sought out vampires and asked to be changed. After the deed was done, she knew that she could never return to Aurelia without facing dire consequences. Instead, she changed her name to Nellie Baker, using her nickname and mother's maiden name as her alias, and made a new home with her vampire friends in the human realm.

"According to the Aurelian constitution, vampires and witches must stay away from one another. For the entirety of its existence, Aurelia has wrongfully excluded vampires from the magical realm." The crowd roars. "Contrary to Aurelian belief, vampires and witches are not enemies. After all, we're cousins, tied together by the demon Xaphan.

"Witch-vampire hybrids or wampires, as they are often called, are known to be the most powerful creatures in existence. Yet, a ridiculous constitution forbids their creation. Again, this law is not only nonsensical, it prohibits the advancement of both of our kinds. Some argue that most witches will not survive the transition. My counterargument is that if more scientific studies were conducted, we'd discover methods for a safe and comfortable transition. At this time, such studies are outlawed.

"This ass-backwards way of thinking must end. For the first time in history, our kinds have banded together for a common cause. This is why I'm confident that we will emerge victorious." Another round of explosive applause shakes the ground.

"For months, we strategized. Our soldiers completed rigorous training courses. We conducted a memory extraction on Nellie, revealing every detail of the original spell. We enlisted participants from each of the royal families, including an original spellcaster, enhancing our likelihood of success. We practiced, rehearsed and memorized every line and motion ad nauseam." Talon taps on the podium. On his middle finger, a skull ring shines. "We're ready. Tonight is the culmination of all our efforts. As soon as that portal opens, we have one objective: take over the throne. Whoever stands in our way will meet their untimely death."

Talon gestures to the woods along the perimeter of the farm. "The portal entrance is about a half a mile through the forest. Let's go."

As Igor pulls me into the thicket, branches scraping my face, I pray for my mother's homeland. If their twisted terroristic plot works, soon I'll be in Aurelia. For the first time in months, I'll breathe the same air as my sister.

Whatever it takes, I'll find Zoe. Dead or alive, I won't return to the human realm without her.

Chapter 40

Saria

I remember this place. I study the enormous tree, the one with the 'A' carved on its trunk. Last time I was here, I was bound to it, endless cords tethering me to the rough bark. Until then, I didn't know it was possible for rope burn to mar every square inch of my body.

Vaeda places a black cauldron on the grass. Nellie lights a fire beneath it. Licinia slips a large glass vial out from between her breasts. "There isn't a Nightingale able to join us in person tonight. Their blood will act in their absence." The blood sizzles at the bottom of the cauldron.

Six spellcasters stand in a circle, chanting words that I cannot understand. They sway in unison. They lift their arms to the sky. Caleb tosses herbs into the cauldron.

Someone screams. Gunfire rings out. Soldiers scatter in every direction. What the hell is going on?

A young man in an Adidas sweatshirt and jeans punches a DOX soldier in the jaw, knocking his head back. As the soldier steadies himself, the man plucks a stake from his back pocket and drives it into the soldier's heart. Poof! The soldier vanishes in a cloud of black dust.

More people in street clothes attack soldiers. Bones crack. Blood splatters. Cries echo.

Licinia turns towards the bloodbath, her red lips an 'o'. "Don't lose focus," Talon shouts. "We're almost there."

The six spellcasters continue to chant. DOX soldiers close in around them, guarding them against the street-clothed invaders.

Igor's fist tightens around my arm. He pulls me away from the crowd, sprinting uphill. We take cover behind a tree. I duck beside him, panting, my breath white clouds that give us away.

An arm seems to materialize from behind the tree. A dagger glints in the moonlight. Blood spews from Igor's throat, splattering all over my dress. Igor's grip loosens. He collapses on the ground. I'm free.

Above me, Red holds the bloody dagger. "What are you doing?" I ask.

"What does it look like?" Red's fingers lace through mine. He pulls me to my feet. "Rescuing you," he says, his breath in my ear.

"But," I shake my head, confused. "Aren't you dating Licinia?"

"Of course not." Red's thumb traces my cheekbone. "I only entertained her flirtations so I could find you."

A body flies through the air and thuds on the ground beside us. The DOX soldier is lifeless, blood leaking from his crushed skull. "What the hell is happening?" I whisper.

"Someone might've tipped off the slayers on where to go. The slayers understand the urgency: that this spell could end the world as we know it," Red says.

My eyes widen as they meet Red's. "You?" I ask.

He nods. "Now let's go. I'm taking you home."

Keisha leaps in front of us, blocking our way. Her mouth opens. "Saria?" She stares. "Oh, thank God, you're alive! Stay very still. I'm going to save you from that monster." Wooden stake in her fist, she pulls her arm back, aiming at Red's chest.

"Keisha, no! He's not hurting me," I say. Keisha stops, her brown eyes wide.

Another slayer steps beside Keisha, sneakers caked with blood. "It's called Stockholm's Syndrome. Don't hesitate. Kill that vampire."

Keisha throws the stake. "No!" I shout.

Red catches it mid-air, inches from his heart. "I don't want to hurt either of you. Please don't make me." Keisha and the other slayer inch closer. "I'm warning you," Red says.

Behind us, a male voice calls out. "She's a witch! There's a crown on the back of her neck! Kill them both."

Red's eyes flash as he turns around. The slayer who ordered my death screams, hands over his ears. He drops to the ground. Thump! Drool pools around his mouth.

"Back up or you'll be next." Red points from Keisha to the slayer who diagnosed me with Stockholm's Syndrome. The latter lurches towards Red. One wave of his hand and she crashes to the ground, limp as a rag doll. "Keisha, I don't want to hurt you. I know you're Sari's friend. Please get out of our way."

Keisha's gaze moves between us. Lines crease her forehead, her expression stricken.

"Keisha, you heard what they said. When they see the mark on my neck, they'll kill me. Is that what you want?" I ask.

Keisha bites her lip, squeezing the stake in her fist.

"You've known me since pre-school. You know that I'm not evil. He's not either." I touch Red's arm. "Trust me. It's a lot more complicated than Fawley even knows."

Keisha's hand twitches, almost like it has a mind of its own. Her internal battle's written all over her face. Her mouth opens and then snaps shut.

Without a word, she takes off, running back towards the war zone. She jets around a tree, and then she's gone. "Be safe," I whisper.

"Let's get out of here," Red says. "Your parents have been worried sick." Red leads, and I follow.

I look back one more time. From our vantage point, up on a little hill, I can see most of the battlefield.

As I watch, the ground opens up. Dirt and rock splits apart. The ground shifts beneath my feet. I stumble. Red steadies me, holding me tight against his chest. We stare, open mouthed as the crater widens. Light shines from underneath. A strong wind blows, hissing through the leaves.

Licinia swan dives into the portal. Talon leaps next, white button-down shirt billowing. Dozens of DOX soldiers follow, their arms and legs swallowed up by a gleaming hole in the earth.

"I need to go." I race towards the portal, my legs propelling me down the hill.

"Are you out of your mind?" Red's footsteps pound behind me.

"I need to find Zoeli," I say. "I can't go home without her."

Red grabs my waist and pulls me against him. "This is a really bad idea."

I wriggle out of his embrace. "I have to do this."

"Sari, please," Red pleads, raking his fingers through his hair. "This is insane."

"For months, I've spent every moment, asleep and awake, thinking of my sister. All I want is to bring her home, safe and sound. I don't know where she is or what she's been through—" I choke on the words, tears welling in my eyes. "Separated by worlds, I almost lost hope that I'd ever see her again. Now could be my only chance. I'd be a fool to miss it." I wring my hands. "If I don't go and something happens to her, I'll regret it for the rest of my life."

Red's blue eyes are smoldering. "Alright. Let's go."

"I know that this is dangerous and probably stupid."

"Both," Red says.

"I don't want you to feel, um, obligated to go with me. If you really think it's a bad idea—"

"Stop talking so much and get moving before I change my mind," Red demands. "We both know that I could carry you out of here kicking and screaming if I wanted to. If you give me long enough, logic will prevail and I'll do just that."

"I can go by myself."

"If you think I'm letting you go alone, you're even crazier than I thought."

We stay low as we maneuver our way through the battlefield. A murky mixture of dirt and blood coats the ground. My stiletto heels sink in with each step. When a slayer poises to attack, Red stuns him with a flash of blue light.

Finally, we stand at the edge, looking down into the portal. It's different than I remember. The last time I stood here, the swirling colors were more vibrant: blues, purples and gold. Tonight, I stare into a red abyss, as if the bloodshed stained the passageway. It looks like a tunnel to hell.

"We don't have a plan, a map or a place to stay. This is by far the dumbest thing I've ever done," Red says.

I raise my chin, feigning confidence. "Blame your undeveloped brain."

"I've done that before. I have a feeling this time won't be as much fun." Red takes my hand.

"On the count of three." I swallow hard. "One, two, three."

We jump.

Chapter 41

Damian

Colson marches into my bedroom, shrugs his black leather jacket off and tosses it on the floor. A lifetime of maids picking up after you will have you believing that's normal. "I heard about you and Cali." He sprawls out on my velvet couch.

"Yeah man, I shouldn't have led her on. I'm surprised the guards haven't locked me up already."

Colson's brow creases. "Why would they do that?"

"Cali's so mad. She threatened to expose my relationship with Zoeli and ruin my life."

"Nah, man, she was just pissed off." Colson shakes his head. "She won't do that."

"How do you know?"

"She loves you, Dame." A cold gust ruffles Colson's platinum hair. "Why's it so damn cold in here?" His gaze follows the direction of the breeze. "Why's your window open? It's freezing."

"I'm not cold," I lie.

"If you're trying to kill yourself, there's easier ways. Hypothermia's slow and painful."

I shrug. Nothing could be more painful than losing Zoe.

Colson stands up and waves his arms. "Snap out of it! Get over that girl already. Every time I ask you to hang out, you have another lame excuse. I'm worried about you, man." Colson paces across the room, hands in the pockets of his black jeans. "If it would help you, I might be able to find out what happened to Zoeli."

I raise my eyebrows. "Really?"

"Well, there's this witch who I dated for a little while. She might know something."

I pull my shoulders back. "Who?"

"This witch who lives over in the human realm. She has a little obsession with the Crowe sisters."

My fists clench at my sides. "An obsession?"

"I mean, obsession is a strong word. She just doesn't like nimwits, that's all."

"How come you never told me about her?"

Colson shrugs. "Come on, man, it wasn't that serious. It was just a fling. I haven't talked to her in a while, but I could reach out and find out if she knows anything."

A vein twitches in my neck. I stand up, cracking my knuckles. "If you know someone who wants to harm Zoeli, I'm going to need their name, address and phone number."

There's a bang on my bedroom door. "Prince Nightingale, I must speak with you." Elric's voice calls from the other side.

I lean against the wall, arms folded, annoyed by the interruption. "Come in, Elric." The door bursts open.

"Your Majesty." Elric's beady eyes dart from me to Colson. "Your Grace. I have urgent news." His voice wavers. "There's been a breach at the portal."

"A breach?" Colson's eyes look like they might pop out of their sockets.

"That's correct. DOX has invaded Aurelia. At least a dozen of our border guards have been killed. One group of DOX soldiers is moving west through the Elysian Forest. Another is working their way through the outskirts. Our intelligence believes that the groups intend to reconvene—"

"Here," I finish the sentence for him, a chill snaking down my spine. "At Nightingale Palace."

Chapter 42

Zoeli

I perch on the window sill at 13 Opal Moon Road, peeking between the curtains. As the guests shuffle in, the food alone makes me want to throw all caution to the wind and join them inside. Most of the guests brought a dish to share. Kian's dining room table is piled with delectable delights: fruit salad, meatballs, artichoke dip, cookies and more.

My stomach groans. For someone who's subsisted off worms and seeds for months, this is torture. Kian dips a mozzarella stick in marinara sauce and pops it in his mouth. A Metallica t-shirt exposes Kian's arms, and for the first time, I notice his full-sleeve tattoos. A dragon coils around his forearm, its scales etched into his muscles. A doe-eyed girl rides on the dragon's back.

"I'm going to be a bad girl and have my dessert before dinner." My beak drops when I hear Layal's drawl. Her green eyes twinkle as she bites into a brownie. She flips her bright red hair, clearly flirting with Kian. "These brownies are divine."

"They're pretty good." Kian seems oblivious to Layal's advances. He turns his back on her and writes the meeting's agenda on a dry erase board.

At least a dozen guests mill about: chatting and snacking. I guess I shouldn't be so surprised about Layal. She admitted to being an anarchist, after all. I can't tell if she's a friend, a villain, or just addicted to chaos.

I search the room for more familiar faces, but find none. If I walk inside, would they shake my hand? Or would they turn me in to the highest bidder?

Before I have time to mull it over, I hear a ruckus down the street. I fly up onto the nearest tree limb.

About a dozen black-clothed soldiers march on the road. Curtains open. Wide eyes peer out. A little boy in blue overalls plays with toy trucks in his front yard.

"Timmy!" A woman in an oversized cardigan hisses. "Come inside, now!"

"Aw, Mom. I want to play."

"Timmy, NOW!" Her voice is shrill.

When Timmy looks up, he turns ghost-white. Eyes damp, he rushes to his mom. He clings to her leg as the door slams shut.

Two men, one in ripped jeans and another in a suit, approach the terrorists. "Who are you and why are you in my neighborhood?" The man in ripped jeans adjusts his red bandanna.

"We're the Descendants of Xaphan. We're here to free Aurelia from the corrupt and oppressive Nightingale regime."

The man in the red bandanna rolls up his sleeves. "Terrorists aren't welcome here."

"We're not here to attack civilians." A DOX soldier says. "Move out of our way and no one gets hurt."

"I have kids." The man in the suit says to his friend. "I'm sorry, but I can't get involved." He jumps over a white picket fence and almost trips over a flower pot before he disappears inside a white brick house, the door banging shut behind him.

The man in the red bandanna is on his own. Arms by his sides, his fists clench shut and then flare open.

A group of neighbors gather on a nearby lawn, huddled close, whispering to each other. Using my powers, I ramp up my hearing like I did when I listened to Damian and Caliah in the woods.

"What the hell is Axel doing? He's going to get himself killed."

"I think we should help him. Stand up there together."

"I'm not that stupid."

"I called the cops," A woman says. "They're on their way."

Sirens blare. Three police cars careen around the corner. Brakes screech. Rubber burns. A voice calls over a megaphone "Civilians go home."

Two military vehicles roll up alongside the police cars, blocking the roadway. "I repeat, civilians, hunker down. Find a safe place." The voice booms over the megaphone. The man in the red bandanna goes inside a rustic ranch.

Policemen jump out of their vehicles. Gunfire blares. Some police hold magical devices that produce rings of light. When bullets enter the ring, they disintegrate, ashes raining to the ground.

Even though police try to stop all the bullets, some evade their shields. One pierces an officer's chest. The officer keels over, blood soaking through his shirt. He looks so young, with his soft curls and chubby cheeks. I wonder if, like Kian, he got the job right out of high school.

An older officer rushes to his aide. Kneeling beside the wounded officer, he puts pressure on the gunshot. Focused on his healing efforts, he doesn't notice the DOX soldier creeping up behind him. The black-clothed soldier swings his dagger. The older officer's head flies off his body, rolling on the ground beside his bloody colleague. I gasp in horror.

The battle rages on. A blast of magic from an Aurelian soldier lights a DOX terrorist on fire. Gunfire and magic attacks blaze from both directions.

As much as I'm itching to go down there and kick some DOX ass, I decide to scope out the situation first. Flying as fast as I can, I swoop over the Elysian Forest. Another brigade treks through the thicket, unopposed at this time.

In the outskirts, a brigade marches northbound. Some Aurelian 'duds' (I hate calling them that) gape in their windows. A young woman wearing jeans and converse sneakers hums to herself, ponytail swaying, strolling down the dirt road. When the DOX militia turns the corner, she freezes.

They surround her, demanding her pocketbook. Hands shaking, the woman hands over her black leather purse. A soldier slaps her ass. As she backs away from him, another gropes her breasts. She begs them to let her go. A soldier spits at her, then shoves her aside. She sprints away, red-faced, tears streaming down her cheeks.

In the outskirts, there's no Aurelian police or army presence. As usual, the Nightingales leave their most vulnerable population to fend for themselves.

In Nightingale City, a dozen Aurelian soldiers, clad in blue-and-gold gear, approach the enemy systematically. Some launch defensive spells. Others shoot fatal beams. A blast of energy decapitates a DOX soldier. Up on a rooftop, an Aurelian sniper looks through his scope.

Despite being riddled with bullet holes, a DOX vampire throws an Aurelian soldier across the street. He crashes through the window of an office building.

I've identified four separate groups of DOX terrorists. Even though they're far apart, they're all heading in the same direction. It doesn't take a genius to figure out where they're going.

Nightingale Palace.

I scream so that only one person can hear.

Damian!

To Be Continued

Under Talon's rule, humans are kidnapped from the human realm and transported to Aurelia to serve as slaves. If captured, half-breeds Zoeli and Saria will be treated just as badly. Talon deploys teams of soldiers to hunt the twins down, intent on exacting revenge.

As more Aurelians come together to oppose Talon's brutality, Kian's resistance group grows. Zoeli admires Kian's courage and integrity, character traits that her soulmate Damian seems to lack. As Zoeli and Kian build a strong bond, she's torn between their connection and the magnetic pull that Damian has over her.

As the sisters prepare for battle, there will be lies told, lives lost and hearts broken. In the end, will the twin flames save the magical realm? Or will their flames blaze so brightly that they burn Aurelia to the ground?

Pick up your copy today! Available at Amazon, Kindle Unlimited, Barnes and Noble and many other online retailers worldwide.

https://www.amazon.com/dp/B0F788SSZ1

Want more YA fantasy romance from Faith Prince?

Check out Wild Souls

"A heart-warming story with incredible character development, Wild Souls isn't just about falling in love. It's about finding someone loves you for who you truly are, regardless of who the world perceives you to be. It's about overcoming your fears and facing your inner demons. Deep, meaningful, well-written, and at times laugh-out-loud funny, Wild Souls is a must-read for all ages."

Ethan sees right through skin and bone, his visions exposing the true nature of each person he meets. In his town, he's known as a freak and a liar. Completely ostracized, he keeps his head down and avoids people. After all, there's no point in uncovering the truth about people if no one believes you anyway. Everyone says he's insane. Yet, Jenna likes him.

Jenna has no idea that Ethan can see straight through to her soul. She doesn't know why he accuses upstanding citizens of heinous crimes—spurring hatred towards him throughout their small town. All Jenna knows is that he gets her offbeat humor and fascination with the paranormal. Spending time with Ethan is a welcome escape from wondering why her dad won't answer her calls…

Until Ethan's sixth-sense opens a gate to their souls—literally. As they face their inner-most demons, they could either fall apart or fall deeper in love than they ever imagined…

Pick up your copy today! Available at Amazon, Kindle Unlimited, Audible, Barnes and Noble and many other online retailers worldwide.

https://www.amazon.com/dp/B0B8NVNXZL

Faith Prince is the author of The Crowe Sisters Trilogy (Where Magic Begins, Magic Coming Undone, Twin Flames) and the stand-alone novel Wild Souls.

Besides writing, some of Faith's favorite things include: spending time with her family, reading, country music, cats, chocolate, coffee, traveling, and concerts, in that order.

Visit Faith's YouTube channel at
https://www.youtube.com/c/FaithPrinceAuthor

Signed paperbacks are available for purchase on my website.
www.faithprinceauthor.com

Follow me!
Instagram: https://www.instagram.com/faithprincewrites
Twitter: https://twitter.com/FaithPrinceAuth
TikTok: https://www.tiktok.com/@faithprinceauthor
Amazon: https://www.amazon.com/author/faithprince